# The Silent Fort

# The Silent Fort

## Fay Sampson

ROBERT HALE · LONDON

ISBN 0 7090 7455 7


Robert Hale Limited
Clerkenwell House
Clerkenwell Green
London EC1R 0HT

2 4 6 8 10 9 7 5 3 1


Typeset in 11/14½ New Century Schoolbook
Derek Doyle & Associates, Liverpool.
Printed in Great Britain by
St Edmundsbury Press, Bury St Edmunds, Suffolk.
Bound by Woolnough Bookbinding Limited.

# CONTENTS

Dumnon is an ancient name for Devon. At the time of the Roman invasion, the Celtic kingdom of the Dumnonii extended across Devon and Cornwall.

# CHAPTER 1

## THE DARK SAIL

Light from the river flashed between the leaves, like a spear to the heart. Wild garlic underfoot was pungent as healing ointment. The girl stopped dramatically on the woodland path, so that the shorter boy following almost bumped into her. Cairenn gazed all around her, as if to paint this scene on her imagination for the rest of her life.

'Before the next full moon the Romans will be masters of the Exe.'

'Never!' Melwas shouted back at his sister. 'The Romans will never even set foot across the Stony River, let alone here. The people of Dumnon would die to the last man and woman before they let that happen. Warriors will come from the high cliffs, and from the slopes of Dartmoor, and even from far Penwith where the sun sets, and we shall drive them back.'

At the sound of his ringing voice, Crab, the little whippet at his heels, barked excitedly. But Cairenn did not turn her head to look at either of them. She stood framed by hazel trees, where the small, pale green nuts were setting. She kept her back to Melwas, tall and slender in her crimson gown. He watched the dappled sunlight shimmering on the rich golden fall of her hair. He was more scared by the shadows between the trees than she was. They were approaching sacred territory.

'They will come,' she said calmly. 'But I shall not see them take the Forest Fort of Idwal Goldenshield. Only six nights are left, and it will be time for me to leave our foster-father and go home to our parents' dun. But it makes no difference. A few more days and the Roman soldiers will be there too, at the Red Deer Fort. Soon there will be no place left where the British can be free. Our time is over. The glory we knew is coming to an end.'

She shook herself free from brooding thoughts and began to walk along the sandy path. Melwas hurried after her.

'You're wrong. We won't let it happen. We shall fight to the death.'

'The warriors of Dumnon can't fight the legions. Celynen says so.'

'Celynen is a druid. What does he know about fighting matters?'

'Druids have taken the sword before now. And Celynen is the wisest man in Idwal's dun.'

'Well, he's wrong this time. Aidan says we must fight them. He says there will be a great battle. He says the hosts of Dumnon will gather at the Stony River . . . .'

'Aidan?' Cairenn turned her head quickly at the name of Idwal's only son, their foster-brother. Melwas saw the rush of foxglove colour to her cheeks. But she quickly recovered herself. She would not admit defeat, even then. 'Aidan is very brave. But he is also young. He can't understand yet that it's hopeless.'

'Young? Aidan's years older than you.'

She tossed her mane of hair. 'A little. But, remember, I'm fourteen. Girls grow up earlier than boys. I count as a grown woman now. Old enough to be given in marriage,' she added shyly. 'And women grow old in wisdom earlier than men.'

Melwas hurled a stick angrily into the bushes. Crab raced after it.

'There are plenty more as brave as Aidan. They all want to fight. *I* want to fight. Tomorrow I'll ask Idwal to shave me as my chief and give me my weapons . . . .'

'You?' Cairenn burst out laughing. 'You're only twelve years old! Who would shave a boy without a hair on his chin? It will be five years before you can carry weapons into battle.'

'I can cast a spear and wield a sword and balance on the yoke-pole of a chariot! Why shouldn't I carry arms? Why shouldn't I fight, when the land of our fathers is in danger?' shouted Melwas.

Cairenn shrugged. 'Ask him, then. It will do no good.'

They came out of the trees into the silver light of late afternoon. Water was slipping softly past on either side of the headland. The wide, shining estuary of the Exe, the Salmon River, more than a mile broad, spread like a great lake towards the sea. On their left, the smaller Clyst, the Quiet Water, wound slowly through the reeds to empty itself into this tidal reach. Where the two rivers met, a low sandstone cliff rose from the mud. On the tip of this headland stood a dark knot of pine trees. Cairenn moved towards them. The boy's face clouded with doubt, on the edge of fear.

'I still don't understand why you had to come here,' he grumbled. But she stayed him with a quick movement of her hand which was oddly commanding.

'Hush.'

Melwas fell silent. Crab, trotting at his heels, licked his hand with a warm tongue and the boy smiled down at him. He was glad of the companionship. This was not a place to walk lightly. The two of them followed Cairenn, who was breathing quickly now with a strange excitement. They entered the cold shadows of the pines and their feet trod softly over the fallen needles. Then they were through, and the world was lighter again. Still Cairenn walked on to the

9

very edge of the bluff. She knelt and looked over. Her face was hidden from him.

*The face of a woman in the water. A face I know, and do not know. A face I have always known, and must never know.*

*She could almost be me.*

*No! Strike out that sacrilegious thought!*

*I am kneeling on Her territory. We come to meet Her at the boundaries. Here, where the land meets the water. Here, where one river flows into another.*

*She is the Lady. She is all of this. The land and the water. I am nothing.*

*You will be Her.*

*A shudder, that is fear and ecstasy. Is this how it feels when the Goddess touches you?*

*The eyes in the water widen. She is drawing you in. Lean closer.*

*Her eyes are dark and dangerous.*

*When I stand here again, it will be as Aidan's bride. I shall be the Lady of my tribe. I shall be my tribe.*

*Why not now? It must be now.*

*I am kneeling on the boundary of time. Between the day when Dumnon was ours, and the day it will be the Romans'. Between the sunrise when this river is the Lady's, and the sunset when it will belong to foreign gods. Between the dear life of this world and the Otherworld.*

*Lady, help us! Help me.*

*Her hair is a redder gold than mine, even in my bronze mirror. The banks of the Clyst are still deeper red beneath Her. Will this water run redder yet with our young men's blood? With Aidan's blood? . . . No, no, I cannot bear even to think it.*

*There! Her face writhes in the ripples. Is She angry with me? Her land is in mortal danger. I would not have him different. I would not have Aidan a coward.*

*Protect us. Protect him. Protect Dumnon.*

*She is smiling now, and hair spreads all around Her as the tide widens. She is coming closer, under me, deeper, fuller. She will accept me. She will accept my gift.*

*How am I daring to do this? Without the tribe, without the drums, without a druid? How do I dare to act alone?*

*Who am I?*

*I am Cairenn, the princess. Our mother is wise. She has druid blood.*

*When Aidan is chief, I shall be his queen. I shall stand here and sacrifice to You for the tribe . . . If Aidan lives.*

*Help us, Lady!*


Shallow water was sliding up over the mud as the tide rose. Each ripple crept a little higher towards the foot of the cliff. Cairenn waited. The wind sighed through the pines. At last the first wave lapped against rock. Cairenn drew from her arm a heavy bracelet of red gold. Melwas watched wonderingly. That bracelet had encircled his sister's white arm ever since the far-off day when they had left their parents' home to be brought up as foster-children with Idwal Goldenshield and his wife Beath. It was a massive thing, two golden serpents twisting their shining coils around each other, but ending curiously in the horned heads of rams. She held it on her palm for a moment, weighing the solid, precious thing. Suddenly she flung her arm upwards in one swift, free movement.

'To the Lady of Meetings!'

The bracelet arched into the sky, spinning and flashing its sunset colour across the silver waves. Then it dipped, splashed once, and was gone.

Something hurt inside Melwas. He had arm-rings of his own, but nothing as splendid as that, and here was Cairenn throwing it away for ever into the salt water and the mud.

'What did you do that for?' he said indignantly. But the indignation masked a growing terror. He had heard her invocation, which surely only a druid priest should make.

She was still kneeling on the lip of the low cliff. Out there in the estuary the ripples from the bracelet's fall were spreading in ever-widening circles.

'It is my offering.'

Melwas backed away from the brink. The meeting-place of two rivers was a sacred place. He did not want to think about the spirit she might have woken.

'That's a druid's work.'

'*She* is a woman, and we don't have a woman druid in the Forest Fort. She will understand. There is no more time left. Soon I shall be gone from here, and the danger is very near. There is . . . there are . . . people . . . I might never see again. What I need to ask cannot wait.'

'Aidan?'

She did not answer. He followed her gaze, trying to trace the sacred spot where one river married into the other. Was it really there, where Cairenn's bracelet had vanished? There, in the still centre of all those spreading circles? Was *She* there?

A gust of wind blew over the surface of the water, shattering the circles into a thousand cat's-paws. The little waves raced towards them, bursting in tiny sprays against the cliff. A cold wind clutched at them both and rushed on. The shining afternoon fell calm again. But Melwas found his heart knocking against his ribs, and under his hand the hairs on Crab's neck bristled stiffly. Beside him, Cairenn let out her breath in a long, smiling sigh. She got to her feet and shook out the folds of her dark red dress.

'There. It is done.'

'What did you ask for?'

'As if I'd tell you! It would never come true. Let's go; it's a long walk back.' Her teasing smile softened, and she said quickly and shyly, 'Thank you for coming with me, Melwas. That was important to me . . . Come on, Crab, you lazy hound!'

She ran ahead, and the whippet bounded after her. Suddenly Melwas felt as though life was cheerful again, as though they were both little children and no danger threatened their playful world. He tore after them, easily outstripping his sister, and reached the wood panting and victorious. He turned to wait for Cairenn, and as he did so a movement on the water caught his eye. He was just in time to see a dark sail slipping out of sight behind the pine trees.

He stared after it with a curious feeling. That ship must have been there on the Salmon River all the time, moving slowly upstream. But against the blue-wooded hills they had not noticed it.

The hazel wood was a small one. Before they were through it, the sound of the Marsh Town reached them, the knocking of hammers on wood, the shouts of the slave-drivers, the barking of dogs. Soon the smoke and thatch of its houses were in sight. Cairenn would have gone past the port, on the road that led back to the Great Forest and Idwal's dun. But Melwas could not resist the lure of the quays and their cargoes. Besides, if a new ship was coming up-river . . . .

'Let's just go to the quay.'

Cairenn glanced uneasily at the straggling lines of houses. 'Oh, Melwas, no. I shouldn't be here. I don't want to meet anyone. Let's go straight home.'

'That's not fair. We've done what you wanted. Now it's my turn. I only want to go down to the waterfront and back.'

'There won't be any ships today. Who'd want to trade with us when we're about to be invaded?'

'There is a ship!' he pleaded. 'I saw it. We won't stay long,'

'It's all right for you; you're a boy. But suppose someone recognizes me and tells Beath and Idwal I came here without my woman?'

13

'Don't be silly. You've got me and Crab to look after you. And we've often been out on our own.'

'I know. But it was different when we were children. I shall be a full woman next week.'

'What does that mean? I thought we were supposed to be free Britons. Anyway, I'm going. If you don't want to, you can stay here and wait for me.'

'No!' she cried in distress. 'You can't leave me alone. I'm coming with you.'

The road into the Marsh Town was much trodden. The wheels of carts and the hooves of cattle and horses had ploughed it into furrows that were never quite trampled flat by the slap of feet. But today it was half deserted. A few small children crawled about the doorsteps. Women stared out through the smoke of cooking-fires, their eyes flickering over each stranger, measuring the wealth they might bring to the town. There was a gleam of interest as they took in the bronze clasp on Melwas's shoulder and the silver girdle round Cairenn's waist. But there was little of the busy coming and going, the bustle of trade, that usually made Melwas's heart lift to the excitement of a wider world beyond the shores of Dumnon. Here, too, they were waiting – waiting for the day when the Romans must come, waiting to learn what fate that would mean for them. This was no time for traders to risk a valuable cargo upon an uncertain shore.

Between the houses, where the road ran out on to the quay, only one ship lay moored in the river. Melwas quickened his pace towards her for a closer look. She was a Phoenician galley, long and swift, already loading her cargo to catch the next morning's tide. A line of slaves, fettered by the neck with an iron chain, trailed sullenly down the road towards her, with the driver's stick threatening their heels. They were British, like Melwas and Cairenn, but from another tribe. Once they had set out for Dumnon with high hopes in the joy of a cattle-raid. But they had failed. Now, their leader's head

'They're going to Idwal's dun!' Melwas spun round to look for Cairenn, his eyes bright with eagerness. He found her close behind him, but she raised a swift finger to her lips.

'Ssh! Don't let them know who we are,' she begged.

The foreigner raised his hand in thanks and the dark brown sail moved slowly on round the bend in the river. Melwas wondered if the breeze would last them up the winding tidal river before the sunset calm. Close to the Red Quay lay the edge of the Great Forest, which hid the dun of Idwal Goldenshield. He realized that he and Cairenn must still go all that way back on foot. He tugged at the girdle round Crab's neck.

'Move yourself. I want to get back before those Armoricans arrive. If they're not trading, what do you suppose they want at Idwal's dun?'

'Probably nothing that concerns us.' But he could see she was alive with curiosity, too. Visitors from overseas had become a rare sight in these dangerous times.

He rushed on eagerly, 'Do you think it's a plan to beat the Romans? There could be anything in that ship. Perhaps they've brought hundreds of warriors to help us fight them? Or maybe they're plotting a rising in Gaul? Just think of it! Vespasian and his legions would have to go rushing back across the Channel to put a stop to it. Dumnon would be free. The Romans may never even get here!'

'You're talking like a child,' said Cairenn, in that stately grown-up manner he detested. 'Vespasian will march to the Exe, and nothing can stop him.' Her voice fell quieter. 'All this would be Rome's . . . . Now, please, can we hurry?'

They walked the rest of the way as fast as they could, through level meadows where the sun shone golden on the reeds and the voices of the field-slaves sang the cattle home for milking. The sun was already low as they reached the foot of the forest-covered hills. The track climbed steeply upwards through the trees. They fell silent, knowing that they must hurry. There would be no breath left for talking. Crab's little head drooped as he panted along behind Melwas. The forest twilight closed about them, trapping dark caves of silence under the sweeping boughs of beech trees. They seemed to climb alone, but both of them felt that they were watched. Deep in the forest, Idwal's men guarded the path to his dun. And though they knew the sentries were of their own people, they could not escape a feeling of guilt at being spied on from the silent shadows.

At last Cairenn grasped a trailing branch and leaned against it. Her fair face was uncomfortably flushed and she struggled to catch her heaving breath. Melwas waited impatiently for her. Soon it would be sunset, the gates of the dun closed and the guard hounds loosed for the night.

'I hate it!' Cairenn gasped, when she could speak. 'I hate hiding away here in the forest, and having to climb so high, and being watched all the time by sentries. I feel like a prisoner. I was so happy when we lived down by the river, with the farm and the cows, and everyone friendly. Now it's spoilt, and all you men can talk about is war.'

'If you want peace, you'd better hurry up. It's nearly sunset, and Beath will cane you for being out after dark, with or without your woman.'

Cairenn struggled on, till they saw a gleam of sunlight through the wide spaces of the beech wood. On the open crest of the hill, the sunset was turning the flowering grass to gold. The level light from the west struck full on the rearing ramparts and palisade of the Forest Fort, the war dun of Idwal the chieftain. The gate was open.

Melwas sighed with relief. They were in time. He knew that Beath would not really have beaten Cairenn very hard, if at all. There was a compelling dignity about her, even at fourteen, that made people treat her as though she were already a queen. One day, she would be. When Idwal died, Aidan was bound to be chosen as the next chief, and Cairenn would almost certainly be his wife.

But Idwal was unlikely to show the same mercy towards Melwas. He was about to run forward over the open playing-ground before the great wooden gate when Cairenn caught him by the arm.

'Look!'

His eyes followed her pointing finger. There was a movement on the palisade, round to the side, out of sight of the watchman at the gate. They saw a man leap over and drop into the shadow of the ditch below. For a while, everything was still – no shout of alarm, no sudden stirring. Then, as they watched, the man climbed nimbly out of the ditch and dashed across the grass into the shelter of the trees.

Crab broke away from Melwas and tore after him. Melwas gave chase, not daring to call out. He caught the flicker of a blue cloak and red-gold hair between the branches. A twig snapped under Crab's paws. The man turned, and for a moment Melwas was looking straight into the blue eyes of the chief's son, his foster-brother.

Aidan's startled face creased into warm and mischievous laughter. He raised his finger to his lips, and his blue eyes smiled a promise of shared conspiracy. Then, without a word, he turned and was gone, streaking into the shadows like a surprised fox.

Cairenn stood on the slope to the gate, her hand stifling the betraying cry from her open mouth.

# CHAPTER 2

## STRANGERS

In the great round hall of Idwal's dun, the warriors were gathering for the evening meal. Cairenn slipped quickly into the shadowy alcove where the other girls were already seated around a table. Some looked up curiously at her, as though they wanted to ask where she had been. Yet something about Cairenn's bearing stifled questions.

Melwas crossed to the other side of the hall, sniffing hungrily as he passed the fire, where rich-smelling clouds of steam billowed from the great cauldron. A fat-faced, merry boy of his own age waved to him from where he squatted on the piled hay. It was Coel, who had been sent to the Forest Fort to learn the druid craft from Celynen, High Druid of all the Forest. Melwas dropped down beside him.

'Oh, here you are at last,' Coel said cheerfully. 'I was beginning to hope you'd miss supper and then I could have your share. Where have you been all day?'

Melwas remembered Cairenn's need for silence. 'I was down at the Marsh Town,' he said vaguely. 'There's a new ship coming up the river.'

'What's so interesting about that? There are always ships at the Marsh Town. Who wants to walk all the way just to look at one?'

'You're just lazy. Anyway, this one was different. From Armorica. I've never seen anything like it before. A leather sail, and chains instead of ropes. And it wasn't just bringing cargo, either. There were men on board, asking the way to Idwal's dun. Who would be coming here from Gaul at a time like this, with the Romans about to cross the Stony River and invade us?'

'How would I know? But if the ship came from Gaul, let's hope there was a good supply of wine in the cargo. It's going to need plenty to sweeten Idwal's temper by the look of things.'

Melwas glanced up through the fire-smoke to the high dais of the chieftain. Idwal was crouched morosely over the table, tearing a hunk of bread to pieces. Beath, his wife, sat beside him, plump and concerned. Melwas ran his eye around the hall. Celynen the druid, the older warriors of Idwal's household, Peryf the harper. He found the alcove where the young men sat. One face, more striking than all the rest, was missing. Aidan. Did Idwal know? Had he himself sent Aidan into the forest at nightfall on a mission so urgent it could not wait till daybreak? Why then that elaborate gesture of secrecy?

The servants began to carry the steaming meat to the high table. Suddenly Idwal's voice, deep and angry, cut across the hubbub.

'Does my son Aidan not eat with us this evening?'

Everyone looked round in surprise. There was a stir among the young men in their alcove, a little ripple of uneasy laughter. Then one of them, Elaeth, got to his feet.

'My lord, Aidan the Red Fox sends his apologies. He has the belly-sickness. He will not come to supper tonight.'

Again that burst of laughter from his friends, quickly suppressed.

'Hmph!' Idwal snorted, and bent his head to the food, biting the pork from the bone with his strong teeth. The chatter faded to the steady sounds of eating.

21

Melwas accepted a bowl of broth, almost without noticing. He stirred it slowly with his bread. So Idwal did not know where Aidan had gone. But some of them did, Elaeth and his friends. Dinogad's scarred face was grinning.

'Here, pass me some bread. I've asked you twice!' said Coel at his elbow.

'Sorry.'

'Look, if you're not going to eat that broth, I'll have it. It's hungry work learning poetry. Twenty times Celynen made us go over it today, and I still can't get it right.'

'Well, you can keep your hands off my supper. I haven't had anything to eat all day. I was just thinking.'

'I don't know why Celynen bothers,' Coel went on gloomily. 'Once the Romans take over, we'll all be learning Latin.'

'Don't talk like that!' snapped Melwas.

'Why not? It's true, isn't it?'

'No, it's not true. It never will be true!'

After the food, the wine went round, filling the cups over and over again, though Melwas and the other boys drank beer with the servants. All round the hall laughter rose, free and noisy, with quick bursts of quarrelling. As the warriors sprawled back upon the hay, white-haired Peryf lifted his harp down from the wall and brought it into the centre of the hall beside the fire. There, in the leaping light of the flames, he began to play. His fingers were old and bent, yet they could still coax a sure, sweet music from the strings, like fresh milk running into a pail. But when he lifted his voice in song, the notes came thin and quavering. His first song was of Idwal, of his gold-emblazoned shield, of battles long ago and cattle-raids.

After a while, he passed the harp to one of Idwal's warriors. Thrumming the strings, the man began to sing. He sang of war. The harp passed round the circle, and one by one the men of the Forest Fort raised their voices in song. Some of them had made new songs. They sang of the Roman eagles, of armies on the march; they told how the hosts of Britain would rise and sweep the legions into the sea; they praised the rolling chariots and the clash of swords. The songs were awkward and homespun, but there was a vigour in them that made the blood beat faster with a surge of hope. Melwas, flushed with beer, looked up at Idwal, whose face was half-hidden behind bushy grey eyebrows and drooping moustache. In the morning he would do it. He would demand a sword and a spear and a shield. He would fight the Romans. He would be a man!

At last Peryf held out his hand and the harp was given back to him. He folded it in the crook of his arm and stroked the wood lovingly, as though he calmed a frightened bird. His fingers lightly touched the highest strings. Then he, too, began to sing a new song.

He sang of the land of Dumnon – of the heron standing one-legged out of the morning mist, of wide rivers like blue silk under the dawning, and golden evenings when the cattle wade thigh-deep among the reeds, of red stags in full flight across the purple heather, of twilight shadows blue as wood-smoke under the forest pines. The hall hushed to his singing and men leaned forward to catch the jewelled words. It was a song that first brought tears to Melwas's eyes, and then a fierce loving to his heart, and last the high courage that would fight and fight and fight again to the death, for the soil that he loved and the soil that his ancestors had loved.

The last notes curled away up into the rafters, leaving a breathless silence. Then the noise broke, roar upon roar. Beakers pounded on the tables, feet stamped the floor. Voices shouted again and again, 'Dumnon! Dumnon! Dumnon!' Melwas was on his feet, shouting with all the rest. Only Celynen the druid sat silent, watching the face of his chieftain. Idwal rose to his feet, unsteady with wine. He loosened from his waist a rich belt, fashioned from plaques of bronze embossed with red enamel, and held it out towards the harper.

Over the frenzy of shouting and stamping, few people heard the fresh commotion outside. But suddenly, those nearest the door were on their feet and rushing to peer out. Idwal dropped the belt into Peryf s outstretched hands and stood glaring at the door. Outside, the guard hounds were barking furiously, and the watchmen shouted a challenge as they ran to the gate, their voices sharp with suspicion. Everyone's hand flew to their knife. The warriors, too, would have rushed out into the night, but Idwal stayed them with a raised hand. And now they could hear the dogs being called off and the tramp of approaching feet. Out of the darkness seven strangers crowded through the doorway and stepped into the firelight.

Melwas craned forward, but at first he could see little. The newcomers were wrapped in heavy, hooded cloaks. Idwal sent his voice rumbling across the hall.

'You come late to our dun, when the meat has been eaten and the wine has been drunk and the guard dogs loosed for the night. But we bid you welcome. It shall not be said that we turned a stranger from our door without food and drink and shelter.'

Beath rose from her seat beside him. She looked flustered, her face beneath the grey plaits as pink as apple-blossom. She hurried across to the tall wine jar.

One of the strangers moved closer, throwing back his hood. Melwas saw a small man, with fierce, dark eyes in a white face.

'We had heard that we should find a good welcome in Britain. We thank you. We come to you from a long voyage and a weary walk, and my men will accept with gratitude whatever food you can offer.'

Idwal turned to the women's side.

'Beath, see that they are fed. Cairenn!'

Melwas started with surprise. From the other side of the room he saw his sister half rise from the shadowy alcove where she sat, as if uncertain that the call had been really for her.

'Cairenn. You will be a woman next week. Come here and pour wine for my guests.'

Cairenn came forward, and Beath handed her the gold guest-cup ringed with jewels.

*My hands around it for the first time. It is surprisingly warm from the grasp of my foster-mother. Warm as her love for me throughout my childhood.*

*And heavy! A shock to my heart as she transfers the full weight to me and I almost drop it. I should have known that solid gold would be a heavier burden than the wooden beakers or hollow horns that children use.*

*Idwal called me a woman. And so I feel, though I have still not passed through the druid fires into my womanhood.*

*Next week. And then I shall be fit to be betrothed.*

*Hard to restrain my head from turning. Where is Aidan? Certainly not ill. I have this vivid picture, like a painting on a wall, of his face framed in the leaves. Blue eyes wide with surprise and merriment. Aidan means mischief.*

*And my heart turns over in a different way, painful and delicious.*

*I want him here. I want him sitting at this table, only a few steps away. I want him to see me tall and womanly, the centre of all eyes. I want him to see how gracefully I carry the cup across the hall, how lightly I walk, how winningly I will offer it to these disturbing strangers, modest yet proud.*

*Surely I am everything a woman of Dumnon should be? Slender and firm-muscled. Hair flowing in waves down my back, where I have released it from its braids. My face freshly bathed from the dust of our expedition, so that the skin glows. It will look rosier in the firelight.*

25

*Come, Aidan. See me now.*

*Next week, I shall enter into my womanhood. Next week, my father will come to make his quittance with Idwal and Beath for their care of me, and take me home, full-grown.*

*Next week, I shall be ready to be betrothed.*

*Where are you, Aidan?*

*The gems are biting into my fingers. Whoever decorated this goblet did so for show and not for comfort. It is a splendid chalice, but it is not easy to hold.*

*I will hold it proudly, though it wounds my fingers.*

*The wine pours from the jar in a red stream. Hold it steady. Let not the bright drops spatter the table. Keep it all safe.*

*The cup is full. A darker red inside the hollow gold. The moment of danger, when I must start to move.*

*A little smile for me from Celynen, that lightens his grave, druid face. Celynen is wise, and I have drunk wisdom from him.*

*Will I dare to tell him what I did at the Meeting of the Waters? Would he understand the need? Would he forgive me?*

*And the brimming surface of the wine shakes just a little. Concentrate.*

*When I am Aidan's wife – if I am ever Aidan's wife – this is what I shall do at his table. This is what I shall be, in the name of our people. Wine-bearer, life-giver, peacemaker.*

*How can there be peace now?*

*If the Romans come, this may be both the first and the last time I shall do this.*

*Why are you not here to see me, Aidan?*

Her cheeks were flushed, but she held the cup steady as she poured the wine, so that not one drop was spilt. Then, bearing the guest-cup in both hands, she came back down the hall towards the strangers. As she stepped into the open space before the hearth, the flames leaped up and the light flashed full upon the flowing golden-brown of her hair. A murmur of appreciation ran through the group of foreigners. Idwal's young warriors, too, were leaning forward with a sudden interest. Melwas found himself staring at his sister as if she were someone he had never seen before. Cairenn had been right, after all. For her, childhood was over. He saw her for what she was – a tall and beautiful young woman. His sister was suddenly a stranger.

When the guests had drunk, she took the cup back to refill it. Servants hurried forward carrying armfuls of fresh hay, and bringing bread and cheese and the leavings of the pork. Idwal sat down again. The seven men ate in silence. No one questioned them. Not till their meal was over did Idwal speak again.

'Now. You have eaten and drunk. Will you tell us who you are and what brings you to this hall when the gate has been shut for the night and the feasting is almost over?'

Their leader rose to his feet.

'My name is Rieuk, High Druid of Armorica. And my business is with Idwal Goldenshield, chief of the people of Dumnon.'

'The people of Dumnon have many clan chiefs,' replied Idwal cautiously. 'I am Idwal. What does a druid of Armorica want with me that makes him cross the Channel at a time like this?'

'Can there be more than one thing that would concern the people of Dumnon now? What else would it be but the Roman legion that is waiting even as we speak to cross the Stony River and take your land?'

'And what has that to do with the druids of Armorica?'

'Much!' The man spat out the word. 'It has much to do with every druid and everyone that speaks the tongue of the Britons, north of the Channel or south.'

'How is that? I have heard that even before my father was born, the Gauls had fought their last battles with the Romans and lost. Now it is the turn of the British to face the

27

legions, and what is it to you whether we win or lose?'

'Then you will fight?' Rieuk asked eagerly.

'I did not say so.'

Celynen rose beside Idwal. His calm, thoughtful face studied Rieuk.

'It is not for Idwal Goldenshield to say. The matter has not been decided. When it is, it will be by the council of the chiefs of Dumnon, with their druids and their warriors and their bards. It is a matter for Britain, and not for Gaul.'

Rieuk's eyes took in the druid robes, the wand of peeled hazel.

'You say that? You, a druid, who have most to lose?' He turned to the chieftain. 'Listen, Idwal Goldenshield. I have not come here to speak for myself alone, but with the knowledge and consent of all the druids of Gaul – and the gods of our land know how few there are of them left and in what danger they walk. I bring a warning to you that this is what it means to be under the heel of the Romans. You think it is your land that they will take, and you grieve for that. You fear for your women and your cattle and your gold. But it is more than that. When they come they will take the soul out of your body, and the heart out of your people and your reason for living. They will destroy the old ways that made your tribe strong. They will cut down the sacred groves. They will murder your priests. And when the gods of Britain are dead, you will be nothing.'

Idwal shifted uneasily on the high dais.

'I am no druid. I'm a warrior, and the chief of this dun. If the Romans come, I shall still be a prince among my people.'

'There were many high duns in Gaul – great, walled fortresses. But how many of our chieftains live in them now? They wear the toga and live like Romans in their painted villas. You should see them in their bath-houses; it would make you sick. Their bodies have grown soft, and their eyes dull, and they have forgotten how to lift a sword!'

28

Rieuk looked round the crowded hall with flashing eyes.

'I tell you, people of Dumnon, when the old faith dies your glory will be gone for ever. Britain is the last hope of our kind. Was it not always here that the druid-fire burned most brightly? If you bow your necks to the Romans, your gods will desert you. And without them, Britain is a rotten apple, ready to fall.'

'Britain is not Gaul. She is no rotten apple!' A voice rang out from the doorway.

*He is here.*

*And there is no one else in the hall, and the distance between us is so short it could be crossed in a heartbeat.*

*Aidan has come.*

*Did he see me carry the cup? Will he look my way? Am I too far from the torchlight?*

*Aidan has more important things on his mind.*

*There is no one else in the world who carries his head so lightly, yet so proudly. No other man's eyes flash such a challenge, turning my limbs to water. He is angry now. Terrifying as a polecat. Commanding silence.*

*My magnificent Aidan.*

*Next week . . . I can feel the eyes of the girls around me, shooting between us. Cairenn and Aidan. It is what everyone is saying. When my father comes . . . .*

*He frightens me. He spellbinds me. What will it be like to be married to passion like this?*

*He is in love with Dumnon. With honour, with glory.*

*He will fight the Romans, whatever Celynen says.*

*The hall spins.*

Melwas turned, startled. How long had his foster-brother been standing there beyond the reach of the firelight?

Aidan stepped forward, his stiff, red mane of hair thrown back in defiance. He looked round at them all, and his face was warm and eager.

'Tell him, my brothers! Tell him what kind of men we are. Seven years we have waited for the Romans to come. Seven years the legions have marched northwards and westwards, conquering the tribes of Britain. Every day for seven years we have cast our spears and wielded our swords and raced our chariots till our muscles are like iron and our wrists like hardened bronze. Now we are ready. We can fight the longest day. We can march without food or sleep. And our hearts are as strong as the heart-wood of the oak. We will not yield one foot of Dumnon's soil to the Romans!'

Swift as a hawk, Rieuk turned back to Idwal.

'The young man speaks well! I have waited a lifetime to hear such fire on the tongues of my own people. While you have warriors like this, then here the flame of the gods still burns, and here the Britons may yet make such a stand that they will drive the legions back into the sea! What do you say to him, Idwal Goldenshield? Can you tell him to pass under the Roman yoke without a murmur, and let the name of Dumnon be forgotten for ever? Or will you swear a great oath tonight, by the club of the Good God, by the black Raven of Battle, by the spear of the Silver-Handed One, that the tribe of Dumnon will fight to victory?'

'The oath! The oath! Victory to Dumnon!'

Uproar broke out anew as the warriors leaped to their feet, clashing their beakers and pounding the floor. The girls were screaming as hard as the men.

Aidan shouted above all the rest, 'Swear it, Father, swear it!'

Cairenn's hands were clasped to her throat, her face shining with adoration. Melwas looked up at his foster-brother's face, his own eyes alight with admiration. Rieuk had caught Aidan by the hand. The two of them were laughing in delight at the frenzy all around them.

Amidst the tumult, Celynen rose to his feet. He raised his

hand, and out of long habit men gave way to him even in their drunken excitement. The shouting subsided, and the warriors sank back on to their haunches.

Idwal commanded, 'Speak, Celynen.'

For a moment, Celynen stood silent, looking down at the table till the last sound was hushed. Then he began in his slow, clear voice that reached without effort to everyone in the great hall, and yet seemed as though he spoke with Idwal alone in a private room:

'Idwal, my chief. We speak of life and death. Not the brief life of a man, who is born one day and spills his blood upon the battlefield the next. But the life of a whole tribe, the life of the people of Dumnon. Is it so far from here to the mighty ramparts of Mai-Dun of the Durotriges? Do you not know what Vespasian did there, and how the hosts of that tribe went down in red slaughter before the enemy? And we, who never built so high a fort, who never massed such a war-host, shall we fare better?

'And I, Celynen, Druid of the Great Forest, say to you that this is no matter to be settled after the wine jars have gone round and our eyes are heavy with sleep. You are a chieftain, the father of your people. You shall not cast for their future among the spilt wine, as though you played at knucklebones. We shall all of us think more clearly in the morning.'

A loud murmuring broke out at this, and argument. Around Idwal, the older men nodded their grey heads in unwilling agreement. But from the alcove where the young men sat came the loudest shouts of protest. One of Aidan's friends, drunk with wine, the scar-faced Dinogad, burst into a loud clucking like an anxious hen.

This was too much even for those who were hottest for the fight. A gasp of horror shivered round the hall. No man mocked a druid and lived unscathed. Melwas looked quickly at Celynen to see what he would do, It was always hard to tell from that calm, clever face what Celynen was thinking.

Just now it was impossible.

Slowly, unhurriedly, he reached out his hand towards his druid wand. Slowly, deliberately, he stretched out his arm until the hazel rod pointed straight at the young man's heart. Then the terrible words began. Cold, strange words, like nothing Melwas had ever heard before. They filled his soul with darkness. Chillingly, separately, one after the other, each word fell through silence like a stone dropped from a cliff. And with each ice-cold word the young man shrivelled where he sat. He shrank into the shadows, further and further back until he could bear it no longer. Whimpering, shielding his distorted face with his arm, he crept from his place, out past his friends, past Melwas and the boys, past the servants, around the dark edges of the hall towards the door. As he reached the threshold, the last word hissed towards him, leaving the air threaded with menace.

'. . . Banished!'

Dinogad turned then, thrown out of his tribe into the darkness, and ran for his life. Melwas listened to his footsteps thudding away into the night.

He looked back at Celynen. The druid was not an old man, but he looked old then. Old and tired. The wand trembled a little in his hand as he laid it gently down.

Rieuk was the first to recover.

'It seems that the druid-folk are not held in high esteem in the dun of Idwal Goldenshield,' he said, raising his eyebrows.

Celynen did not answer. Instead it was Idwal who sent his fist crashing down on the table.

'Enough! Is it not bad enough that I have Vespasian and his Roman legion on my doorstep? Must I also listen to druids quarrelling at my feast table? We shall talk more of this in the morning. I am going to bed!'

Beath rose hastily from her seat and shepherded the girls towards the door. Slowly the others began to move out of their shocked stillness. Families straggled out to their huts, hushing tearful children. In silence, the rest pushed the tables out of the way. They began to settle themselves for the night in the dark recesses of the hall beyond the ring of roof-poles. As she passed beyond the firelight to the door, Cairenn's face was still turned back to gaze at Aidan, as though she could not bear to let him out of her sight. The young men stood in a close group, heads together, muttering resentment.

Melwas snuggled down into the hay beside Coel, with Crab at his feet. He no longer felt the safe, warm comfort of familiarity. Too much had changed, too fast. He lay there, watching the servants smothering the fire with turfs. The last little flames sparkled through the cracks before they too were covered over. High overhead, the smoke-hole slowly cleared and a few stars shone down.

'Tomorrow,' thought Melwas. 'Tomorrow I'm going to do it. I'll go to Idwal and ask him to give me my weapons.'

# CHAPTER 3

## THE CHIEF'S RAZOR

Melwas paced nervously between the huts of the dun. The earth was dry at the end of summer, and the grass had been trodden into a brown stubble like an unshaven beard. A murmur of voices came from Celynen's hut. Melwas glanced in. Celynen was not there, but his pupils chanted on and on, an ancient poetry that could not help but sound like music, even on the limping tongues of boys like Coel. This day was strange, for in fine weather it was Celynen's custom to lead his boys out to some quiet spot in the forest, and there, under the oak boughs, or beside a running stream, to teach the druid wisdom. Melwas, too, should have been at weapon practice on the chariot-field, not idling his time away in the fort with the sun bright in the sky.

He climbed to one of the watch-places on the ramparts and leaned over. The treetops billowed below him in every direction. To the north they reached as far as the eye could see. He looked down. Far away, at the foot of the hill, the Salmon River reflected the summer sky. Here, above the reach of the tides, it looked no wider than a band of blue silk embroidered on the hem of a tunic. The other boys would be down there now in the level field that ran alongside the river. He could see the black specks of chariots, weaving their swift way through imaginary battle-lines, and the glint of sunlight on horse-bridles and weapons.

Melwas sighed impatiently and turned away. Aidan was not there, urging his team with bloodcurdling yells or balanced, legs apart, in the flying chariot. All the important people were in the great hall now, with Idwal and Celynen and the Armoricans. He could not understand what there was to argue about. Surely they must fight the Romans? What other choice could there be?

But it was not only that which troubled Melwas this morning. He had another reason for waiting. As soon as this meeting was finished he must brave Idwal in his hall and ask for the weapons of a man. And he had been waiting for so long that he was beginning to wish he had never thought of it. He was too young. Five years too young, by the custom of his people. But he had boasted that he would do it. The boast had been only to Cairenn and to Crab, but he had made it. There could be no going back.

Would their meeting never be over? As he sat, drumming his feet against the palisade, he heard the faint, sweet notes of the harp drifting across the grass towards him. He twisted round to look. At the back of the dun, a smaller gate led out towards the forest. In the clearing beyond, a single tree had been left standing. It was an ancient hawthorn, low-spreading, with a trunk twisted with age. Beneath the green foam of its leaves Melwas could make out the figure of Cairenn, resting Peryf's harp against her knee, with the other girls in their bright gowns sitting around her. The old man had been teaching her to play. Idwal's people now called her Cairenn of the White Fingers. She moved those fingers now over the strings, and music, pure as birdsong, sang through the sunshine.

Something was happening outside the great hall. Melwas turned back quickly. People were coming out. He saw Rieuk and his followers walk swiftly towards the great gate, but he was too far away to read their faces. He jumped down and started to run between the huts. Women looked up in surprise as he dodged past them. He caught a glimpse of Aidan and other young men hurrying after the Armoricans, but before he could reach the hall they had passed out of the dun and disappeared down the forest track.

He stopped. Idwal had appeared in the doorway with a knot of older men. They raised their hands in a farewell salute to their chieftain. He heard Bearrach Horse-Thief, Idwal's sword-master, shout to his servant to bring his weapons. Melwas felt a sudden urge to race out of the back gate and down the track to the practice-field. He could be there before Bearrach discovered his absence.

But he stood his ground. Idwal and Celynen turned and went back into the hall. Some women who were bringing water from the spring for the great cauldron turned away again in annoyance. Melwas took a deep breath. In a way, it was better for him to do it like this, when he had Idwal cornered in one place with few onlookers. Easier perhaps than trying to catch up with him as he strode about the dun, or make him stop and listen when he was shouting encouragement to the warriors in the field. But it was frightening, too. It was not like Idwal to spend the bright hours of morning lurking indoors like a wounded bear in its den. Melwas knew he must act at once, before his courage failed him.

He ran swiftly across to the private hut of Idwal and Beath, and ducked under the doorway. Idwal's personal possessions would be over there, ranged on wooden shelves beside the bed. His hands began to search quickly through them in the half-darkness.

*They've finished their meeting.*

*Too quick to jump to my feet. A twang of protest as the poor harp hits the ground. Not like me to be clumsy. The other girls are looking at me in surprise. Feena rescues the harp. Well, let*

36

*her stare. She's only a slave.*

*The Armoricans are striding out of the gate, looking angry. Does that mean Idwal has refused them? Are they going back to their ship?*

*Are we not going to fight?*

*I should be glad. Celynen says the only wisdom is to make an accommodation with the Romans. Let them build their camps and their towns, while we withdraw to our hills and our forests. Nod when we see them, pay their taxes. Cherish our way of life in secret. Guard the flame.*

*Cowardice, treachery. That's what Aidan says.*

*I should be angry. Melwas is angry, but maybe a child sees clearly.*

*Aidan is angry.*

*If Aidan fights, the Romans will kill him.*

*There he is. The young men are almost running to the gate, with Aidan loping in front. And my feet are moving, too.*

*It's nothing. They're going back to the chariot-ground for weapons practice.*

*They're going after the Armoricans.*

*I'm almost running now.*

*He didn't see me. The woods have swallowed them.*

*And I stand here in a fort that feels suddenly emptied of all its joy, its courage, its hope. Only the old men left, and the women, and children.*

*What will be left of us if Aidan dies?*

*What will be left of Aidan, if he does not fight?*

*What do I want?*

*I turn and see it all, as if I was a stranger. The wide circle of the great hall, with its sweeping thatch. The girls who were listening to my harp under the hawthorn tree, still staring at me. The women returned from the Council have carried their looms out into the light and have started to pick up the pattern. The bright wool flies, bright finches flutter down to peck at the spilled corn in the doorway. Somewhere the boys and girls of the druid school are starting to sing.*

*But where is Celynen, and where is Idwal? The shadows are dark in the great hall. They have not come out.*

*I am not a child. Soon I may sit in the council as Aidan's wife. It is not presumption to ask what has happened.*

*I feel I should stoop in under this doorway, though it is taller than I am. This hall is a place of feasting and drunkenness and laughter and song, and yet it is more than that. Larger, now it is almost empty. Darker in the morning, without the torchlight. More awesome with authority because only two men stand in it alone.*

*Am I as foolish as Melwas? What did I want to ask?*

*'Cairenn?'*

*I am only a distraction. Idwal Goldenshield has the future of this country heavy on his heart.*

*But Celynen is looking at me as though I really matter. He says nothing to help me.*

*'What's going to happen? What did the Council decide?'*

*'It is too big a thing for us alone. I've summoned the Great Council.'*

*'Here?'*

*Is that a flash of anger in Idwal's face? He must know I mean 'You?' Why does Idwal Goldenshield have to call the Great Council to the Forest Fort? He's not our High Chief.*

*Celynen speaks calmly, to reassure me. 'The times are strange, Cairenn. Old certainties are falling. We stand at the boundary.' He does not reassure me. I feel the floor unstable under my feet.*

*'Why is Aidan ... Where is Aidan?'*

*Anger now in Idwal's face, even in the shadows. 'He'll be back. If Dumnon decides to fight, it must be with thousands. He must see that.'*

*'He knows they will not fight.'*

*Did Celynen say that, or my heart?*

*My head turns, though I have given it no command. A*

*rectangle of light and then the gate of this high dun, the tops of billowing trees, the empty sky. Aidan has not been excommunicated from the tribe. Has he exiled himself? Would he be so rash, so brave, so stupid, to fight the Romans with a handful of comrades?*

*My heart falls further than I would have thought possible.*

*'I have summoned your father, with the other chieftains, of course.'*

*The words mean nothing to me at first. And then I see the level, kindly, troubled way Idwal is looking at me, as though the words sadden him.*

*'My father?'*

*'I had thought ... when he came to fetch you home next week ... Beath and I had hoped we might reach an agreement. Your clan and ours. You and Aidan.'*

*This should have been the climax of all my joy. The peak of my dreams, from as far back as I can remember. I think I have been in love with my foster-brother since the day I came tripping into this dun, a child of eight. Aidan, the red-haired glory of this family. Aidan, the clever, dashing, brilliant Fox.*

*Aidan and I. Aidan, my betrothed.*

*I savour the sweetness of that confirmation, and find it turned to bitterness by the past tense. 'Had hoped.'*

*I cannot bear these dizzying heights and plunges. Celynen moves so swiftly, I think he must magic himself from one place to another. His hand is under my arm, strong as steel, for a man who carries no sword.*

*'It is hard for Aidan to bear, diplomacy. He is too young to care more for his people than for his honour.'*

*'All our honour.' I sound like Melwas.*

*'If all that was dear about Dumnon was warfare. If song and story and art and worship could be defended by the death of a whole generation. Be a different guardian, Cairenn. Live, and teach them to your children.'*

*What children will I have, if Aidan dies?*

39

*I turn and leave the hall, desperately dignified. And then I run to find a place to sob.*

A shadow blocked the doorway. 'Who's in there?'

The voice was Beath's, Melwas's foster-mother.

'It's only me. Melwas.' He thought quickly. 'I . . . I'm fetching some things to take to Idwal.'

'What does he want? He didn't ask me for anything after the council.'

'No . . . but when everyone had gone, he went back into the hall with Celynen.'

She was twisting a handful of her gown. 'What sort of temper was he in, after Aidan went?'

Melwas grinned up at her. 'I'll tell you that after I've been to see him.'

She came further into the hut, trying to force a smile for him. 'What is it you're looking for, dear? Can I help you find something?'

He had his back to her again. He wished she would go away.

'No, thanks. I think I've got them.'

His hands had found the dark red cloth which served Idwal as a towel. Beside it were a small bronze bowl, a razor and a mirror, also of bronze, highly polished and incised with delicate, curling patterns. He hesitated over the mirror and then laid it aside. His hair was as red as Aidan's, but he had no wish to see the youthfulness of the face beneath it, mocking his claim to manhood. He quickly bundled up the other things in the cloth and made for the doorway with them.

Beath was watching him. He felt a pang of remorse as he approached her. Did she guess what he was going to do? Plump, soft Beath had been a good foster-mother to him. He remembered his own mother only as a beautiful stranger, rarely seen. For the first time he wondered what would happen to him if his wild dream were suddenly fulfilled and

Idwal granted him his weapons. First, of course, there would be the great battle against the Romans. But after that? Would he have to leave the Forest Fort and go back to his father's dun as Cairenn was soon to do? Would he have to live in every way from now on like the man he had boasted he was? He felt suddenly very small and childlike. He was close to Beath now and he yearned to put his arms round her and be hugged like a little boy for the last time. But it was not possible. There was the bundle which he was keeping half-hidden at his side, and the need for haste before his resolve could weaken.

Beath gave him a sad half-smile, as though she too would have liked to kiss him before he went. But she stepped back from the doorway and let him pass. She watched him run the last few yards across to the hall.

Inside it was dark, for the fire was smouldering low. Idwal and Celynen sat talking on the high dais, where they had sat last night, though now the trestles were stacked away, and the clean, bare boards propped against the wall. The great cauldron stood empty. Idwal's body-servant squattted beside the hearth, idly twirling a length of firewood between his fingers. His face showed nothing. He might have been dreaming, his mind far away. Or he might have been listening intently to every word that was spoken.

The talk broke off abruptly as Melwas entered. Celynen smiled and raised his eyebrows.

'The Red Fox has gone, and the foxcub comes in his place.'

But there was no smile on Idwal's face.

'Well?' he called impatiently. 'What brings you here, boy?'

Melwas's mouth went dry. He found it was not a matter that he could shout across the empty hall. Perhaps if he had been truly a man he would have done it the proper way. He should have come dressed in his richest garments, striding into the feast hall in front of all the clan and shouted out his request. Now, confronted by Idwal's sour, morning frown and

41

---

the cool smile of Celynen, he could not make such a show of it. He started towards the high dais.

It seemed a long way across the hall. He found himself walking faster and faster in his anxiety to get it over with. Then he remembered Cairenn. Had she felt like this last night as she came to fill the stranger's guest-cup for the first time in her life? And yet, how well she had carried herself, with the eye of everyone in the hall upon her. Not once had she trembled, or hung her head, or stammered as she spoke. She had not spilled a drop of wine. And were they not of the same blood?

Suddenly he was there, before the dais, and the blood beat high in his throat and the fire came back to his eyes. He dropped on one knee before Idwal and spread out the cloth on the floor. Then, flinging back his red hair, he held out the bowl and razor to Idwal.

'My chief!' he cried, and the voice, that he had been afraid would crack, rang true and clear to the rafters. 'I ask a favour.'

'Ask it.'

How could one ever read the twist of Idwal's mouth behind that drooping grey moustache, or the glint of his eyes under those bushy brows?

'I ask that this day you shave my chin and cut my hair and give me the weapons of a man!'

Celynen started, and then sat very still. There was a heavy silence, while Melwas stared his chieftain full in the eyes, determined not to drop his gaze. He saw him move, and hope began to rise, soaring up and up like a lark into the sky. Idwal stretched out his hand and took the razor.

Then, without warning, he hurled it with all his powerful strength. It whistled past Melwas's ear, across the hall, and twanged into the roof-pole on the further side, where it hung quivering with the spent fury of its flight. Idwal rose, crashing a stool over, and towered above the crouching Melwas.

'What day is this,' he thundered, 'when puppies with their eyes half-open come staggering into the lair of wolves? Is there not enough blood on Roman swords, that we must dirty them also with the entrails of our children? I have a son already that would drag a whole tribe down into the grave. Must I now take my foster-child, hearth-son of my closest friend, and throw him into the burial pit also? No, boy, I will not give you weapons today, or any other day! Go back to the women and ask them to wipe the milk from your chin, and do not come babbling to me of a man's razor!'

Melwas flinched under the cruel tongue. Tears of outraged pride scalded his eyes, filling them till they could no longer be held back. Choking with rage, he sprang to his feet and tore across the hall, with Idwal's voice still lashing about his ears. He ran stumbling through the great gate and into its shadows.

The forest was a green blur, like weed on the river-bed. He blundered on, staggering over fallen trees, tripping on brambles, with magpies clattering away in fright as he passed. No voice pursued him now. Still he ran blindly, leaving behind the wreck of his fragile honour, which Idwal had crushed into the mud like a bluebell trampled underfoot.

At last he dropped to the ground, exhausted. The tears were still wet on his cheeks, but he was too bitter to find relief in sobs. He told himself fiercely that he was not a child, or he could have cried like a child, weeping on the breast of the Earth-Mother as once he might have wept against Beath's large bosom. But he was a man, whatever Idwal might say, and he could hate like a man for the hurt that had been done to him.

He lay face downwards, with his chest heaving. His fingers dug into the loose soil, twisting viciously as though there were someone there he could hurt. There was a pattering beside him. Out of nowhere, Crab appeared, snuffling through the dried skeletons of last year's leaves. He thrust

43

his narrow muzzle under the boy's hand. Melwas stopped his convulsive movements. He sat up. Crab sprang into his lap and licked his face. Suddenly Melwas enfolded him in a great hug. He buried his face against the little grey dog and sat there for a long time, silently rocking back and forth.

He did not know how long he had stayed there. The distant sparkle of the sun was hard to gauge through the thick tree-tops. At last he got to his feet, tipping Crab off his cramped knees. He began to walk, dragging his feet listlessly through the leaves. He felt hungry now, a cold emptiness that came more from the heart than from the stomach.

'If we keep going across the hillside, we should find a path sooner or later, Crab.'

He came upon one sooner than he expected. He was surprised to find that it was the broad main track that led from the great gate of the Forest Fort down to the Red Quay. His wild flight, which had seemed to last half the years of his childhood, had not, after all, been so very long. An elm had blown down beside the track and lay there now, still garlanded with ivy. Melwas sat down on it. His restless fingers picked at the white ivy-roots that clung like starfish to the rutted bark. He wondered what to do next.

Presently he heard the thud of many running feet. He jumped up. They were coming from higher up the track. He drew quickly back among the trees and hid behind a trunk. The runners came into view, lean, sinewy men, the chief's messengers from Idwal's dun. Some were turning grey as they approached their middle years, but were still hard and spare of body and able to run the longest day through heat or storm. Others were young men, in the pride of their strength. Last of all, but with as free a stride as any of them, came a girl of sixteen. Beath's messenger, Tegan, with her green gown kilted up above her knees.

Melwas stepped out of hiding and hissed sharply as she passed.

'Tegan!'

The girl ran on a few steps, reluctant to break the rhythm of her downhill flight, then turned. Melwas liked Tegan. He knew that Cairenn and the other girls laughed at her behind their hands, because she was much darker than any other girl in the dun, with her curling black hair, and her bright green eyes, and her skin burnt brown by the wind. But Tegan never seemed to care what anyone thought. She could run like a deer, faster than any boy of her age, and she could cast a spear or jump a stream as well as most. When she was not busy serving Beath she would come down to the battle-prac-tice, bold and laughing, and if Bearrach was in a good humour he would let her practise her swordplay against younger boys.

She stood now with her hands on her hips, the laughter in her face telling of health and joy and the glad freedom of running across the hills.

'Well, foxcub, what do you want?' she smiled.

His own troubles were momentarily forgotten.

'What's going on? Where are you all going? Did Idwal send you, too?'

Tegan lifted her head proudly.

'I am a chief's messenger under orders, not a pedlar spreading gossip to earn a meal.' But she was still laughing.

'Oh, go on, Tegan! It must be very important for Idwal to send all the messengers out at once. It will be all over the dun by the time I get back, so there's no harm in telling me now.'

'If you're so sure of that, you can wait till you get back and find out for yourself.'

She looked down at Melwas's pleading face, and her smile began to fade as she took in the dusty tracks of tears on his cheeks. She asked him no questions, but her eyes softened.

'Oh, all right. I suppose there's no harm in it . . . . We have been sent out to summon every chieftain east of the High

Moor.'

'A hosting! The warbands of Dumnon gathering here!' Melwas's face blazed with sudden excitement.

But Tegan was frowning. 'N-no. Not yet. Idwal's calling a council to decide whether they'll make war against the Romans or not.'

'But they will, won't they? They must!' He sounded shocked.

'Don't look so upset, little foxcub! There are many more who feel like you. Me, for one!'

'We can't go down without a fight! Even losing would be better than that.'

'We won't lose. But I mustn't stop. My message is to the High Dun of the Ridgeway itself! And if I had my way, I'd go on from there and swim the Stony River and creep into the Roman camp. I'd leave a score of their soldiers dead with my dagger in their hearts before they knew what had hit them!'

And then, with a grin and a wave of her hand, she was gone, leaving Melwas alone on the path. He found his heart racing with hope again.

'If the chieftains vote for war against the Romans, then anything could happen! When the legion gets to the gate of Idwal's dun, they're not going to stop and ask if I'm a sworn warrior, if I'm holding a sword, are they? I'll show Idwal! What will he say when they tell him it was the spear of Melwas that pierced Vespasian's heart? Or that it was my body sealing the gate that made the Romans stumble and turned their attack into a rout? Crab! I'm going to make a new song for Peryf s harp. He shall sing the deeds of Melwas Mighty-Heart!'

# CHAPTER 4

## INVASION

Melwas started to run up the track. He could not wait to get back to the fort, to find the others, to plan for the coming battle. A council of war tomorrow! For it must be war. It must. It must . . . .

And then he remembered. Even if the chiefs decided to fight, he would be left behind. They would march away to the east with their chariots and their spears and their trumpets, and he would be left in the dun with the old men and the women. To them he was only a child, and a child who had been spurned and humiliated by his chieftain. He could not go back.

'I wish I was Tegan,' he muttered to Crab. 'Why couldn't I be sent out to the furthest fort?'

He could have raced all through this hard, bitter day, wearing his anger into the ground with every pounding stride. But he was not good enough, even for that. A girl like Tegan was more use to Idwal today.

A girl . . . . Suddenly he gripped the loose skin on Crab's neck.

'*Where* did Tegan say she was going? To the High Dun of the Ridgeway? Idwal has chosen a *girl* as messenger to the greatest chief in all Dumnon? *Why?*'

47

Now more doubts came crowding thick and fast. Why was the council not there, in that High Dun towering on the ridge above the Stony River? Why was it only Idwal who was sending out messengers? Why had no summons reached them from the east? What was happening on the boundaries of Dumnon? When Idwal and Celynen had chosen to send Tegan to the High Dun, instead of the chief messenger, what had they known, or guessed?

A sick fear clutched at Melwas's stomach. Next moment, he was running down the path after Tegan.

*We have sentries enough. I do not need to stand on the ramparts, make myself tall enough to peer over the palisade, scan the country around in every direction. I am making myself ridiculous, pacing this walk, circling the fort. Gazing north over the Forest rolling on and upwards to where the rivers rise. West, where the trees run out and the moor climbs bare and blue, tors stacked against the sky. South, and the river spilling silver from her skirts as the estuary opens, all the way to the sea. And east. Heart stops. This is where they will come from. The spreading plain too gentle to slow them. The ridges beyond have not resisted them. Mai-Dun has fallen. The greatest fort of them all. And no word from our own High Chief in the Stony Fort. Idwal fears what that silence means. I think we all know.*

*Nothing between us now, and the Romans. No one between us now, and defeat.*

*Except Aidan.*

*It is tearing me in two, this pride, this grief.*

*I would run to him in whatever way-camp is hiding him. I would snatch him to my breast like a mother with a wayward child. I would cradle his head, red as the soil for which he is fighting. I would stifle his sobs. I would hush his pain.*

*Would I unman him?*

*It is tearing Beath in two, but she is braver than I am. She will hold her head high, the mother of a warrior-martyr. Idwal is furious, but proud too. His heart is breaking. They are taking his land, they are taking his son, they are taking his hope.*

*Celynen is steelier, though they think him soft. Celynen sees further than the rest of us.*

*Here's Beath now, climbing the steps to the rampart, panting a little. Run to her. As a daughter to a mother, twice over. Foster-mother, mother-in-law . . . if Aidan ever comes back.*

*'I've looked all over for you. No sign of them?'*

*I shake my head.*

*'When they come back, it will be with Roman heads swinging from their sword-belts,' she tells me stoutly.*

*Smile agreement for her. Like a grinning skull, it feels.*

*Her eyes, like mine, find it difficult to tear themselves away from the cleared space of the hill slopes, from the last shelter of the trees, from the thousand hiding-places from which they could break out to surprise us. It is Aidan and his company we are hoping for. I do not think the Romans will come upon us stealthily. We shall know when the legion begins to march across that plain. They have no need of subterfuge. They will overwhelm us with their might.*

*Who are we, the British, that we believe so little in ourselves? That we are already composing laments before a weapon is lifted?*

*Aidan believes he can defeat them. Or does he know the truth and would rather die despairing than live despairing?*

*He will be our champion. If he dies for Dumnon, my harp shall sing his death, brave as the great heroes of the past whom the gods welcome to the Otherworld with joy and honour.*

*'I've got something I want to show you.'*

*I look down, and realize I am taller than Beath now. Her plump face creases like a winter apple, squeezing back the tears from the corners of her eyes. She is brave, too.*

*She turns, and I must follow her. We cross to her hut, and she is looking to either side, almost nervously, as though she feels guilty at what she is about to do.*

*We stoop and enter. This is a fair house, fit for a chieftain's wife. Beath rules here as firmly as Idwal. Even in all our turmoil, there are fresh reeds on the floor. The shutters are open to the morning. Women are spinning outside.*

*She leads me up the stepladder to the half-floor which is her storeroom. The chest is heavy, the iron locks ornate. The key on her girdle echoes their scrolling pattern.*

*Will I have keys at my girdle like that one day?*

*I cannot help gasping as she lifts the lid. I did not know even a chief's wife would have so much treasure. From the deep litter of brooches and buckles and arm-rings and pendants she uncovers something more massive, as I have delved for the shell of a crab half-buried in the beach.*

*A golden torque. A hoop of solid gold, twisted like the braids of my hair, with two proud finials, studded with garnets, rich and red as dragons' eyes. I have seen her wear this, perhaps four times a year, at the greatest ceremonies. She hefts it now, and it weighs down her small, plump hands. Then, with decision, she rises and faces me, so that I am left kneeling before her.*

*'Cairenn of the White Fingers,' she says 'it was my dearest wish, and Idwal's, that you should marry our son. I had planned that next week, when your father came, we would hold the betrothal feast. But now . . . .'*

*'Aidan will come back! They can't catch the Red Fox. They'll never kill him!' My voice is too desperate to convince even myself.*

*'I'm not a fool. We shall never see him again.' She looks down at the torque between her hands, as though she had almost forgotten about it. 'Idwal's mother gave this to me on my wedding day. I have no other son left alive. My daughters are married and far away. I'd as soon see it round your*

*neck this once, than leave it lying there for the Romans to loot.'*

*She raises it now so that it hovers in the air, almost like a diadem. Then she forces the finials apart and it slips round my neck. Cool as a snake. And heavy. Heavier than the cup I carried yesterday. This is rich, this is wealth, this is power and beauty.*

*This should have made me Aidan's wife.*

Melwas paused to snatch breath at the foot of the hill, where the green waves of oak and ash broke against the fields in a scattered surf of hawthorn bushes. In the lush meadows the red-brown cattle were grazing in the sunshine. Here, the way divided, going west and south and east. On the next slope, a flash of green amongst the fields of hay, he could see Tegan running hard for the east.

Sickles glinted in the sun. Bondmen and women were cutting the long swathes of hay, each armful of golden grass starred with wild flowers, like the garlands which the girls weave in their hair for the feast of Beltane.

One of the reapers straightened his back and called out that the cattle were trampling the hay. Down in the meadow, a cowman with a crooked back picked up his switch and limped in among them, thwacking the cows on the hindquarters and calling to them in ringing, wordless cries. They shook their great horned heads and ambled out of the hay on stiff, ungainly legs. Melwas could hear their strong teeth steadily munching as they moved closer.

He trotted forward. The cowman respectfully touched his forehead with his stick, as though this were just a normal day.

'Good morning, sir.'

'Have you heard any news?' Melwas asked eagerly.

'News, sir?'

'News from the east. About the Romans?'

'No, I can't say that I have, sir. But it's a funny thing you should ask that question.'

'Why?,

'There was a pack of foreigners with long faces here not long since, asking me that very same thing.'

'Foreigners? Armoricans?'

'That I couldn't say, sir, only that they talked funny. But they were wanting to know if we'd heard any news of the Romans, and would we fight them if they came?'

'But of course you'll fight! You told them that, didn't you? We'll need more than our noble warriors against the Roman army. If they invade us, the whole tribe must rise and drive them out of Dumnon!'

The cowman put a juicy stem of grass into his mouth, chewed it slowly and spat.

'I told him the truth, sir. We're bondmen, not warriors. It's not our business to fight. But if Idwal Goldenshield says "fight", then we fight.'

'But you want to, don't you? You *must* want to. Even if you only had sticks and stones, you'd fight them!'

The man's eyes met his. Melwas might almost have thought there was pity in them, if it had been possible for a bondman to pity a high-born Briton.

'Well, you see, sir, it's like this. I look after the cattle for your foster-father. That's my life.'

'I know.'

'Now. These Romans. They eat beef, don't they?'

'I don't know. I suppose so. But what difference . . .'

'And they drink milk?'

'Yes. But . . . .'

'And their soldiers use leather?'

'Yes.'

'And I'm a cowman. I do what I'm told.'

And with that, he hobbled away after the cattle, swishing at the red poppies with his stick.

Melwas stared after him. He's only a bondman, he thought bitterly. What does he care, as long as he's got his cattle? But I'm not a bondman; I'm free. It's my country. And I care!

He choked down a lump in his throat and looked round angrily. The long blue line of hills swung across his vision. Across that ridge, and another, and another, a Roman legion lay waiting to invade.

'We can't just let it happen, Crab. There has to be *something* I can do.'

Suddenly he realized Tegan was out of sight. Before he had time to think, he was running again, east, on the track she had taken.

He settled to a steady jog-trot. Crab bounded beside him. He did not know how far he would run, or what he hoped to do. He only knew he could not go back to Idwal, who had so hurt and shamed him. Not yet. The sun would set, the gate would be closed, and he would not be there in the hall. The chief would realize then what he had done. And Melwas? . . .

'I don't know, Crab. Somehow I've got to show him I'm a man. And there's only one way for that – where Dumnon's enemies are.'

As the miles fell away under his feet, Melwas began to feel better. He forded the Quiet River with Crab swimming frantically behind him. He toiled up the sun-dappled slopes of hidden valleys. Sometimes he was running over open ground through waist-high summer grass, with blackberries and rosehips ripening all around him. The long blue line of hills drew steadily nearer.

When he reached the foot of the ridge his legs were aching and his throat was dry and panting. A stream ran chuckling between hazel trees, and he knelt to drink cool water from cupped hands. Then he rose and pushed his way through the last of the trees.

The hillside towered above him. Tall, bleached grass rippled in waves before the wind, and all across it blossoming gorse sent up a shout of bright gold. Melwas looked slowly up, and a strange shiver of excitement ran through him. High on the crest, against the summer sky, reared the red earthworks of the Silent Fort.

There was no movement on the walls. The gateway gaped unguarded. Only the young pines growing within its circle lifted dark heads like watchful sentinels. Along its ramparts, the palisade had rotted into brown stumps like decaying teeth. For as long as Melwas could remember, and longer than his lifetime, the Silent Fort had stood there deserted. Grass overhung its ditches. Brambles straggled across the soil. Every year the trees within it grew a little higher. But still the raw, red earth of its ramparts frowned down upon the world.

He climbed towards it. To the south, the ridge dipped. Through the gap, Melwas caught the blue shimmer of the sea and the high, red cliffs of the coast, and further off, marching across the skyline, another band of hills. His way to the east lay through that gap, and down the long slope towards those hills. And yet . . . .

The Silent Fort brooded on the ridge like a huge, red spider. He could feel its power reaching out to him, gathering him into its circle like a gnat into a web.

All about him, the afternoon fell silent as he climbed. The ramparts waited for him. Was this all he would find inside their circle? Silence and emptiness? Or would there be warriors from the past? An ancient chief seated under the pines with sword and shield, waiting for a boy to come, a youthful hero who would claim those weapons, and use them to save his country?

He was startled out of his dream by a running figure. Up the grassy slope from the east a girl in a green tunic came panting. Her black hair streamed back from her shoulders and her face was crimson with heat. It was Tegan Mare's-Daughter, not loping with her easy stride, but running hard, as though the hounds of the Otherworld were after her. She was heading for the low gap in the ridge, making back to the west. Melwas started to run down the slope towards her, calling.

'Tegan! Tegan!'

She turned. Her tanned face was frightened. Then, as she recognized Melwas, she laughed with relief. He came up to her and she clutched at him for support. He saw that beneath the laughter she was shaking.

'Oh, foxcub, thank the gods it's you! Whatever are you doing here? I thought you were a Roman!'

'But what about you? You can't possibly have run to the High Dun and back already. What's happened?'

'No. I didn't even come within sight of it. There was no need. The whole countryside's full of people fleeing west. Families carrying away whatever they could save. Foxcub, the Romans have crossed the Stony River. They're in Dumnon!'

Melwas's eyes blazed with joy.

'Then the fighting's started! Quick, we must get back and tell Idwal! But why didn't the chief of the High Dun send for help sooner? There's no time for a council now. Idwal must gather the warhost as fast as he can and . . . .'

But Tegan was shaking her head.

'No, foxcub, you don't understand. It's worse than that! There won't be any fighting. The chief of the High Dun has sent messengers to Vespasian. They've surrendered!'

Melwas felt his heart grow cold. The High Dun of the Ridgeway! The greatest stronghold in all Dumnon. As long as the harps had sung at the chieftains' fires, so long had it stood defiantly on the edge of the spur, its mighty defences proof against every enemy, even the fierce Durotriges from across the Stony River. And it had surrendered without one blow, without a single Roman head rolling in the dust. With the High Dun fallen, the whole land of Dumnon as far as the Great Forest now lay open to the enemy. What hope was there now for the smaller fort of Idwal Goldenshield or the dun of his own father to the west?

'How close are they? Did you see them, Tegan? Did you see the Roman army?'

'See them? Not me! I didn't wait, once I'd heard the news. Oh, foxcub, I'm a terrible coward! There was I, boasting I'd swim the river and burst into their camp and kill them, and what do I do? I turned tail and ran, like a frightened hare.'

Melwas drew himself up taller.

'Well, I'm glad they've come! We've waited long enough. Now we've *got* to fight them. And we *will* fight, Tegan! I don't care what they do in the High Dun of the Ridgeway. This is our land; we won't let them take it from us and not draw one sword to stop them!'

She clapped him on the shoulder.

'Yes, foxcub, we'll fight them. You and I, and Aidan, if no one else. Though I doubt it's a fight we can win . . . . And now, will you race with me back to Idwal Goldenshield? I'll tell you honestly, I'd rather not run alone today!'

'I'm with you.'

He felt a surge of pride. He was, after all, to be the chief's messenger. He, Melwas, would come flying into the Forest Fort, bearing the news for which they had waited so long. It would be his shout that sent Aidan leaping for his spear and Bearrach calling out the chariots.

'Tegan?'

'Yes, foxcub?'

'Wait just a minute.'

He turned and looked up at the ramparts towering on the crest of the ridge.

'What is it?' She shifted her feet impatiently. 'This news is urgent. I ought not to be wasting time.'

'It won't take long. There's something I have to do. I just

need to go up there. To the Silent Fort.'

'The Silent Fort?' There was a scared look in her eyes. 'Why?'

'I don't know why, I just have to. As though it's calling me. There *is* something special about it, isn't there? You can feel it, can't you?'

She backed away. 'No, don't, Melwas. It's time I was on my way.'

'I'll be very quick.'

He turned and made uphill as fast as he could, hoping desperately that Tegan would stay for him. He had only gone a few strides when she came running after him.

'All right, wait for me. I'd rather not be on my own.'

But as the gateway loomed before them, dark and awesome, she gripped his arm.

'No, come away, Melwas, come away! I don't like this. It's no place for us to be! This is a haunt of the . . . Fair Folk.' Even to speak the name was an act of terror.

Melwas was trembling himself, but he walked on. In an agony of indecision, Tegan let herself be dragged forward, still pulling at his arm.

'It's too uncanny! They say when night falls you can hear the smith Govannon hammering out weapons for the gods. We shouldn't be here.'

He shook her off. Perhaps Tegan was just a common girl, after all. Cairenn would never have shown her fear.

The great timbers of the gate were rotting away. He walked steadily closer, till the huge ditch yawned at his feet. He stared down to the bottom, which lay far deeper than his own height. Its brown shadows were full of leaves. Here and there, curious patches of white gleamed through the gloom. What could they be? Suddenly he knew, and his heart knocked against his ribs. Skulls. Long ago, the people of this dun had spiked the heads of their enemies around the ramparts. The wood had decayed, the palisade had fallen,

57

and the skulls had tumbled into the ditch.

He looked round quickly, praying that Tegan had not noticed. She stood close behind him, her eyes half-shut, muttering a rapid string of charms against evil.

In front of the gateway the ditch was bridged by a solid ramp of earth. They passed over it, on between the walls, and came out into an open space. Crumbling mounds, with blackberry bushes sprawling over them, showed where once huts had stood. The dry grass whispered in the wind. Here and there, scattered stalks of barley ran wild among it. Young trees were pushing up through the sandy soil, some of the pines already twice the height of a man.

Melwas drew a deep breath and smiled. It was not so very frightening, after all. He climbed the rampart. All around him Dumnon lay dreaming in the sunshine. Heather was showing purple on the hills, vying for glory with the golden gorse. Between wooded shores the estuary spread its sheet of silver. All around, as far as he could see, the world was ringed with blue. Blue of the arching sky, blue of the summer sea, deep blue in the enfolding arms of forested hills.

Crab whined. Tegan begged, 'Hurry up, Melwas. What did you want to do?'

'I don't know.'

Cairenn would have known. He remembered how she had cast her golden bracelet out to the Lady of the Watersmeet. She had not needed anyone to tell her what to do. She seemed to know inside herself what the gods wanted, the actions which were fitting. He must try to do the same.

Slowly he began to walk forward. His eyes were fixed on a group of pines at the centre of the fort. He would walk right up to them. He would go down on his knees. And then . . . .

The sun was shining in his eyes, dazzling him. He walked in a strange, dazed dream. Surely there was a brightness, there, in front of the trees. He gazed at it as he walked, till the world seemed dark about him and he could see nothing but the light beating back at him from that shining thing in the long bleached grass. He stopped and stared down at it.

Suddenly he started back in terror. Behind him, Tegan let out a sharp scream as her hand flew to her mouth. Crab growled in alarm.

There, at his feet in the bloodstained grass, lay a man. The sunlight sparkled on his breastplate. His helmet had slipped sideways from his head, showing the hair cropped unnaturally short and the blunt, clean-shaven face. His right hand was clenched in the act of drawing a strange, short sword. His left was cloaked with blood. The silver chain it was reaching for had been severed, along with his throat.

'Is that . . . ?' whispered Tegan.

'A Roman soldier.'

# CHAPTER 5

## ESCAPE

He was the first Roman they had ever seen, and he was dead. There could be no doubt about that. He lay in the grass with his head hacked almost from his neck and the blood still seeping away among the heather. Why had he been left like that, when the neck was so nearly severed? One stroke more, and it would have rolled free, a fine trophy to swing from the victor's chariot. Though how could you tie a Roman head to anything if it had not enough hair on it to make a decent handful?

Melwas was used to blood, but the sight of this dead soldier sickened him – the shorn head, the blunt, dark features, the grim uniform of iron and leather, starved of gold, ungraced by the rich-flowing patterns of British art.

Tegan said wildly, 'How did he get here? Oh, Melwas, I'm scared! I knew we should never have come! The gods have punished him.'

Melwas dropped on one knee beside the body. His hand soothed the trembling Crab. He was remembering days of his childhood that now seemed far away. When he had followed the hunting party through the forest to come at the end of the day upon the kill. So often his short, boy's legs had failed to keep up with the chase. Yet still he had run on, his eye picking up the trail of men and dogs. And he had stumbled at last upon the hunters, to find them sitting at their ease, the deer trussed to a bough, the blood drying and sticky and the flies already busy. It was not like that now.

'Tegan,' he said wonderingly. 'I think this man has not been long dead. So whoever killed him . . . .'

He scrambled to his feet and swung round. The fort looked empty. But could he be sure? Those mounds of blackberry bushes . . . He found he did not want to go and look behind them. He climbed the rampart quickly and his eyes searched the hillside. No movement but the wind in the long white grass. Close below the ridge to the west, the woods began, cloaking the long slope down to the Salmon River. Anyone might be hiding there, under the screening branches. Watching.

He shivered. 'You're right, Tegan. This is no place for us to be now. Where there's one Roman soldier, there may be more. I wish I knew who killed him.'

Tegan was hitching up her tunic. 'Come on, foxcub, let's run. I shan't be easy till I'm back in the Forest Fort. Let's see how you match your pace against Tegan Mare's-Daughter with an invading army on your heels!'

'I'll try . . . Wait.'

He nerved himself to do it. This was a day like no other in his life. He should have a trophy. He could not take the soldier's head, but he would have something else. The sword? The blade was trapped under the heavy body.

'Hurry, Melwas!'

He did not want to stay. Changing his mind, Melwas grabbed the thing the Roman had reached for when he knew he was dying. The broken chain came away. From the dead man's curled palm emerged what he had been grasping. A lead pendant. Under the smear of blood it seemed to be marked with signs. Melwas dropped it into the pouch at his belt.

They started off at a run, with Crab bounding eagerly in

61

front. Back to the gateway they sped, over the dark ditch and
through the outer walls. The countryside lay bright before
them all the way to the Great Forest. Soon they were off the
crest of the ridge and running down the long slope to the
north-west. Melwas took his stride from Tegan, trying to
match the reach of her longer legs. It was fine to be racing
like this, downhill without effort, almost like flying, with the
wind sweet in his lungs and his long red hair streaming back
from his shoulders. No sound but the thud of their feet on the
sandy soil.

Then ... a loud shout behind them. Everything stopped
abruptly – their flying feet, their hearts, even the sun in the
sky seemed to stand still. Melwas looked back, but his terrified eyes could not travel fast enough over that wide expanse
of hillside. He forced himself to concentrate on the fort. It
must be there. Someone had found the body.

He strained his eyes. No movement. He could not bear to
wait any longer. But as he started to run again, Tegan cried
out:

'Look, Melwas!'

This time he saw them clearly, looking over the ramparts.
Helmets. Six of them, at least. Shouting broke out again, and
sudden movement. They disappeared. They must be running
for the gate. He pulled at Tegan.

'Run!'

But she dragged her hand away and pushed him off in
another direction.

'Not this way! Make for the wood! And may the Horse-
Mother lend speed to your heels!'

And she was off, racing away from him along the side of the
ridge, heading for open country.

'Tegan! Tegan!' he called after her. 'Take cover!'

She looked back once over her shoulder, and he saw to his
astonishment that she was laughing.

'Run, foxcub! Run for your life!'

He let her go. He could not help himself. As the Roman soldiers came bursting out of the gateway he took to his heels and fled, hurtling towards the edge of the wood which lapped so thick and inviting along the foot of the ridge. He heard more shouting behind him. A spear whistled over his head and plunged among the leaves. Now he was under their shade, crashing through fallen twigs, and the air was suddenly cool and dark.

He glanced back just once. The pack of soldiers was break- ing up, half veering aside to follow Tegan. Another spear flashed out behind her. She swerved like a hare and streaked away, a splash of brilliant green through the pale summer grass.

He saw her no more. He rushed on into the darkness of the woods. All the time his training as a hunter was telling him to move swiftly but silently, slipping between the trees. But he could not control himself. Never in his life had he been himself the hunted, and a wild panic was on him. Several times he forced himself to check and listen for the crash of footsteps behind him. But while the echoes of his own head- long progress were still pounding in his ears, fear drove him to flight again.

At last he could run no further. His knees felt as weak as frogspawn. The blood was thudding in his head and his breath was torn from his chest in shaking gasps. In front of him a small stream ran deep between earthy banks. He stag- gered down to it and bathed his burning face. Crab lapped noisily beside him. Melwas lifted his dripping arms from the water and found they were trembling. Already he felt cold.

The stream bank was steep. His legs shook with weariness as he hauled himself up it, smearing his wet skin with mud. Then he fell exhausted on to the soft earth. Crab lay panting too, with his pink tongue lolling sideways. Presently Melwas reached out a hand and rubbed the grey whippet fondly behind the ears. Part of his mind was still listening for the sounds of pursuit, but by now he hardly cared. He was too tired to run any further. Too tired even to fight. His hand moved towards the dagger in his girdle, but fell slack again before he touched it. The wood was silent. He lay on his back, not thinking about anything, staring unseeingly up at the thick canopy of yellow-green leaves. This was all he wanted – not to be running, not to be thinking, to forget why he was afraid.

His breathing relaxed, his pulse steadied. He sat up and brushed away the twigs that had pressed into bare skin. A sparkle of silver caught his eye. He frowned, puzzled by its unfamiliarity. The broken end of a chain dangled from his pouch. He unbuckled it and drew the thing out. It was the pendant he had taken from the dead Roman. Gazing down at it, he felt reality return.

An instinct of fury made him want to hurl it away. It belonged to the invader. It was evil. Then he remembered he had taken it as a trophy, even though he had not killed the soldier himself.

'He's dead,' he said out loud. 'So will they all be. Aidan will kill them.'

The pendant was lead, softer and greyer than its silver chain. There were marks on it. Some were straight lines at different angles, like the language carved on twigs that Coel was learning to read in the druids' school. But there was something else, two lines curving above and below, then crossing. You could almost imagine it was a fish.

He started to slip it back into his pouch, then changed his mind. It was a trophy, of his first brush with the Roman army. Now that he had escaped with his life from them, he was entitled to wear it. He knotted the broken chain around his neck. The pendant swung against the neck of his tunic, then dropped inside.

With a sigh, Melwas stood up.

'It's no good staying here, Crab. I'm a chief's messenger

now and it's urgent. We've got to get this news home.'

Home? With an ache of weariness he realized how far that must be. He must have fled miles out of his way. But he had a new responsibility. He was no longer a hurt child running away from a cruel foster-father. He had a report that must not wait.

'Though I guess Tegan will have got there long before I do. Unless . . . .'

Suddenly he felt sick. He did not want to think about Tegan. He must not let himself still see that flying figure in green, the Roman chasing her with javelin poised to throw. He knew there was another picture waiting in the corner of his mind, but he could not face it. Instead he stood up and looked about him.

This wood was unfamiliar. In the Great Forest, giant beeches made wide caverns under their sweeping boughs. But here the oak trees clustered thickly together. Their branches grew beards of lichen and there was a smell of damp about the leaf mould. Few birds sang. But in his ears there was still that high tinkle of running water. He thought about it. That little stream must run downhill into the Salmon River. From it he could judge his way northwards.

He took fresh heart as he began to run again. His muscles ached, but the rest had revived him. He could feel the strength coming back to his limbs.

'We did it, Crab. Our first meeting with the Roman army, and we outwitted them. I've got away safely with my message.'

He pushed his way forward through the branches. How strangely knotted the trunks of oak trees were. Glancing sideways at them, it was easy to imagine he saw a face. A branch, half-seen, loomed like a clawing arm. He pushed on faster, glad to have Crab's faithful grey shadow behind him. He was a man now, not a child. He must not let himself be frightened by fancies.

But it was into the oak woods that the druids led them to meet their gods.

It was a long way, and still the wood stretched out in front of him, dark and silent, as far as the eye could see. He forced himself on, always hoping to see a gleam of daylight ahead. And now he knew that the day was dying. It was harder to be brave as the evening shadows deepened and the rustlings began. Adders slipped homeward across his path, startling him. He saw where a bear had scored the bark of a tree-trunk, clawing down the wild bees' honey. He knew that he would not reach the Forest Fort that night. He must find himself a safe hiding-place in which to spend the hours of darkness. He would rather it had not been in this wood.

He stumbled on, as if in a dream. By now he scarcely knew whether he was even walking in the right direction. His legs seemed to be possessed by an evil magic. He wanted with all his heart for them to stop, to let his tired body sink to the ground and rest. But still they plodded, one after the other, rhythmic as drumbeats, dragging him with them.

Without warning, he staggered over something small and solid in his path. It let out a piercing squeal, leaped to its feet and dashed away through the undergrowth. A whole chorus of squealing broke out, followed by the crashing movement of some larger animal. Across his glazed vision a litter of young pigs with their sow went galloping away from him through the wood. Crab broke into a frantic yapping and tore after them. In a few moments they had all disappeared among the trees.

Melwas swayed in his tracks. He could not find the strength to whistle Crab back. With a last effort he plunged after them, following the distant sounds of their progress.

The crashing ceased, though Melwas hardly noticed it. He could hear Crab still barking furiously in the silence. Suddenly he was on the edge of a clearing. The whippet stood stock-still, his thin legs planted stiffly on the grass, yapping defiance at a high wicker fence.

For a while, it meant nothing to him. Across a level clearing, the fence that encircled a grove of oak trees, yet kept the rest of the wood at bay across a level clearing. The open gateway. The sharp smell of wood-smoke lingering under the boughs. Then, all at once, a great wave of thankfulness swept over Melwas and he felt he had found safety. He summoned Crab to heel with a flick of his hand, and walked through the gateway.

Around the great oaks the grass grew green and sweet. At the foot of one were the pigs, now munching quietly at the fallen acorns. Three huts stood to one side of the enclosure, and from one of them a thin smoke stole upwards. But it was to the very centre of the grove that Melwas's eyes were drawn, and, having once seen what stood there, he could not look away.

A tall wooden pillar reared up towards the first pale stars of evening. Its wood was black, and there were things shaped out of its surface. Melwas drew slowly nearer. His footsteps made no sound on the soft grass. The grove was still. Nearer and nearer. Now the pillar towered over him and he lifted his face to look.

Where the blade had bitten fiercely into the wood, the gashes were filled with blackness. As he peered at them, these shapes in the dark wood emerged as human heads. Long, shadowed slits of eyes stared down at him. They had no mouths.

He was afraid. His eyes were hurrying. He was scared to gaze at them now, yet he dared not look away. His eye slid downwards. One. Two. Three. Now the heads were clustering more thickly. Six ... nine ... eleven ... and .... His heart stopped. At the base of the pillar hung the twelfth head, upside down. Below it, a deep hole gaped in the ground.

Melwas stood gazing down at it while the world rocked

about him. He could not begin to understand its meaning. But he felt the power of it cold upon his heart. He knew that it *had* a meaning, dark and deep and dangerous to know.

'Welcome, Melwas Mighty-Heart! What does Idwal Goldenshield's young foxcub come seeking at the Oaks of Seiriol?'

*They are starting to come. From the nearer duns between here and the moor. The chiefs, the nobles, the wise, the bravest of the warleaders. The most honoured men and women of Dumnon. We are a proud people, even now that we are staring at conquest. Horses' hooves spattering dust in the gateway. A flying of chequered cloaks. Chariot wheels clattering. The flash of jewels and gold. And I put my hand up to the precious thick, cool gold collaring my neck. The gift that should have made me one of Aidan's family.*

*Where is he?*

*Beath is sending me in a hundred directions, overseeing with her the preparation of sleeping-quarters, the seething cauldrons of pork, the kneading and baking of still more bread. As if I were already her daughter-in-law.*

*The young men have not come back.*

'*Where's Melwas? I need him.*' *Beath looks hot and worried.*

*I shrug. 'Down by the river, I suppose. Practising his weapons with the other boys. They're all playing at being the hero who defeats the Roman army singlehanded.'*

'*The boys were back long since. It's getting late.*'

*We both look to where the low sun makes long-legged shadows of the cows on the hill slope. Far, far away the line of silver that is the sea, before the southern sky stoops down to finger it. And between them, the darker billowing waves of the Forest.*

*Something in Beath's face calls my attention back.*

'*He was acting strangely this morning, after the Armoricans left. I caught him in our sleeping-hut, looking for something.*'

'What?'

'He wouldn't tell. And when he found it, he made off fast, with the things wrapped in a towel.'

'A towel?' Memory plucks, as though a harp string ran deep through my guts. 'Not a razor and a bowl?' It is rushing back to me now, the flood of certainty. 'He said he was going to ask Idwal to shave him and make him his warrior. He's like all the rest of them! He just wants to fight the Romans. Even if it's throwing his life away!'

I stop and we stare at each other, Beath and I. My brother. Her son.

'Well, Idwal wouldn't do it, of course. The boy's only twelve.'

'He's very proud. He'd set his heart on it.'

'I'm going to find Idwal. Why ever couldn't the man tell me about this?'

She marches off, formidable, though she is not a tall woman. I follow. As yet, I will not admit to myself what it is we are fearing.

It is not easy to beard Idwal. Beath understands well enough why he has had no time to talk. He stands surrounded now, by his own advisers, by these noble newcomers. They are arguing, as though tomorrow's Great Council had already begun. These are older men, chewing their moustaches, women twisting their plaits with angry fingers. What can they do? Do Aidan and Melwas imagine their elders do not want to fight? This is our land, our home, our past, our future.

What will be left of it, if we fight? What will be left of us? Will we have a future?

What can our future be, if we do not fight?

Beath has got Idwal by the elbow. I cannot hear what she is asking. But Celynen is behind me. His voice makes me turn. There is something protective about the druid's tall form standing over me, his part-shaved brow stooped forward, the long silvered hair flowing free down his back.

'Cairenn?'

'We're looking for Melwas, Beath and I. Have you seen him?'

'What you are afraid of has indeed happened. He came to Idwal, carrying a razor, a bowl and a towel.' He smiles at me thinly. 'The third pillar in the hall bears the marks of that razor blade. Idwal has a good arm.'

'Idwal didn't shave him?'

'Melwas is still a child. But a hurt child now. It was the lack of a razor blade that cut him. He ran away.'

I stare helplessly. 'And he hasn't come back?'

'So you tell me.'

'But ... Father will be coming tomorrow for the Great Council. He'll expect to find us both here.'

'Then Idwal will have more wounds than one to carry. I think his own son will not be there.'

'But Idwal's responsible for Melwas. He's his foster father.'

'Idwal Goldenshield is responsible for the whole tribe, if what I fear has happened, and the High Dun of Dumnon has gone down in the east.'

There is pain in his eyes for more than Melwas. But I cannot stop myself.

'We've got to find him. We've got to get him back before Father comes.'

I am responsible, too. I am his elder sister. I am an adult, even without the ceremony. The torque round my neck says so. Beath gave me what Idwal would not give Melwas.

Celynen's grey eyes are unfathomably sad. 'There is a kind of freedom, for those who are about to lose their freedom. The freedom to rebel against all they say they want to defend. Tribe, family, custom, law. Melwas has gone to seek his manhood from someone else.'

'From Aidan?'

'Perhaps.'

'But where is Aidan?'

The druid shrugs. 'East of here. West of the Romans. And the gap between us is closing.'

*'But what if Melwas doesn't find Aidan? Anything could happen. There are wild beasts in the Forest.'*

*'Anything could happen to us if we stay in this dun. There is no certainty any more.'*

*'Aren't you worried about him?'*

*'Of course. And about you. About all of us.'*

*'What can we do? The sun's going down.'*

*There is a long silence. Celynen's silences are unquiet. Winds of the Otherworld are raging through him. We wait for the whisper of wisdom that finally creeps through his lips. It comes at last, as though forced out against his will.*

*'Tomorrow, when the Great Council is gathered, I shall sacrifice the white colt.'*

*I hear the words, but cannot understand them. There seems too great a gap between the question I have asked and his answer. What has Melwas, heartbroken and alone in the Forest, to do with the Great Council and the sacrifice of the white colt?*

Sacrifice the colt?

*At last the words penetrate to my very core. I am staring up at Celynen. My face must look aghast. The white colt, not one year old, that runs free and has never known saddle or halter. The foal of the Mare. The spirit of the tribe. The pure, unblemished Son.*

*Celynen is going to sacrifice the Colt.*

# CHAPTER 6

## THE SHEARING

The voice was pure silver, with laughter running under it, cool as a stream in springtime. Melwas turned. A woman was coming towards him, tall and spear-straight over the grass. The voice was young and her red hair flowed loose down to her waist like a girl's, but it was streaked with grey and the brightness of youth had gone from it. Yet still she carried herself with a proud grace, as though she were so used to admiration that she made men believe she held her beauty still. Her dress was blue, shimmering with silver embroidery. In one hand she held a honey-cake, and in the other a gold-tipped drinking-horn.

Melwas stared at her and licked his dry lips. She had called him *Melwas Mighty-Heart*. Who was she, who knew not only his name but even his secret dreams?

She was laughing as she came.

'The evening star hangs on the horns of the moon. Soon the Wild Hunt will ride the sky. It is late for a little foxcub to be so far from his earth.'

'I couldn't help it. I was chased by the Romans. They're here! At the Silent Fort! They chased me into the wood.'

His tone was pleading, begging her to excuse him for being here.

'I know it!' Her mood changed. She almost spat the words. Then she quietened and looked at him long and thoughtfully. Her eyes travelled past him to the pillar of heads.

'So. You went seeking a sword, and the way has led you to our Lords, our Ladies.' Her grey eyes were fixed intently on the pillar behind him. Slowly Melwas felt himself impelled to turn and face it, too. Those dark, unfathomable eyes gazed back at him unwaveringly. They seemed to be waiting for him. Hesitantly he took a step forward. The blood began to quicken in his pulse. He was aware of Seiriol close behind him. Her right hand touched his, pressed something into it. He found himself grasping the horn of wine. Then his left hand, and the rough stickiness of a barley-cake mixed with honey.

'We are hungry.' Her voice breathed softly in his ear.

Melwas looked down at the food in his hands. The pillar was very close to him. Even without looking he could feel those eyes gazing down at him. But his own eyes were trapped by that awful twelfth head, staring upwards with a dark despair.

The grove was silent. Melwas lifted his head. High over-head the sky was turning grey and the stars sparkled more brightly. He let his eyes come slowly downwards past all those shadowed heads until they rested once more upon the twelfth. Slowly still, as if in a dream, he stretched out his left hand. The barley-cake began to crumble between his fingers. Fragments dropped, one by one, into the black pit at his feet. His right hand began to move. Then, with a sudden jerk, he swung the horn forward. The wine arched through the air and splashed into the pillar, staining its dark wood darker still. He watched it trickle slowly downwards over that mouthless head, over the dry ground and on into the hole.

The last drops had ceased to run. Still his left hand felt sticky. He lifted it to his mouth and solemnly licked it clean of crumbs.

Behind him, Seiriol laughed once more, very softly.

'It was well done, little foxcub. It was well done. I think they shall drink redder wine yet at your hand.'

Melwas remembered all at once how tired he was. He looked round for Crab, and found him just inside the gateway, still sniffing suspiciously. But before he had time to whistle, Seiriol had snapped her fingers. At once, Crab came trotting over to her knee. She knelt down to fondle him. Then she ran her hand appraisingly along his slender body, and there was a gleam in her grey eyes that pierced Melwas with a sharp, unreasoning fear.

'Crab!' he cried out in a sudden, high voice.

The little dog turned and sprang up at him, wagging his tail, and Melwas rubbed his ears in a burst of jealous affection.

Seiriol became suddenly brisk and practical.

'Now it is time to eat and rest. Come with me.'

She led him across the enclosure to the smallest of the three huts. It had a stout door hung upon iron hinges. Seiriol pulled this open and motioned him in.

'Sit down. I will send you food.'

The hut was dark. Melwas felt about and found a mound of hay, clean and sweet-smelling. He lowered himself on to it. Almost immediately his eyes began to close.

The doorway darkened again. A serving-woman Melwas had not seen before came in. She was carrying a bowl of stew, fragrant with herbs. Melwas put it to his lips and sucked hungrily at the food. When the dish was half empty he fished out some morsels of meat and offered them to Crab. But he found that the whippet was already gnawing contentedly on a bone the woman must have given him. Melwas ate the meat himself.

As he licked the last drops of gravy, his fingers began to be aware of the texture of the bowl. This was no common thing of wood, but polished metal, with a richly beaded decoration round the rim. He turned it in his hands, wondering how such a thing came to be here in the heart of the wood, with a pair of women and the pigs and those strange carved pillars out there in the darkness.

'Who is Seiriol, Crab? Where are we?'

Without warning, Seiriol herself appeared in the doorway, her silhouette looming larger against the shadowed background.

'Sleep soundly, my foxcub.'

She threw him a bed-covering. The heavy door shut upon him. The darkness intensified.

Melwas reached out and felt for the covering. His fingers sank into deep, soft fur. Wonderingly, he explored the great size of it. It could be nothing else but the huge, dark skin of a bear. He would lie soft tonight.

But it was too much effort to think. All he wanted to do now was to sleep. With Crab nestled against his stomach, he pulled the bearskin up around them both and closed his eyes. For a moment he knew an ache of longing for the Forest Fort, for the empty space in the hay beside Coel, for the familiar snores of Idwal's warriors all around him. And then he was asleep.

He was awakened out of his first sleep by the sound of voices and a burst of laughter. He sat up quickly. That heart-warming, reckless laughter! He would have known it anywhere.

'Aidan!'

He threw off the bearskin and ran to the door. He tugged at the latch to open it. It did not move. Thinking it must be jammed, he pulled harder. Still it would not budge. He put his shoulder against it and tried thrusting it outwards. But nothing that he could do would shift it. It was securely barred.

There was another peal of laughter outside. Melwas shouted at the top of his voice:

'Aidan! Aidan! It's me, Melwas! Let me out!'

The voices ceased at once. He thought he heard Seiriol hushing them. Then came the muffled sound of people moving away across the grove.

'Aidan!'

No one answered. Melwas felt his heart sink with disappointment. He stood in the darkness, uncertain what to do next. If he really wanted to, he could tear a hole in the wattle of the hut and force his way out. But he was not sure that he would dare to do that. This hut lay within the circle of the high fence. It was all one with the sacred oaks and the pillar of heads. No one lightly damaged a druid sanctuary.

He felt his way back to the bed and crept under the bearskin with his arms tight around Crab for consolation.

*This is the morning I have longed for, and now dread. When my father will come from the Red Deer Fort in the west and acknowledge me as his daughter, full-grown. When he should have taken me from the hand of Beath, my foster-mother, and handed me back as a betrothed woman to Aidan, her son.*

*Now I have lost everything, before we have even seen a Roman.*

*I have lost Aidan. I have lost Melwas, and my father is coming.*

*I do not want him to see me. I have taken off the torque that made everyone stare at me, and hidden it in my chest in the hut where the girls sleep. I try to hide among the other young women, to busy myself with domestic necessities. The dun is full. There is much to do before the Council.*

*And still they come. The hill is steep from the river crossing. I know they walk their mounts and their chariot teams up through the trees. But when they break out of the leaves then their heels are drumming the horses' sides, the goads are pricking the ponies' flanks. The horsemen come storming up the cleared space, as though they would charge down our palisade under their hooves. The chariots bowl and bounce on the uneven ground, lucky not to lose a wheel. We are a proud people. We will make a show and a sport of this Council, even as we face defeat.*

*Will they really not fight? Can Celynen convince them?*

*Somewhere in the Forest, or beyond, is a small brave band of young men who will never surrender.*

*And tears fall with the bitter herbs into the brew I am stirring. Tiny bubbles begin to rise and glint on the surface. The steam thickens. The dark mirror is heaving. I feel my nostrils prickle and my throat smart, but I will not pull back. Beath and Celynen have given me instructions for this. It is an honour that they trust me. Stir on, and add the slow handfuls of powdery leaves. The steam envelops me. It is soothing. I want to weep still, but now it is as if I grieve for something already over, settled, irreversible. Is this how we shall all feel when we drink from it, that there is nothing we can do, our fate is sealed? Is this what Celynen plans? Am I his tool? And still I stir, slow, rhythmic, chanting the secret words Beath has taught me.*

*'Cairenn.'*

*It is Beath herself. Why did she not send a slave, when she is so busy?*

*'Your father is here. I'll finish that.'*

*'It's done.' The bronze bowl beside me is empty. I heave the cauldron sideways, settling it among the ashes to simmer.*

*I turn to face her. 'Has Idwal told him?'*

*'I did it.' For all the plump softness of her face, Beath is no coward. 'Idwal has problems enough.'*

*I want to ask her how my father has taken it, the loss of his child, his son. Her face tells me nothing. I must be like her. I am a woman now. I straighten my long red tunic, brush the powder of crumbled herbs from it, put up my hand to touch my hair. I wish I had put on the torque. I will wear it for the sacrifice.*

'You look beautiful.' The immeasurable sadness in her voice tells me how much she wanted me for a daughter. I move impulsively to hug and kiss her.

Then I am outside and stepping quickly through the crowd, willing them to part before me. Head high, proud as any of them. A princess of Dumnon.

He is there. A shorter man than I remembered, and older. Idwal is beside him. I cross the last space and make my reverence. Then he is raising me to my feet and gripping me strongly. His embrace tells me this is a man whose life has been warfare, cattle-raiding and skirmishes, hunting and horse-racing. His muscles know nothing else. What will men like him do under the Romans? Will they take our weapons away?

What weapons does Melwas have?

We separate now, and look into each other's eyes. Can neither of us acknowledge what is tearing us apart?

'I'm sorry. I'll find him. I'll get him back,' I say, blindly, foolishly. Words that make no sense.

'The boy has courage.' He gulps back a sob.

But we are swept up in something greater than personal grief. The tide is surging to the great hall for the Council. I realize I am not, in law, a woman yet. The ceremonies have not been performed. I must wait outside.

I turn away and see what I never would have wished to. Celynen has had a corral made on the other side of the dun. The fence looks small to me. Surely our treasure could soar over it and go galloping free? But he stands, innocent of his fate, exquisitely vulnerable, leaning his long pale nose over the roped stakes. The Son of the tribe. The White Colt.

I move on dreaming feet, the steam of the cauldron still clouding my brain. His eyes are huge, luminously brown. He trusts me. No one has ever laid a restraint upon him. My hand caresses the side of his face. This white hide feels rougher than the grey fur of Melwas's whippet. There is power here, as well *as delicacy. I fold my arms around his neck and he nuzzles my shoulder. If he could understand me, would I tell him what is going to happen to him?*

*'Save us,' I whisper. 'You can, can't you?'*

*His breath is roaring in my ears.*

*Suddenly he leaps from my hold, bruisingly. Flinging up his glorious head so that the mane flies white against the bright blue sky. He is cantering now, bucking, galloping. He is free, he is alive, he is wonderful.*

*The corral is small. A few bounds brings him back to me. And still he gallops, round and round, as though he cannot believe his world has contracted to this tight space.*

*His life cut short to a single year.*

When he woke again it was broad daylight. He rubbed his eyes. The door stood slightly ajar. Melwas hurried over to it. It swung freely at his touch. He ran his eyes around the enclosure, longing to see the flash of Aidan's red hair, or one of the young warriors who followed him everywhere. He was disappointed. The oak grove was almost empty. Only Seiriol was there, carrying a bucket across the grass.

She looked older in the light of morning. The weight of the bucket dragged her sideways so that her tall form appeared shortened. Under the cloudy sky her hair showed more grey than red.

Melwas stepped outside the hut. He was still more than a little afraid of her. He called out, 'Good morning.'

She passed him by. At the foot of the pillar she poured milk, muttering words he could not hear. He followed her at a little distance as she went towards the largest hut. Before he could reach it, she came out again quickly and shut the door firmly behind her. She leaned against it, and now she was drawn up tall and straight again, lifting her head like a young woman and smiling at him.

'Well, Melwas Mighty-Heart?'

'Last night? Aidan was here, wasn't he?'

She lifted her eyebrows and her smile widened, but she said nothing.

'Where is he now? I need to find him.'

Still she did not answer.

'Please, tell me if you know. I can't waste time. I've got to get back to the Forest Fort as fast as I can and tell them that the Romans have invaded us!'

Now her face split into a scornful laugh which had no warmth.

'So you want to run back to the Forest Fort, do you? Back to the skirts of your fat foster-mother? Back to that white-livered old fool who calls himself High Druid? What would you do in the dun of cowards?'

'But my news! The Romans are *here*!'

'And do you think they won't have heard that by now? Do you think they didn't know weeks ago that the High Dun of the Ridgeway would surrender? Why do you think Idwal Goldenshield has waited till now to call his Council, if he really meant to fight?'

Melwas lowered his head. It was true. He had known all along that it must be so, but he could not bear to admit it till now.

Seiriol's voice came down to him more softly, comforting him.

'No, little Mighty-Heart. There is no hope for you back there. But Dumnon needs you. While such as you and Aidan live, the old spirit will not be conquered . . . . Let me test what metal you are made of.'

Melwas glowed with pride that she should rank him with Aidan, the Red Fox of the Forest. He watched her go into the third hut, whose door he had never seen opened. When she came out he gasped. She carried in her arms a treasure-hoard of weapons fit for a king. Behind her, her woman carried a second set.

Now Seiriol was holding out to him a wooden shield, stout enough for battle, yet bound in bronze and studded richly with red and blue enamel. Next, a long iron sword in a scabbard laced with twining patterns of gold. Lastly, a long casting-spear. Her fingers buckled the bronze-plated sword-belt at his waist, and he slipped his arm through the leather thong of the shield.

As he took the weight of the shield upon his arm and hefted the spear in his hand, he could feel them changing him. No longer was he a twelve-year-old boy. Bearing such noble weapons he could believe himself a grown man, a hero, a prince. He felt his blood beating high with excitement and the breath coming fast to his lips. Before his eyes there flashed a dream, glorious and dangerous. He was charging into battle with spear upraised. His enemies were falling about him at every stroke of his sword. Yet still he rushed on, unable to stop himself . . . .

Seiriol looked into his shining eyes and a light began to blaze in her own face, too.

'So!' she whispered. 'Let us begin!'

She took from her woman a mighty spear and a sword so long she could rest the point of it upon the ground without leaning. She girded herself for battle, throwing back one sleeve of her blue and silver gown. Melwas saw for the first time the great white scar that scored her arm from shoulder to wrist. He stared at it with respect and wonder. Not even Bearrach Horse-Thief could boast such a battle-scar as that.

'Throw!' she commanded.

He sent the spear hurtling from his arm. Her own went streaking after it, whistling under the leaves of the oak trees twice as far. The pigs went squealing in fright out of the gate. He tried a second time. Again hers shot beyond, to the wicker fence of the grove.

All through the long morning she worked him, in the weirdest weapon-practice of his life. One after the other they

81

cast spears and swung their great swords and parried with shields which seemed too extravagantly rich for such brutal work. With every stroke and every throw Melwas realized how much was being asked of him. Gradually, painfully, his arm steadied, his nerve tightened and his whole being became concentrated on showing her the best that he could do. Never had he fought like this. As the hours passed he grew amazed at his own strength and skill and endurance. He had not believed that he was capable of anything remotely like this.

After each new effort he rested his aching limbs and saw with despair how Seiriol far outstripped the best that he could do. He watched her with awe. He was used to seeing Tegan, laughing and bold on the weapon-field, wielding a sword with lusty enjoyment. But this was utterly different. Seiriol fought the empty air like a woman possessed. With every stroke she grew in power and frenzy. Her two hands gripped the huge sword and whirled it above her head, higher and higher, faster and faster.

The sun stood high at midday. Seiriol lowered the point of her great sword to the ground and leaned on it, panting. Sweat ran down the wrinkles of her face and her grizzled red hair fell forward.

'It was good, Mighty-Heart. It was good,' she managed to say.

It seemed to Melwas that her voice came from a long way off. He saw the clear day darken in spots before his eyes. He longed to sink down on the grass and rest his spent body. He could not remember ever having felt so drained of energy. But Seiriol had not finished with him yet.

'Give me your sword,' she commanded.

He handed it to her. She took it back with her own into the hut from which she had brought the weapons. Her woman, who had been watching cross-legged, followed her. He heard the sound of iron being sharpened against stone.

Soon Seiriol came back, carrying their swords. Her servant had an armful of hazel wands. Some of these she set upright in the soft turf. When she had finished, two straight rows made an avenue that led from Melwas to the strange carved pillar at the centre of the grove. Seiriol handed him his sword and stepped back.

'Now,' she said. 'Let us see what a shearing you will make upon the heads of your enemies!'

Dumbly, Melwas grasped the sword. His arm felt impossibly weak. He did not think his wrists could even raise the weapon now, let alone strike. But Seiriol was staring at him. He saw the light begin to blaze in her fierce grey eyes and the breath rise faster to her lips. He felt his hands tighten involuntarily about the hilt.

'Now!' she shrieked.

Her voice impelled him forward. He ran. Right! Left! Up. Down. With sweeping, chopping movements the hazel rods fell, clean-cut at each blow, like ranks of headless warriors. His sword swung on and on.

He had reached the end of the row. The pillar stood before him. He could feel the dark faces staring down at him. His strengthless wrists lowered the sword to the ground and he bowed his head. He was too tired to feel truly afraid.

Seiriol was beside him.

'Now,' she said softly. 'It is my turn. Stand you here.'

She set him before the pillar. The serving-woman made a circle of fresh hazel wands around them both, there on the grass between the sacred oaks. When all was ready Seiriol picked up her sword and raised it high. Melwas thought it was him she was saluting. Then he remembered the twelve mouthless heads at his back.

'Keep . . . very . . . still.'

Flash! He blinked as her blade swept through the air, severing a hazel rod. Flash! Another fell. Faster and faster. And at each stroke she spun around so that the grove was full of whirling blue and silver edged with a glittering band of iron. Faster and faster, flying rods, streaming hair, whirling sword . . . . The headless circle was almost complete. The last wand snapped. With a wild scream Seiriol flew at Melwas, seizing him by the hair.

His neck was jerked backwards, choking off his cry, as the blade flashed down past his eyes.

Seiriol stepped back, holding aloft her trophy. A thick red stain dripped from between her hands. Through a hundred pounding heartbeats Melwas could not make himself realize that the stain on her hands was his red hair and not his life-blood. She dangled the bright locks before his eyes with joyful laughter.

'See, Melwas Mighty-Heart! You have had a shearing to remember, have you not?'

He nodded weakly. He could not trust himself to speak.

Her eyes sharpened. 'What's that you're wearing?'

He did not understand at first what she meant. Her hand reached out and grasped the pendant round his neck. He wanted to stop her, but he did not dare. She peered at the signs stamped on it, in the dappled sunlight.

'Do you know what these marks mean?'

'No. I took it from that Roman. A trophy.'

'Romans!' She flung it back against his breastbone.

His hand flew to the pendant, just as the dying Roman had reached for it. It felt oddly like a protection.

She took the sword from his unresisting hand.

'Come with me.'

She led him towards her own hut. This morning he would have been curious to see what lay inside. Now, he was too weary even to turn his head to look, though he could not help noticing the gleam of skulls around the walls.

Obeying her instructions, he knelt in the shadowed circle. The servant held a bowl and a towel. Seiriol picked up a razor. She bent over him and went through the motions of shaving his chin, though there was nothing on it but down. Then she turned to her woman and dipped her hand into the bowl. When she lifted it out, it was dripping with a sticky white paste. She began to massage it into his hair, which was now shorn off above the shoulders. As she worked, he felt the light softness he was used to grow stiff and caked. When his whole head was saturated with the stuff she took a golden comb and began to draw it through his hair, so that it stood out from his head in a stiff mane. He winced as she dragged the comb through the clotted strands. Then her fingers went to work again, squeezing the tip of each lock into a sharp point. Melwas could feel the stuff already growing dry and hard. At last Seiriol sat back on her heels and studied him. She nodded with satisfaction.

She raised him by the hand and led him out into the sunshine. The serving-woman followed with a mirror of polished bronze, which Seiriol handed to Melwas.

'Now you are indeed a warrior. See for yourself.'

Melwas took the mirror and looked into its cloudy surface. The face that stared back at him was gaunt with weariness. Around the head the spiky hair stood back in hedgehog points, all caked and white with lime towards the tips, but still showing red around the roots. It was a sight to terrify an enemy.

Melwas looked long at it.

'That's me,' he thought. But it did not make any sense. He did not know this fierce, proud warrior.

Seiriol's servant was ready with the studded shield, the heavy sword and spear. The druid held them up in front of Melwas.

'These are yours now. The weapons of your manhood,' she said. 'I will bring them to you when you need them. And that will be very soon.'

Dumbly, Melwas touched the weapons, owning them his, and let her take them back. She had made him a man. It was over. He understood that she was dismissing him, that it was time for him to go. But where? And whose man was he? He opened his mouth to ask. But a noise from the wood made them both lift their heads and listen.

It was the sound of singing. A boy's voice, unnecessarily loud, and quavering at the end of each phrase. The song drew nearer, and broke off abruptly. Slow, stealthy footsteps approached the gate. Melwas recognized that feeling with a rush of sympathy. How often had he himself broken into loud singing in some strange place to scare away the sense of evil lurking all around him? And he, too, had stopped short like that, suddenly afraid that his noise would draw down upon himself the very powers he sought to ward away.

The footsteps stopped by the gate. There was a rustling in the grass. Now the steps were hurrying away. A little farther off the singing began again, more cheerfully now, as though the singer were glad to be hastening homeward.

Seiriol seized Melwas by the arm and hurried him to the gate. He had just time to glimpse a fine salmon wrapped in dock leaves lying in the grass, and a loaf of barley bread beside it.

'Hu!' she called down the path, in the high, silvery voice that had first greeted Melwas.

Quick as a twisting fish, she pushed Melwas out through the gate and slipped back behind the fence.

The song choked to a halt. The boy turned, very slowly, as if afraid to look behind him. When he saw only Melwas standing there, he gave a start of surprise. His face relaxed into a grin, quickly suppressed. He touched his forehead. Melwas stood by the gate staring back at him, unsure what to do next.

Hu seemed to be waiting for him to move first. He was shorter than Melwas, with black hair, and he wore the rough, brown kilt of a peasant. Melwas walked slowly down the path towards him. This boy looked only a little younger than himself, but suddenly Melwas was conscious of how different he must now appear to Hu. He was a high-born chieftain's son, and from today he boasted the proud hairstyle of a British hero. He was an initiated warrior. Only he wished the druid had let him keep his sword. He wished she could have granted him a moustache. He wished he was a little taller, and Crab a wolfhound.

If Hu had any doubts about this small new warrior, they did not show. As he watched Melwas approach, his nut-brown face creased into a wide grin again.

'Another one!' he cried. 'Come on! I'll take you where there's a fine welcome ready for you.'

With a summons of his hand, he set off at a trot down the woodland path.

# CHAPTER 7

## REBELS

Hu's way lay down a narrow trail so lightly beaten that Melwas might have mistaken it for a deer-run. They walked in silence, though Hu looked round from time to time with a quick, encouraging smile. Melwas smiled back, feeling an eager bond of shared adventure, the promise of secrets to which he would soon be admitted. He wondered where Hu was taking him.

Suddenly he stopped. Crab! His heart seemed to drop sickeningly into his bowels. How could he have come this far without one thought for the slender grey dog that always ran at his heel? And now that he thought about it, where had Crab been all that strange morning? Melwas was seized with a nameless terror at the idea of his whippet left alone in that brooding grove. He remembered with panic the gleam in Seiriol's eye as she ran her hands along Crab's body, and the black hole before the twelve carved heads that had no mouths and yet were so insatiably hungry.

He shouted desperately, as loud as he could:

'Crab! Crab!'

His cry echoed back to him from the silent oak wood. Hu turned, curious and alert. Melwas gave a piercing whistle. He repeated it again and again. High overhead, a startled blackbird burst into a torrent of defiant song. The two boys waited. There were faint stirrings and rustlings in the undergrowth. Nothing more.

In an agony of fear, Melwas was about to whistle again when Hu caught his arm.

'Listen!'

Melwas strained his ears, afraid to hope too much. But Hu was right. He heard a distant snapping of twigs which came rapidly nearer. Then, out from a clump of ferns raced Crab. His tail wagged furiously and his thin paws scrabbled wildly as he jumped up at his master. Melwas hugged him in delight, while Hu grinned at them both with understanding.

'That's a fine dog,' he said.

'The best in the world.'

'Then you were right not to leave him behind with that one.' He jerked his head back in the direction of Seiriol's grove, and his eyes were clouded. 'I wouldn't trust her — though it scares me even to say it. I wish I didn't have to go near her. But we've no choice. She lives so close, it would be more dangerous to stay away. If we didn't feed her, she'd turn the ewes' milk sour, and blight the barley, and put a curse on every salmon in the river so that we'd never catch one.'

'I'm glad to be away from there,' Melwas agreed. But he felt uneasy saying it. For had not Seiriol given him the things he wanted most in all the world?

The two boys went quietly on their way, with Crab running eagerly in and out of the undergrowth on either side of them. Presently, the little trail opened on to a broader path that led downhill. And now Melwas could hear the sound of running water close beside them.

A little way down this track, Hu suddenly halted. Behind him, Melwas too was instantly still, laying a restraining hand on Crab's neck. From somewhere to their right, a branch had cracked loudly, followed by the angry scolding of a chaffinch. The boys listened, holding their breath. There was no further sound, but they could both feel a prickling sensation as though unseen eyes were watching them. Hu looked uneasily at Melwas. The older boy took his hand from Crab's neck.

'Go. Seek,' he urged.

Crab bounded away through the trees. He was soon lost to sight, but they could still hear him scuffling among the leaves. Then silence. Anxiously, the boys looked at each other. Melwas was just about to go after Crab when the little grey dog came trotting back. He licked Melwas's hand in passing and padded on down the path, sniffing about him as though nothing had happened.

Hu frowned after him. 'Would he have barked if he'd found someone?'

'Well, yes, I think so. He would if it was a stranger.'

'It's not likely to be a friend who skulks in hiding.'

They knew that neither of them was reassured, but there seemed nothing for it but to go on. Only Crab seemed unconcerned. Melwas was still listening intently as he walked, and Hu kept glancing suspiciously into the leafy shadows and sniffing the air as though he scented danger. But they heard nothing more.

It was a long walk before the trees thinned out at the head of the valley. A brook rushed downwards, singing over its pebbled bed. On its grassy banks grew scattered rowan trees. Beside this brook, where the ground levelled briefly, was a cluster of small huts, bent branches mounded over with turf. From them, smoke was going up into the evening air. Up the steep slope came the murmurous bleat of sheep being folded for the night. Melwas looked beyond into the pale blue distance and glimpsed the silver reaches of the Salmon River, with dark spots at its edge that might be fishing coracles. This was a poorer place by far than the dun of Idwal Goldenshield, and yet it had a feel of home.

'This is my village,' said Hu proudly. 'Welcome. Tonight you will be our guest.'

He led Melwas towards one of the turf hovels. There were children of all sizes, women preparing food, and a group of men squatting beside the fire. As Melwas approached, they rose and touched their foreheads respectfully. The women were grilling fish, and the smell made his mouth water.

Then he heard men's voices raised loud and laughing on the other side of the village. He walked on faster towards the brook and came out from between the rowan trees. He saw the men clearly now, and his heart leaped with gladness. These were warriors, like himself, some twenty of them, supping on bread and fish. He ran eagerly over the grass towards them, his face stretched in a smile.

The men turned curiously at his approach. Joyfully he recognized Elaeth, Aidan's closest friend, sitting with his back to a slender tree-trunk. Elaeth stared back at Melwas as though searching his memory for some lost recollection. At last he dropped his knife and broke into uproarious laughter.

'It's the foxcub! Just look at him! What's a baby doing here, with hair like a warrior come to manhood?'

The boy stopped, trying to swallow his hurt pride. He stood looking carefully around the group of dauntingly full-grown men. Most of the faces he knew, the young men of Idwal's dun who always followed where Aidan led. He recognized also three who had been among Rieuk's Armoricans who had come to Idwal's hall. He turned back anxiously to Elaeth.

'Where's Aidan? Isn't he with you?' he managed to say.

Now the men were crowding round him, clapping him on the shoulder, drawing him into their circle and offering him food to eat. Elaeth, with his mouth full, pointed down the stream.

'There. He's coming.'

Melwas went forward, slowly and softly over the wet turf, to greet his foster-brother, drawing himself up as tall and manly as he could. Aidan had just straightened from washing his face in the brook. He shook himself, and drops of glistening water flew from his face and arms. His red hair stood out around his face like tongues of flame. He had dressed himself in his finest gear, as though for a festival. A gold torque encircled his neck, there was more gold about his strongly muscled arms, and round his waist he wore a sword-belt enamelled in a blue as bright as his eyes. Women paused in their cooking to look at him as he passed, and he flashed his warm, brilliant smile at them all. As he strode nearer, his eye fell on Melwas. He frowned in puzzlement. Then a burst of laughter set the valley sides ringing with echoes.

'Melwas! By all the gods! So Seiriol's made a man of you at last!'

A friendly blow on the back sent Melwas staggering. Then, clasping him warmly about the shoulders, he led the boy into the circle of his friends.

'See what luck this day has brought us? The Romans should tremble now, when even the cubs come running from their dens to fight beside the dog fox. Dumnon will never go down into slavery while there's spirit like this in the hearts of her youngest sons.'

Melwas looked up at his foster-brother, feeling his own face hot with pride and admiration. He crouched down on the grass beside Aidan and burst out eagerly,

'Did you hear my news? The Romans are in Dumnon! The High Dun of the Ridgeway has fallen. Idwal's sent out messengers to call a Council at the Forest Fort! You should be there. If you're missing, who's going to stir the old ones to war? They're all cowards. You must go back, Aidan. Tell Idwal Goldenshield he's got to fight!'

'Idwal!' Aidan snapped a dead twig between his fingers and hurled the pieces from him. 'My father's no true chieftain. It's Celynen the Druid who rules at the Forest Fort. If he says surrender, then that's what my father will do. Rieuk warned me how it would be. We haven't got time to wait for their Council. If we're to stop the Romans, it must be now, before ever they reach the Salmon River!'

He lifted his head, and his blue eyes were shining.

'We'll fight them, brothers, won't we? No Roman shall pass here while there's a drop of red blood left in our veins.'

'Never! Never!' yelled back his warriors.

Melwas blazed with excitement.

'Then you're not going to wait for the Council? We're going to fight them? Tomorrow?'

Aidan swung round laughing. 'Listen to the cub! He can't wait to taste enemy blood. But where's your sword, little warrior? Are you going to march against the Roman eagles with only a dagger in your belt?'

'Seiriol's keeping my weapons. She said she'd bring them to me when the time came.'

'Aye . . . Seiriol.' Aidan gave a quick shudder. 'War makes strange allies. But I tell you this: there's ten times more courage in her than in the cool heart of Celynen, or in my father and those grey fools round him. There's no fire in any of them for battle, or for life itself. But Seiriol is all fire and fury. She may be a woman and a druid, but she can wield a sword from sunrise to sunset and still give back stroke for stroke with any man.'

'I know,' said Melwas fervently.

Aidan's smile was swift with understanding.

'Aye, little brother. It was no light thing to be alone with Seiriol under the sacred oaks. And hear this,' he added earnestly, 'you must have shown courage too, or you wouldn't be standing here with us today. If you'd given her the slightest cause to believe otherwise, she'd have had your head from your shoulders there and then, and your life-blood poured out before the heads of the dark gods.'

Melwas felt himself go white. His hand flew to his throat. He remembered crying out in fear as her sword swept past his eyes. Yet Seiriol had spared him. Had there been others before him who had not stood their ground so well? Had that sword edge been red with more than hair?

The hand at his throat felt cool metal. It took him a second to remember what it was. He had knotted that Roman soldier's broken chain and hung it round his own neck. He thrust it out to Aidan.

'Look! I took this from a Roman soldier. At the Silent Fort. Someone had cut his throat!'

There was a moment's silence among the men, then a bark of coarse laughter.

Aidan's eyes danced. 'Aye, brother. That was a close thing. But it was first blood to us.'

'It was you . . . ?'

Aidan laughed louder and clapped Melwas on the shoulder. 'Cheer up, foxcub! Don't look so startled. You were very useful yesterday, you and the girl. Elaeth and I ambushed their scout, but then we saw six of his friends coming. We'd have given them a hot time, mind you. Only you happened along and led them nicely off the scent.'

Melwas stared back. He remembered the spear darting behind Tegan, the terror of his own heart as he pounded into the wood. Aidan had been there, among the trees, watching it all?

'But Tegan . . . What happened? Did she get away?'

Aidan shrugged. 'We didn't see her body. Don't look like that. Tegan Mare's-Daughter could outrun the whole Roman army.'

Melwas hoped it was true.

Proudly, at Aidan's invitation, he sat down with the men. Hu fetched more fish and hot bread. He seemed pleased to be entertaining such princely guests in his village. Melwas fell upon the food, burning his fingers on the crisp, charred fish skin. It was very good. A little girl came, carrying sweet ewe's milk in a wooden bowl for him. Her hair was black and her brown face crinkled into a smile like Hu's.

'Does Crab like fish-heads? I've saved some for him.' She

clicked her fingers at the whippet. Crab bounded up and wolfed her offering.

'You've made a friend there, Garwen,' grinned Hu.

The little girl went off to Hu's family hut. As she passed, Melwas saw her reach out her hand to Crab, who wagged his tail and stretched his nose closer for her to stroke. Suddenly she looked up and saw Melwas watching her. Her hand darted back. She looked as though she was afraid he might be angry. He smiled at her reassuringly.

Hu followed her more slowly. He kept looking over his shoulder, as if he wished he could stay with the warriors. The brother and sister stooped through the doorway under the low roof, and disappeared into the smoky interior. Older family members crowded after them. After the great hall of Idwal's fort, it looked to Melwas a very small hut to hold so many people. One was the woman who had cooked the fish for him. Peasant though she was, a strong brown woman with hard hands, she reminded him of his foster-mother Beath.

The warriors were preparing to sleep on sheepskins spread under the hawthorn trees. Shyly, Melwas copied them. He had fled the Forest Fort so suddenly that he had no chequered cloak to roll himself in, but he settled among them, close to his neighbour for warmth. Drowsy with the smoke, and the smell of close-packed bodies, and the day's exhaustion, he felt his eyes closing before the last light had drained from the summer sky.

Fleas jumped from the sheepskin, but Melwas was used to that. It was so good to be back among his people again, even without a roof over his head. Still, the stiff, lime-washed hair was uncomfortable to sleep on. He wanted to run his fingers through it and loosen the spikes, but pride would not let him. He was a man now. Seiriol had made him a warrior. He would suffer any discomfort for that. Now everywhere he went people would acknowledge him as full-grown.

And the Romans? They, too, would have to recognize him

as a man when they met him face to face, sword to sword, on the field of battle. He closed his eyes with dreams of glory crowding through his mind.

He woke early next day to find the village astir and bustling. For a few moments he lay still, wondering where he was. Then, as he saw the man next to him rubbing the sleep from his eyes, joyful remembrance flooded back. He sprang up, unable to contain his eagerness to greet the new morning and find out what lay in store for him. All the questions he had been too tired to ask the night before rushed to the surface of his mind. How had Seiriol known he was coming? What was Aidan planning? How soon would the battle begin? He strode out from under the hawthorn boughs into the sunrise.

Dew lay white on the grass, sparkling like hoar-frost. Far below, the Salmon River was hidden beneath a fleece of mist. The distant peaks of hills floated above it, rising like islands from a fairy sea. Melwas breathed deeply of the cool, gorse-scented air. It was the first dawn of his manhood. With the intoxication of danger, he realized that it might also be his last. He did not care. He felt wild, reckless, gloriously happy. He was a man. It was enough, just to live this day, this hour, this moment.

The men breakfasted quickly on bread and cheese. Aidan sprang to his feet.

'Brothers, let's march! Today, at last, you're going to see the enemy warhost with your own eyes!'

Melwas found himself swept up in the band of warriors. No one questioned his right to be with them, his fitness for the coming battle. He was accepted as one of themselves, a warrior, a man among men. He strode past the villagers' huts, crowded with watching faces, with a proud step and a high head. The little children squeezed aside to let them pass, then crowded after them, round-eyed with wonder.

Near the edge of the village they came to the hut where Hu and Garwen had slept. Crab came trotting out, licking his lips. He nudged his nose apologetically into his master's hand as though excusing himself for his absence. Melwas grinned and patted him. 'Hello, old boy. So you found yourself some breakfast?'

He saw Hu's sister watching fondly from the doorway, and guessed who had fed the whippet.

Aidan called out, 'Hu! Are you there?'

The dark-haired boy slipped silently out of the doorway. He smiled expectantly up into Aidan's face as the Red Fox placed a hand on his shoulder.

'You're sure you can guide us to the Romans?'

Hu nodded vigorously. 'I know where they camped last night, and I know the way they must come from there.'

'Then lead on.'

Hu looked past him at Melwas. 'We can't take the dog.'

Melwas stiffened with resentment. 'Of course he's coming. Crab goes everywhere with me. I'm not leaving him behind.'

Hu's eyes were solemn with understanding. 'He'll be all right. Garwen will take good care of him.'

Melwas turned. Hu's sister had come out of the hut behind him. She gave him a shy smile and held out her hand. Crab sniffed it, and licked her fingers.

'Let me look after him for you, sir. Please! He's beautiful.'

The men were watching Melwas, impatient to be on their way.

Aidan spoke. 'He's right, Melwas. This is war. It's no place for a whippet. He'll be safer here.'

Melwas pushed Crab towards Garwen. He felt a pang of remorse, as though he were betraying his oldest friend. He held up his hand.

'Stay, boy,' he commanded.

Crab sat down beside the girl and wagged his tail.

The men set out, up the valley of the brook and into the

wood. Melwas turned and had a last picture of the village, with Hu's sister waving farewell to them, her other hand resting lovingly upon Crab's neck. He wondered if he would ever see them again.

Before long they turned aside from the way Hu and Melwas had come the evening before, and pressed further uphill through the thickets of the wood. Hu led the way, with Aidan close behind him. Melwas followed near the rear, watching the other men, trying to match his stride with theirs, and wondering what was going to happen. He wished he had a weapon.

The men moved quietly, and he could hear other sounds around him – the trickling fall of water, birdsong, the noises of small animals in the undergrowth. Twenty men. Did Aidan really plan to fight the Romans with only this handful? Surely even he was not so foolhardy?

Or was he? Guiltily he smothered this train of thought. Had he not sworn that he would die rather than see Dumnon surrender without a blow struck in her defence, against all odds? If these men trusted Aidan to lead them into danger, then so would he.

In front, Hu had raised his hand in warning. The column halted abruptly. At the same time Melwas heard it, too. That ominous crack of wood, followed by the scuffling flight of startled animals. All the men were listening, peering through the trees, but everything was quiet now.

Aidan frowned. 'Go on, Hu. We've no time to stop.'

'Didn't you hear it, sir? There's something in this wood. Something large, I think. It could be a man.'

'More likely a boar. And we're after a bigger quarry than that.'

Eager to prove his newfound manhood, Melwas stepped forward. 'Let me go and check.'

At Aidan's nod, he glided swiftly through the trees, trying to use all his hunter's skill. It was hard to distinguish anything in the dappled shadows. The corner of his eye caught a flicker of movement. Was that the shape of a man, vanishing behind a tree-trunk? A glimpse of rags and unkempt hair. He sprang after it. But no matter which way he looked, it was lost immediately. He was not even certain he had seen it.

Aidan's voice called from the pathway. 'Melwas! Come back now. It's not important. We're stalking a more fearsome enemy today.'

Melwas turned back. Already the men were starting to push forward. He met Hu's questioning gaze and shrugged his shoulders. Aidan gave the order to march. No one else seemed worried. Only Hu continued to glance uneasily into the shadows beside the path.

They reached the upper limits of the wood, and Melwas saw suddenly that they were close below the ramparts of the Silent Fort. The red walls reared up, motionless and mysterious as ever. Somewhere nearby must be the place where he had burst into the wood in his panic flight from the Roman patrol. Even now there was a catch in his breathing as he scanned the bare hillside. But nothing moved.

They passed the fort and crossed the ridge, down the long slope towards the east. The wild heath was bare of movement, the very emptiness seemed threatening. They moved fast, as men accustomed to hunt the deer on foot, and stealthily too, running from brakes of gorse to clusters of trees, using every fold of the ground for cover. More woods filled the next valley. But as they drew closer, Melwas could not help thinking how they themselves had waited unseen among the trees, scanning the open hillside above. Was someone else waiting in this wood? Soldiers, watching and listening and fingering their swords?

He raced down the last slope, pursuing Hu. He was determined not to be the last, even though he had only a short dagger in his belt. The woods were still about them. No cry of alarm, only the startled ring-doves clattering away. Their footsteps thudded under the trees. They came out on the bank of a swift river and Hu led them to where it could be forded.

On the further bank, Melwas looked back and saw that Aidan had stopped in midstream. The sunlight was bright on his hair and on the rippling water. He fingered his sword as he looked about him with a smile of mischief. Elaeth called to him, and he came running through the shallows to join them, with the golden water splashing up from his boots. So they climbed out of the trees to the ridge beyond and came at last to the gap in the crest.

The sky widened suddenly away to another line of hills in the east. Melwas looked down into the next valley. And as he did so, a groan of dismay and anger broke from all the men around him. The marching-camp of the Roman legion lay spread beneath them in full view.

The beloved red soil of Dumnon had been slashed into the shape of a giant square, the torn earth thrown up in defensive banks. Within the square, brown leather tents stood in regimented ranks, all evenly spaced, all facing the same way, one after the other exactly alike. There were a few larger tents, placed symmetrically near the centre, and longer ones against the walls. Along the lines of grass between, figures moved, indistinguishable as ants. So straight and precise those paths, and meeting always at right-angles. What rivers, what boughs of trees, what tracks of wandering feet would ever meet like that in nature?

Melwas, looking down on the camp, felt his heart grow cold. He had seen the hosting of armies before, when the neighbouring tribe of the Durotriges had threatened the land of Dumnon. But that had been a wild, high-spirited gathering of free warriors, brother with brother, clan by clan, massing together in their hundreds like leaves swept up in a gale. He thought of the ramparts curving round their British

100

duns. Of the huts clustered together in friendly disarray. But this camp was different. It was not like the work of humans at all. It was disciplined; as though one mind had planned it all, and the rest within it were mindless workers. In only one place could he remember such perfect symmetry, the regular pattern repeated over and over again identically, allowing no variation: the bees' nest. And he was suddenly terrified to think how such men might fight, all governed under the sway of one mind, thousands of arms, thousands of swords, all moving as one like some horrific monster.

Aidan was the first to recover himself. He signed to the others and the men moved back behind the shelter of the ridge.

Aidan's face was wildly merry. 'Well, there's our enemy. Less than a day's march from us!'

He strode up to an alder bush and tore thin branches from it. With his hunting-knife he slashed signs upon them and handed them round with a brief word to several of his companions. The men grasped them eagerly, beginning to catch Aidan's excitement. As though they knew already what they must do and had waited long for this moment, they were off, darting swiftly north, south or west. The east of Dumnon had fallen.

Aidan swung back to the others, his face aglow and blue eyes bright with the joy of danger approaching.

'Brothers, our chance is here! Tomorrow the Romans will try to march west. We'll hit them as they ford the river!'

*I do not want to remember. I do not want to see Celynen, always so calm and considered, standing in the centre of that sacred space with his druid knife upraised. To think that it might be only the brew I made which makes it possible for him to do this.*

*No. Celynen is tougher than that. He ordered me to make that brew. He drank it knowingly. Celynen will do whatever he believes necessary to save the tribe.*

*Was this necessary? Can this save us?*

*I do not want to see that pure free spirit bound and led, almost unresisting, into the circle of the tribe. I think they have drugged him, too. But still he shies a little. His head flings back and sideways, so that the white mane flies. So that we see for an instant how glorious and powerful he should have been, he that is the life of Dumnon. The colt that will now never grow to be a stallion.*

*I do not want to remember how I joined my chant with all the others, consenting to this, begging the gods to accept this dearest sacrifice. To see the knife flash suddenly under the grey sky and know that it is going to happen and no one will stop it.*

*The knife plunges, and I must not see the scarlet tide flowing over his breast unstoppably. Spattering the white robes of Celynen. And now the other druids are seizing sprays of oak leaves, dipping them in the blood, spattering all of us. We are all his children. He is Father as well as Son. He is giving his life for us. There is no other way. We cannot save ourselves.*

*I do not want to see. But I can see nothing else.*

*What have they done to us, the Romans?*

*Celynen tells me he has never made this sacrifice before. Nor has he known in his lifetime any druid in Dumnon who ever did. He thinks this may not have happened for a hundred years.*

*'I believed in the way of wisdom, Cairenn, in a druid philosophy. I believed that the colt and the blood and the fire were symbols only. That we could dance our mock horse in Maytime, and make him die and rise again. That the reality need never happen. Real blood. Real death. The real Colt.*

*'But I was wrong. The forces against us are too great. We cannot fight them ourselves. The blood of the Colt must speak for us.'*

*'Will the gods accept it? Will they help us?'*

'They must. Or all that was Dumnon will go down, unre-membered . . . And yet my heart is sick, Cairenn, at what I have to do. And across the Channel, other tribes have made an even graver sacrifice than this. Human lives. The Romans call us barbarians. I fear it is they who are making barbarians of us.'

I hate the Romans. I see the Colt lying in a welter of red and white. The fire getting ready to blacken him.

Yesterday, he was alive. Yesterday, I held his face between my hands and his luminous eyes looked into mine, so bright with life. Yesterday, he was galloping.

The Romans have done this to us.

It is over, at last. I wander away, still marked with his blood. The chiefs will sue for peace to Vespasian. We shall let the Romans march, unmolested, into the very heart of Dumnon, to camp by the Salmon River, the Exe. We shall trust to the blood of the Colt to save us, where swords cannot. We shall try to remember who we are, and teach our children.

Children? I shall never bear Aidan's children now, I am sure of that. The ache is uncomforted, like the loss of the Colt. I think I do not want to be comforted. I want to tear my hair and grieve. I want to scream aloud.

There is a flutter of green in the doorway of a hut close by the gate. I try to reorientate myself in reality. The armoury, where Bearrach issues weapons for practice to those too young to have earned their own. Something familiar in that tunic that whisks inside.

Why is there no guard, no lock on the door? We are vulner-able.

I step in after her, widening my eyes to peer into the gloom. 'Who's there?'

She comes forward, reluctantly, either shy or sullen. 'Tegan Mare's-Daughter.'

A shock of pain. This is Beath's messenger, the girl who brought the first certain news that the Romans are in

*Dumnon. That she had seen their soldiers.*

*That she had seen Melwas. And lost him.*

*'What are you doing?'*

*She has buckled a long sword round her. It is certainly not hers.*

*Her chin goes up, defiant. 'Fighting for Dumnon.'*

*And she is off, passing me to the door faster than I can catch her. There is a startled shout from the sentries at the gate. Then one calls to the other, 'It's only Tegan.'*

*They are used to her, streaking away with that easy stride on some errand for the chief or his wife.*

*And slowly, too slow, the truth shakes off the drink that is fuddling my brain, and surfaces.*

*Tegan would rebel and fight the Romans rather than submit. But not alone; she would steal a sword and race to join a rebel captain.*

*Then Tegan must know, or guess, where Aidan is.*

*Without another thought, I have hitched up my own skirt and am chasing after her.*

# CHAPTER 8

## SACRIFICE

Melwas, full of heady dreams, hardly noticed the way back. Aidan's little band made good speed. They moved warily and watchfully, but there was no sign of Roman patrols. For all their caution, their hearts were high with an unspoken joy at the coming fight. At last the weeks of tension and doubt were at an end. When they halted at the edge of a wood, they were warm with silent laughter, and a strong knot of brotherhood seemed to bind them closer than before.

Melwas was shocked back into reality when he saw where Aidan had stopped them. They stood once more under the red ramparts of the Silent Fort. This time, it seemed, they were not going to pass it by. Aidan's hand motioned Hu forward.

Hu looked cautiously about in every direction, then slipped out into the open. The men waited silently under the cover of the trees. They saw his brown kilt flicker like a shadow through the tall white grass. Then he was lost to sight and there was silence. Midges danced under the oak leaves and beyond, little white clouds drifted across the hilltop.

There was a whistle from the rampart. At a sign from Aidan the men broke from the wood, running fast and silently up the hill to the shelter of the gateway. Within the earthworks they stopped to draw breath. Some of them began to wander curiously about the deserted fort. Melwas followed them more slowly. Against his will he found himself drawn towards that central knot of pines. As he came closer, his throat tightened. Then he swallowed with relief. The body had gone. There was no Roman soldier lying in the grass now. Only, when he looked harder, he thought he could see a faint discolouration in the sand, which dew and drizzle had not quite washed away. His hand strayed to the enemy's pendant, half hidden under his tunic, convincing himself it had been real. As he stood staring down at it, Aidan came up behind him. His voice was hard, without its usual laughter.

'So perish every Roman who invades Dumnon.'

He squeezed Melwas's shoulder. Turning away, he summoned Elaeth and Hu. The three of them crossed over to the eastern edge of the fort and carefully peered over the rampart. Melwas watched the brief exchange of words as they surveyed the land. He felt a pang of jealousy. It was not fair that Hu should be there among the leaders while Melwas was left out, even after that proud initiation yesterday. Hu was younger than he was, a child still. He had not earned the weapons of a warrior, and, being a commoner, he never would. Yet Aidan seemed to turn to him for guidance and advice as much as to any grown man. He could see how happy Hu was by the shine in his brown eyes and the eager lift of his face to Aidan's.

There was a bustle behind Melwas. More recruits were arriving, as if they had only been waiting for Aidan's signal. They came in little groups, some breaking from the leafy cover of the wood, others darting from furze-brakes on the open hill and skimming like cloud shadows over the golden grass. Here, the sun glinted on an arm-ring or a shield; there a bright cloak flashed for an instant, blue in the heather, red against the vivid gorse.

As the day declined, more men kept coming in. Melwas stood by the gateway, greeting the newcomers with the high pride of being foster-brother to Aidan, the Red Fox. He was startled, though he realized he should not have been, when Rieuk, leading the rest of the Armoricans from the strange ship, arrived. The druid's dark eyes were smouldering with excitement as he grasped Aidan's arm.

As the fort began to fill, Melwas saw at last that victory was possible. A band as brave and daring as this, fierce children of Dumnon, high-hearted British warriors, might challenge a whole Roman legion. They could hold them and harry them again and again, force them to turn back and trouble the land of Dumnon no more. His head was spinning with dreams of glory and his hands longed for the feel of a sword-hilt in his grasp.

There was a rustle of excitement, then a silence. Through it, came the creak of chariot wheels approaching the gate. Two piebald ponies came into view, then, standing tall above the wicker frame, Seiriol the druid. Her womanservant rode as charioteer. Seiriol was armed for battle, more terrifying than ever in breastplate and helmet. She held a spear as tall as herself.

The crowd of men fell back. Aidan went to meet her, with more respect than he had shown even to Rieuk of Armorica. He handed her down and bowed his knee before her. Her hand made signs over his head. For a while they talked, then Aidan nodded and went to the Armoricans.

Melwas edged closer to Seiriol, drawn by his need of what she could give him. She was still standing by her wicker chariot, not far from the knot of pines where he had found the dead Roman soldier. He felt her eyes watching him come.

'Well?' she said when he stood before her. The silent laughter, which was so heart-warming in Aidan, was terrible in her.

'The battle will be tomorrow. I've come to claim my weapons,' he said.

'So, you think you are a man?' Her grey eyebrows lifted in

a face that was still strangely young.

'You made me one,' he answered reluctantly.

She looked long at him, and the mockery faded from her eyes.

'I did indeed,' she said softly.

Neither of them moved. Melwas wondered in panic if she would go back on her promise, if that shearing had been a dream. Then she turned abruptly to the chariot. From it, she lifted the same richly enamelled shield, the long sword and spear that he had wielded before. Melwas felt a lump in his throat when he saw them. Beneath the shadows of the oak grove, these had been strange, mysterious, exciting gifts. Now, in the clear daylight of this, a war camp, he saw them in all their grim reality. These weapons were the scales on which human lives would hang – his enemies', his own.

Seiriol tossed the heavy sword in her hand, testing the balance at the hilt. Then she reached forward and silently buckled the sword-belt round him. At the touch of her muscled hands, he felt that once again her strength and power were flowing into him. He stood very still. She lifted the shield and he took its weight on his arm. Lastly she set the tall spear in his right hand. She stepped back to look at him, and her face softened with a yearning that seemed strange for her.

'Use them well, for Dumnon,' she said gruffly, and turned away.

The arms were heavy. Melwas hardly knew what to do with them. At first he wore them proudly, and flushed with pleasure at the jokes of Aidan's friends. But after a while he noticed that the other warriors did not stride about the camp fully accoutred, though they kept their long swords swinging at their knees. He found a pine tree out of the way of the throng, and propped his shield and spear against it. After that he felt lighter, both in body and in heart.

Towards dusk, Melwas glanced up and caught a flash of

bright green in the gateway. He sprang to his feet with a glad cry.

'Tegan!'

She came running in. She had a borrowed sword at her hip and her face was alight with excitement and alarm. Melwas dashed over to greet her.

'You're safe! The Romans didn't get you!'

She threw back her black hair, laughing and gasping for breath.

'Is that what you thought, foxcub? You surely didn't imagine a pack of foreigners could run down the Mare's-Daughter with the wind of fear at her heels? It'll need a fiercer chase than that before you see me dead with a spear in my throat ... But I never thought I'd come back to the Silent Fort, ever.' She looked around apprehensively, then shook herself and clapped him on the shoulder. 'And what's happened to you, foxcub? You look a sight. Where did you get to? I suppose Aidan found you in the wood and led you to safety?'

'You *knew* Aidan was here?'

'I guessed.' Her mouth twisted. 'Didn't you?'

'No. And anyway, I didn't need Aidan's help. I got myself to Seiriol's Oaks.'

'Seiriol!' she whistled softly. 'That's not what I call safety, if even half the tales they tell of her are true. I think I'd rather take my chances with the Romans, any day.'

'She's not so awful,' he said hesitantly. He could not begin to explain to Tegan the mixture of terror and admiration which the druid inspired in him. 'She shaved me and gave me my weapons. Idwal refused me.'

'Aye, I heard,' she answered more gently. 'So now you're a man. And you'll have a man's work to do, following Aidan into battle.'

She drew her sword thoughtfully from its scabbard and began to sharpen it upon the weapon-stone standing in the middle of the clearing. Melwas joined her, bearing his own new and treasured weapon, till he realized that his unpractised efforts were only blunting the fine edge that Seiriol had already put upon it.

'What about you?' he asked. 'Have you been back to the Forest Fort? Did they hold their Council? What did they decide? And what made you come here?'

'Yes, the High Council of Dumnon is over,' she said grimly, slipping her sword back into its sheath. 'Your father came. Idwal had a hard time explaining to him why you weren't there to greet him, as well as why Aidan and his friends were missing. Cairenn's in a state about you, too.'

'And? Aren't you going to tell me what the Council said?'

'What would you expect? They're not going to fight. Aidan was right not to wait for them. Afterwards, Celynen sacrificed the White Colt, for the safety of the tribe.' Melwas gasped. 'I know. It's desperate. And now they're sending ambassadors to Vespasian to beg for peace. But I knew Aidan would fight, whatever they decided, so I grabbed myself one of Bearrach's swords, and here I am! Aidan may not think much of me for a warrior, but he can't afford to be choosy, can he?' She looked around, eyes still wary. 'This place isn't quite so scary, now it's full of human beings.'

The rasping of iron on stone echoed across the ancient dun. All other sounds were strictly subdued. One man had brought a harp slung on his back, but as the first vibrating note sang out under his fingers, Aidan strode through the ring of listening warriors.

'Quiet, friend,' he said, not unkindly. 'This must be a cheerless evening, I'm afraid. No music, no fire, no wine. We've done well to keep our hosting secret from the enemy so far. It would be a pity to spoil it now. We're out of sight here. But Roman scouts have come this way once, and they may be back again, now they've tasted our steel. If your spirits grow cold, think of tomorrow and the welcome we'll have waiting for Vespasian at the ford. Let your music be the laughter inside you, and dreams of glory warm your hearts for wine.'

There was some muttering at this. The men were young and high-spirited, but they trusted Aidan. They made a cold supper of bread and beer, and not much of either, for they had travelled light.

All the time more men, and women too, were gathering to them as the shadows lengthened. Some were fugitives from the duns of the east who had resisted the Roman advance and learned too late of the High Chief's surrender at the Ridge. They had fled from the ravage of fire and sword, and their mood was dark and bitter. Some had brought families of frightened children. Others came alone, and their eyes were grim and staring. Aidan had a ready smile for them all, but he would allow only those who could fight to remain in the camp. He sent the rest of the refugees off to find what shelter they could in neighbouring villages.

There were other, more boisterous bands – young warriors from the north and the west. Some had travelled for days seeking news of Aidan's hosting. Like him, they had left their fathers' duns, weary beyond endurance of their elders' caution, hoping against hope for a leader who could rally the pride and the flower of Dumnon to one glorious battle, even if it should be their last. Now all of them, clansmen or strangers, hopeful or despairing, set their eyes upon one man – the Fox; tall, red-headed Aidan, son of Idwal Goldenshield.

At the close of the day, some two hundred warriors gathered in a great circle round him. Aidan, with the druid Rieuk on one hand and Seiriol on the other, looked around at them all with joy and pride. His voice rang out on the evening air, despite his own order for caution.

'Warriors of Dumnon, brothers and sisters! It is enough! We are few indeed, compared with a mighty legion of Rome. But we're British. And isn't each one of you worth more than ten of these soft southerners? They're little men, with little swords, and legs too short to run away on!'

A wave of laughter swept round the warhost.

'Rieuk tells me these Romans fight for pay. Will money give them courage when our swords are at their throats? We fight for our land, for our homes, for our families. But strongest of all is the ancient power of our gods, which we can call to aid us in our hour of need. Listen to Rieuk, High Druid of Armorica.'

He squatted down, and Rieuk took his place, his dark eyes flickering over the host and the tip of his tongue moistening his lips.

'Warriors of Dumnon, you make my heart glad tonight. I risked the long voyage from Gaul, escaping from the chains of Rome, for just such a night as this. To see the free people of Britain, who speak the same tongue as us, gathered with hearts made bold to strike the blow which must be struck for their land. To drive out Rome from this island, once and for ever. To save the ancient ways and the ancient faith and the ancient laws of the Island of the Mighty.

'It grieves me bitterly that you are so few. I had wished for thousands upon thousands. But you are the pride of your nation. You will teach your fathers the meaning of courage. The gods look into your hearts and they laugh for joy. In you, the fire still burns. In you, hope is still high. You are heroes. Tomorrow you go into battle. Some of you will fall, and the earth will drink deeply of your blood. But if the gods ride with you, victory shall be yours at the end of the day! What do you say? Would you have the great ones before you and beside you – the Son of the Waves and the Mighty Smith and the terrible Raven of Battle?'

'Aye, we will have them!' roared the crowd.

'And will you do whatever they demand?'

'We will do it!' came back the answer.

Rieuk flashed a quick glance at Seiriol beside him, and she nodded vigorously.

'Hear, then, the tribute they ask. Your land is hungry. Too long you have fed her with wine and milk and the blood of cattle and pigs. She asks for stronger drink. If you would have the favour of her gods, you must give her that which is most precious of all. And what more can you give, in the last resort, than human blood, to pay for the life and freedom of you all?'

His fierce gaze swept round the ring of faces. There was a startled silence. The crowd was uneasy. Such a thing was hardly remembered in Dumnon, since Celynen had been High Druid.

One man said hesitantly, 'We reckon otherwise. With us, the most precious gift to the gods is the White Colt that runs all year in the meadows by the river and has never had a bridle laid upon him.'

Rieuk burst into harsh laughter.

'A horse? The fate of your country trembles in the hands of the gods and you can offer nothing better than a four-footed beast? Better to make no sacrifice at all than so insult them. A sacrifice of cowards!'

Melwas was angry. The Colt was the son of the white mare who was their true queen, the royal bride of the chief, the life of the tribe. How could the life of one worthless man compare with such a sacrifice as that? He clenched his fists, wishing he could stand up and say so. But it was no use. Only Celynen could have matched the eloquence of the Armorican. And Celynen was far away.

'He's right.'

'We've got to do it.'

'There's no other way in the darkest hour.'

Murmurs of approval began to come back from the circle. Some of the men were beginning to gaze at Rieuk with a kind of hunger, almost eager for what must follow. But the stillness lengthened. Rieuk gazed back at them, saying nothing. Melwas looked around the circle, wondering what they were waiting for. As his eyes passed round the circle of faces, he saw, one after the other, the desperate knowledge surface in their eyes. One of them here must be the victim. And now everyone was looking at their neighbour, across the circle, anywhere, rather than be the one, the only one, whose eyes the waiting druid caught and held. Not a whisper broke the silence, but fear ran screaming through all their hearts.

Melwas was caught up in the confusion. He felt his own heart beating wildly. The gods must have a victim. But whom? Gradually, all heads were turning one way. Relief showed plain in their faces as the idea leaped from one to another. In moments, two hundred pairs of eyes fell upon one figure.

Melwas felt the blood drain from his cold heart. The whole warhost was staring at him. His brain struggled to deny it. But even he could see the reason why. He was the youngest of them all, unscarred by any battle, a virgin warrior at the dawn of manhood. Like the White Colt. He wanted to scream out 'No! Not me! Not me!,' but only his terrified eyes cried out for him as they sought the face of Aidan, his foster-brother.

Aidan looked shocked. He bit his lip, and his blue eyes flickered away from Melwas's at the moment of meeting. But he said no word against it. In desperation Melwas turned from him to Rieuk, and in the druid's smile he read the confirmation of his death.

Was it all over, then? The bright adventure. The blazing hope. The glorious dream of manhood. Even this first and longed-for battle would be taken from him. He would never run to meet the Roman host, brandishing his new sword. He would not even see that dawn. He licked his stiff lips and felt his face set rigid in fear.

But he would not cry out. Whatever happened, he must not plead or struggle for his life. He would die like a hero, a willing sacrifice. Though the time of his manhood had been cruelly brief, this was how the tribe should remember him and sing his story. He was a chief's son. A warrior of Dumnon. He was laying down his life that his country might be free.

Rieuk must have beckoned him. He was walking forward, though he had lost the feeling in his limbs. Seiriol and her charioteer had started singing. Surely there should be a fire?

The buzzing crowd seemed far away. He could not see them clearly. He was aware of Rieuk looming closer, loosening the long, bronze knife from his girdle. The druid alone seemed larger than life, filling Melwas's vision, till the knife in his hands grew larger than the man. Melwas's thoughts flickered sideways to inconsequential memories – his mother lifting him in her arms as a little boy, the day when Idwal Goldenshield first took him hunting in the forest, Crab . . . A solitary tear blurred his eye. He must not think about Crab.

There was a sudden stir on the edge of the crowd.

'Hold!'

It was Aidan's urgent shout. He sprang to his feet and lifted his hand for silence.

The ripple of questions eddied away. All faces turned curiously towards their leader. Still Aidan stood with his head cocked sideways, listening. Then the sentry, posted behind the rotting palisade, gave a low cry and pointed. Aidan sprang up the rampart beside him and vaulted over. There was the sound of scuffling in the leafy ditch below. A few moments later, he reappeared through the gateway, dragging a second figure with him. He hauled the man forward by the scruff of the neck and threw him face downward at Rieuk's feet.

'Will you take this for a victim?' he cried triumphantly.

The man was in rags, his hair unkempt and matted with leaves. He rose to his knees and saw the knife in Rieuk's hand. His eyes swung round and saw a great circle of eager faces. A wild look of despair flashed over his face and he flung his arms about Aidan's knees, mumbling piteously. Aidan kicked him off in disgust. Still on his knees the man shuffled

115

towards Rieuk, his hands clasped pleadingly in front of him.

'Spare me! Spare me! I only wanted food. And company. I'll go away. I won't trouble you any more, I swear it. Only spare my life!'

Melwas could hardly believe what was happening. He was free. He was alive. No one was taking any notice of him. All their eyes were turned on the pathetic creature kneeling at Rieuk's feet.

Melwas watched him, too, with mingled pity and relief. But as he looked, a curious sensation came over him of having seen this victim somewhere before. At first he had thought the man old, he was so broken and dishevelled. But now he saw that, beneath the matted hair, he was young. As young as Aidan, though terribly marked by sorrow. And behind that distorted face there was indeed something familiar. That scar . . . . With a shock, Melwas knew where he had seen it before. Surely it could not be? But he knew beyond doubt that it was. He had looked at this face every day and night for years. Only a few days ago it had been the face of Dinogad, Aidan's friend. The young man who had imitated a hen, and whom Celynen had cursed for his impiety. Now Dinogad's face was ravaged by fear and indescribable loneliness. Melwas's mind recoiled in horror from it. The knowledge that a living man could be so utterly destroyed had become more frightening than death itself.

Aidan was explaining to Rieuk:

'He has been stalking us since the night when Celynen drove him out. Wherever we sleep, he crawls close for company. He steals after us and searches for scraps of food where we have eaten. When we take the trail through the woods, he creeps alongside the path, just out of sight. Take him; his life is a burden to him since he was cursed. He has no tribe.'

Rieuk nodded slowly. 'It is fitting. He mocked the servant of the gods and his blood is forfeit to them. They will be satisfied.' He turned sharply to two of the Armoricans. 'Take him!'

His men seized the victim and dragged him towards the tallest tree of the dun.

'No! No!' Dinogad screamed and fought with sudden energy. The Armoricans tightened their grip. Melwas found himself trembling all over. He tried to harden his heart. He told himself that this man was not worthy to live. He had lost all the pride of a British warrior. He, Melwas, would have died with dignity. He had made up his mind not to struggle like that. But all the same, he wished he could shut his ears to those terrible screams.

Seiriol came forward. There was a cup in her hands now. She held it out to Dinogad. He started, then almost grabbed it from her and downed it in one gulp.

The older men rose to their feet and began to chant, uncertainly at first, as if it were something remembered from long ago. But the rhythmic beat was compelling. Soon the younger men were standing too, catching it from them. Their bodies began to sway, hands to clap, feet to stamp. The noise and the movement were heightening, like a wood lashed by a gale.

The two Armorican guards led Dinogad away. He went unresisting now, staggering slightly, as though he were drunk. They placed him against an oak tree, with his face to the bark. They stretched his arms out to branches above his head and held them there so that he could not move. He hung, trembling, exhausted with terror or drugged. Only an occasional sob broke out. 'No!' 'No!' 'No!'

Rieuk advanced, proclaiming the words of power in a strange tongue. Melwas wanted to shut his eyes, but would not let himself; he was a man now. This was for his tribe, his country. He winced as the long bronze knife whipped upwards, glinting coldly in the last rays of the evening sun. Then it plunged down into the victim's back. With a last scream the body leaped convulsively in the air, jerked once, and fell in a twisted heap among the pine-needles.

117

Melwas turned away then, but not quickly enough. Now that it was over, he felt both disgust and pity. He knew that there had been more to the manner of Dinogad's death than a blood sacrifice. He did not have the knowledge to read the signs the druids would in the death throes of the victim . He only knew that that lifeless tumble of limbs might have been his own body. But in the moment of turning, his eyes caught the sharp look of dismay that passed between Rieuk and Seiriol. A new fear woke. Had the omens of that sacrifice been so bad?

Seiriol saw him looking, and frowned with annoyance. Quickly she pulled a sprig of oak leaves from a young sapling and dipped them in the blood which still flowed from the victim's back. She crossed the circle and stood over Melwas. Caught unawares, he flinched as the leaves brushed his fore-head, leaving a hot reek of blood and a warm stickiness that dripped down his face.

'Your first blooding!' Only her lips smiled, while her grey eyes searched his face keenly.

Some of the men cheered, but Melwas scowled back at them. Had they forgotten so easily whose blood they had hungered for first? He knew that what Seiriol had done to him was a mark of favour, but it was too late to mend what he had seen. This sacrifice, dreadful though it was, should have set the seal upon their victory. But it had gone badly wrong. He was sure of that.

The ritual was still going on. There were more prayers, more chants, more pouring of blood and other gifts. At last it was over. The circle began to break up, people shaking them-selves as if out of a daze, moving uncertainly, not quite meeting each other's eyes. The thickening twilight deepened the solemnity.

Melwas looked round for Aidan. Had he, too, seen the look that had passed between Rieuk and Seiriol? If he had, he gave no sign of it. His grin was as warm and confident as ever, as he looked around at his host, and his voice rang cheerfully across the fort.

'Brothers and sisters, we have done what the gods demanded and they have taken our gift. When the morning breaks, they too will rise in all their strength to aid us. Remember, the Romans have no gods like ours. Be worthy of them. And now, let us get what sleep we can. We march before dawn.'

# CHAPTER 9

## CAPTURE

Melwas found a grassy corner to settle himself for the night. Seiriol's charioteer had tossed him a short cloak which he pulled around him. There was a soft footfall, and Hu stood over him.

'May I sleep beside you?' he asked shyly.

In the hall of Idwal Goldenshield, a chieftain's son would not have lain with a village boy, but rules were different on the march. Melwas nodded, glad to have warmth and company. The two boys lay on their backs looking up at the pale sky. True darkness was still some way off. Melwas could hear the men shouting bawdy comments at Tegan, vying with each other to get her to come and sleep with them. His stiff face muscles began to relax into a grin. For once, even bold Tegan must be blushing. She could have gone to sleep beside Seiriol, and then no man would have dared to trouble her. But he had noticed that she always kept a careful distance between herself and the druid woman. He did not blame her for that.

There were running footsteps, and then Tegan herself was standing over them, half-laughing and half-ashamed.

'Can I join you? I think I'll be safer sleeping with you two than anywhere! I wish Beath was here to give the sharp side of her tongue to this lot. They'd never have dared say things like that to me in Idwal's dun. And the other girls all seem to have a man with them. I'm beginning to wish I'd let Cairenn catch me up, after all.'

'Cairenn!'

Melwas started up on his elbow. He saw Tegan's hand fly to her mouth as though to catch back the words. He was on his feet now.

'What's this about Cairenn? She didn't follow you, did she?'

Tegan stared back at him wordlessly, her green eyes wary now. He shook her roughly.

'You know something, don't you? Tell me! Where's my sister?'

She shook her head. 'I didn't mean any harm. It wouldn't have been right for her to be here. You can see that, can't you, Melwas? What would a fine lady like Cairenn of the White Fingers be doing in a war-camp? Aidan would only have sent her away.'

'She was coming *here*?'

'She was worried about you. I told her she'd only be in the way if she couldn't use a sword. I hoped she'd turn back before we were out of the Great Forest.'

'Out of the Forest? How far did she follow you, then? Where is she now?'

'I don't know. She came at least half-way, I think. Maybe more. I lost sight of her after I forded the Quiet River. I never thought she'd follow me so fast and so far. I thought I'd shake her off easily in the woods.'

'And you just left her? On her own? For a Roman patrol to find?'

'It wasn't my fault. Honestly, Melwas. I told her not to come.'

'It's nearly dark. We must find her! Where's Aidan?'

*How could I think I could catch the Mare's Daughter? I have*

121

*kept myself lean and fit, but she has legs like the wind. And still I run, as though this careering downhill slope had taken possession of me and is hurtling me on.*

*Tegan knows. She is going to find Aidan. And where Aidan is, there Melwas may be, too.*

*That's why I'm chasing her, isn't it? My little brother, my parents' precious son. I must find him and bring him back. I must wipe out the look of desolation in my father's eyes, struggling with pride in his son's courage. Idwal and Beath have let him think that Melwas has gone as a rebel like Aidan. Not that he ran away in a temper, a shamed child. What have we left, if we lose our ridiculous pride?*

*Tegan is deep in the wood now, but heading away, I think, from the river. At a turn in the path I look over my shoulder, back up the way I have run. Did the sentries shout at my going, as they did after her? I keep expecting to hear the thunder of hooves, or at least the thudding of running feet. Surely someone will come after me, to stop me?*

*And still I run, and no one chases after me.*

*I am a fool, ridiculous as the rest of them. Why didn't I shout for help at once? Order swift horsemen to catch Tegan and question her? They could have run her down in moments. Why did I think I could overtake her alone?*

*I should go back. Get help.*

*Too late now. Hard enough to keep in sight those glimpses of fleeting green between the trees below me. She is going further and further away. If I turn back I shall lose her. I shall lose my hope of finding Melwas.*

*I shall lose Aidan.*

*No, do not think of him. Do not see the backward tilt of his head, the proud-tossed hair, the gesture that bares his sun-browned neck and the glint of the golden torque he always wears. I finger mine, even while I run.*

*It is not Aidan I need to find, is it?*

*I have no sword. I did not think to snatch one like Tegan. I could have fought alongside him.*

*I do not know how to use a sword.*

*Only the knife at my belt, which we all carry.*

*How does she run all day, over these hills? I am tiring already, and we are still going down.*

*A stream at the bottom, muddy but shallow. I see her fresh footprints. Then up and out of the trees into clouded sunshine. This is meadow land. I gasp with relief. I can see her again, half-way up to the ridge. A tiny bolting figure she seems, no bigger than a rabbit.*

*'Tegan!' I try to shout, but there is not enough air in my lungs. I gasp for more. 'Tegan!'*

*Astonishingly, she checks. She must have heard me. She turns, hesitates, then runs on.*

*Didn't she see me? Doesn't she know who called her? Surely she must have seen my crimson dress and remember I was wearing this when I challenged her in the armoury? Who else does she think would follow her?*

*And anger drives me on, up the grassy slope after her.*

*Every breath is pain. Every step feels as if I had a granite boulder tied to my leg. I cannot shout again. But I will not be denied by a commoner.*

*She is slowing herself now, looking over her shoulder occasionally. The distance between us grows no wider. And the way is dipping again, down to a broader river. This is not our Exe, which can bring seagoing ships. Still, it flows calm and slow between tall reed-beds. It looks too deep to cross.*

*But Tegan knows the way, and her path twists down between little fields to where a gravelled bar runs like a silver ingot just under the surface. She has splashed across ahead of me and now stands waiting, hands on hips, breathing deeply, but not distressed, as I am.*

*My feet sink in the wet silt on the nearer side. There are curious cows moving towards me. It is some time before I can find enough breath to send it out again as words across the water.*

'Where are you going?'

'I told you. To fight the Romans.'

'Who with?'

A defiant silence.

'It's Aidan, isn't it? You're going to Aidan.'

'Who else will fight them, except the Red Fox?'

'And Melwas is with him?'

She starts then. 'I don't know. He might be. Maybe Aidan would rescue a lost foxcub . . . or maybe not.'

I do not know what she means. Of course Aidan would protect his foster-brother, if he found him.

Can Aidan protect any of us now?

'Take me with you.'

'Don't be silly. You haven't got a weapon.'

She should not speak to me like that; I am a princess.

'I'm not going to fight. The Council has forbidden us to resist the Romans. I'm coming to take Melwas home to his father.' I start to wade across the ford.

'No . . . my lady. Don't. A war-camp's not for you.'

'I'm coming anyway.'

'Go back.'

She starts to run again. Despair seizes me. I stop midstream and look back.

The Forest looms huge, strange, from an angle I have never seen it before. I doubt that I can find my way home through that labyrinth of trees. Ahead, the country is open heath, wide and golden with summer grass, and the heather beginning to stain it purple. Pines crown its crest. More distant woods to my right, where a brightness in the sky tells me the sea must run beyond my seeing.

I try not to think that over these hills ahead lies an invading army.

I should go back. I am afraid to go back.

I will not go back without Melwas.

It is not Aidan I am running to, is it? That tall protection of *his strength beside me. The laughter in his eyes that mocks at danger. If we must die, I could do it bravely with his arms around me.*

*He loves me, doesn't he? This is more than a political marriage? I have seen his eyes on me when I sing in the fire-light of the hall. The flash of desire. His hands have reached out and cupped my breasts as I pass him, with that low, wicked laugh. His caress melts the muscles within me, so that I would flow like honey for him.*

*This is war, this is killing, not such sweet swooning.*

*Surely he would want my arms around him, if we must die?*

*Celynen tells me to live for Dumnon.*

*Of course, it is Melwas I have to find.*

Melwas strode across the fort with Tegan trailing miserably at his heels. He found his foster-brother bedding down for the night under the pines. Aidan smiled at them, but wearily.

'Tell him,' Melwas said curtly to Tegan.

'It's Cairenn of the White Fingers,' she said nervously. 'She saw me take a sword and leave the dun. She tried to follow me. I told her to turn back, but she wouldn't. She said she must find Melwas and take him back to his father. She told me there was no sense in fighting the Romans and it would break your father's heart if you were killed.'

'You didn't tell me that!' Melwas interposed indignantly.

'No. Well, I think, anyway, you were only half the reason. I guess she was also worried about somebody else.' She looked meaningfully at Aidan, who flushed and frowned.

Melwas's anger was shifting from Tegan to Cairenn. 'Girls! Doesn't she know yet that I'm man enough to fight without her running after me to fetch me home?'

Still Aidan looked impatiently at the pair of them. 'Why are you bringing this tale to me when you should be sleeping? She's not here, is she? And if she did come, I'd send her back.

This is a war-camp.'

'But she's out there somewhere, alone! And it's nearly dark. What will she do, with a forest full of wild animals on one side, and a Roman legion just over the hill?'

'Where did you see her last?' Aidan asked Tegan.

'I tried to run fast and lose her in the Forest. But she wouldn't give up. She was behind me when I crossed the Quiet River by the Ford of the Hazel Trees. I didn't see her again after that. Maybe she did turn back then.'

'Turn back?' Melwas shouted. 'How dare you say that of my sister? I know Cairenn. She's my father's daughter as much as I'm his son. If she had made up her mind to follow you, she'd never turn back!'

'Oh, hush, foxcub!' Aidan clapped his hands to his head. 'Have you both forgotten we've got a Roman legion to fight tomorrow? Isn't that trouble enough for you? Tegan's right. Cairenn will have turned back and gone home. There's nothing we can do.'

'I tell you she wouldn't! I know her! You can't just leave her. Aren't you going to send out a search party?'

'And risk running into enemy scouts and betraying the whole camp? No, don't worry, little foster-brother. By now, she'll be back home in the Forest Fort and sound asleep. As you should be. We'll need all our strength for the battle in the morning.'

'But you can't do that! You can't just leave her!'

'No one's leaving anyone. This is war. Your sword for Britain above all else. It's people like Cairenn we're fighting for.'

'Then if *you* won't find her, I will!'

Melwas bolted away, straight for the gate. Behind him, he heard Aidan cry out: 'Stop him!' The guards at the entrance of the fort sprang forward, their spears crossed in his path. He swerved aside from them and raced for the ramparts, vaulting over where the palisade had crumbled away.

He tumbled over the bank and rolled down the long red slope into the ditch, thumping the breath from his body as he landed in the thick leaves at the bottom. Then he was on his feet, scrambling up the farther side, no easy task on the slippery earth which rose far above his head as sheer as a wall. As he struggled up, digging in fingers and toes, a spear came whistling over the rampart. It struck the bank, wide of his shoulder. Melwas wondered grimly whether it had been meant to hit him. If so, they could not miss twice at such short range.

Now he was at the top, but he dared not stop to draw breath. He raced on through the heather. There was an echo to his footsteps. He sprinted faster. But those other footsteps were gaining on him, running easily now just behind his shoulder. He darted a glance behind him. Hu's brown face grinned back at him as his shorter legs matched Melwas's flight, stride for stride. The two boys slowed to a halt in the shelter of some gorse bushes and grasped arms in comradeship.

'I'm with you,' said Hu. 'I've got a sister, too. We'll find her.'

There was a cry behind them. They spun round. In the dusk another figure came flying down the slope from the Silent Fort. It was Tegan. In another moment she had joined them, looking defiantly at Melwas to see whether he was still angry with her.

'I can show you where I last saw her. It may save us a little time before it's pitch black,' she said gruffly.

'You shouldn't have come. It'll get you into trouble with Aidan.'

'I don't care.'

She tossed her black hair bravely. But all three of them felt small and alone outside the fort. As part of the warrior host, with Aidan as their leader, they had been brave and high-hearted. They truly believed that he could lead them to victory. They had looked to him to bring back joy to the land, as every-

127

one turned to the midwinter fire to call back the summer and the sun out of darkness. But now they were on their own, almost like Dinogad expelled from the tribe. They would even have welcomed the sound of hot pursuit. But behind them the fort was utterly silent again. There were no more shouts, no sign of the pursuing guards. Aidan had let them go.

They looked around at the glimmer of bare heath. The edge of Seiriol's wood lapped dark and close. It was growing cold in the colourless twilight.

Melwas turned to Tegan, trying to sound bolder than he felt.

'She must be somewhere between us and the Forest. Show us where to start.'

'We'd better go back the way I came.'

'At least it's downhill,' said Hu.

They travelled swiftly, peering with anxious eyes over the open hillside in the fading light. As they searched for Cairenn, they were all of them uncomfortably, guiltily, aware that they too might be targets for unseen eyes. Melwas, most of all, knew that his presence here in warrior's garb could betray the nearness of Aidan's camp, and with it the last hope for Dumnon. Was it right to disobey him? Was it worth the risk, even for Cairenn?

Suddenly Melwas flung back his lime-spiked head and knew that it was. He was a chieftain's son. He had not been brought up to be careful, to count the cost of danger, to set a limit on honour. If he had been like that, he would have followed Celynen's advice. There would have been no battle-camp for him, no hosting of reckless warriors, no splendid sword and shield. The same fierce pride, which had driven him to claim his manhood and fight for Dumnon, was driving him now to find his sister, under the eyes of the whole Roman army if need be.

Melwas was so busy with these thoughts that he did not see Hu's silent movement of warning. All at once he was aware that the others had stopped. Hu was pointing urgently. He looked ahead, and his heart leaped for joy.

In the dusk, a tall figure was walking up the hill towards them. Her head hung down, so that her long hair hid her face. It must be Cairenn. Even as they watched they saw her stumble from weariness.

She had not seen them yet. Melwas raised his cupped hands to his lips, but before he could shout, Tegan had caught his elbow with a low mutter of alarm.

'No, Melwas! It's too late!'

*I have lost her. I was bound to, from that first flying step she took past me through the armoury door. I was a fool not to turn back when she told me. I fear I have brewed my own destruction.*

*I have no choice but to hold to my resolution. I must turn my back on the light. On the sun that is going down in glory across the Exe. Gold and crimson and purple streak the sky, as the chequered wool for a chieftain's cloak cut from the loom of Dumnon's finest weaver.*

*But ahead of me the brambles weave traps across my path. Travellers no longer come this way. The path is shrinking. The eastern sky is grey and darkening rapidly. What shall I do when the sun goes down, if I have still not found them?*

*Yet I trudge on east, too tired to run. East, because that is where the Romans are. And before I see the Romans, I shall find Aidan. I tell myself that firmly, insistent. He draws us all: Melwas, Tegan, me. I must not let myself think that I could have passed him by and be walking into an invading army.*

*Gorse snags at my gown. I stop to free myself. As I look down, I see in the damp sand the print of a bare foot. It is going the other way. It shocks me into uncertainty. Tegan left prints like this when I followed her across the river. I am not a skilled enough tracker to know if this is the same.*

*Am I going the wrong way? I glance over my shoulder. The sunset has faded to a more sullen red, but it is still behind me. This may be the wrong way now. Sense is crying out to me to turn back, while I still can.*

*Back there, I crossed a broader track, and saw the marks of many people all going west. The puddled hollows of the path trampled by men, women, children, even animals, all fleeing one way. Fresh with their fear. It was not easy to make myself walk on over them, impressing my solitary steps in the opposite direction.*

*I would only do this for Melwas, for my little brother.*

*I wish he was here beside me, short though he is, and without a sword.*

*If Melwas was here, we could go home.*

*Where shall I spend the night? The darkness is closing and I have found none of them.*

*Was that a flurry of movement?*

*Heart leaps for joy. Those are ponies trotting over the skyline, heads lifted against the last of the light. There are horsemen, heads high, cloaks swinging. A surge of pride. It's him! Aidan the Red Fox and his warband. He will protect Dumnon. He will protect me. I am safe. He has found me.*

*I start to run towards him. He has seen me. The ponies are stretching their necks out into a canter, gathering their legs up for a gallop. They come storming down the slope.*

*Slowly, horrifically, the truth sharpens into focus, till even the twilight cannot deny it.*

*This is not Aidan. These are not British horsemen. The hair too black, the cloaks too uniformly blue, the bows they are unslinging even as they gallop too unfamiliar. These are foreign invaders.*

*Still, as I turn to dash the other way, my mind is protesting. Is this how Romans look? I thought of massive legions of foot soldiers tramping in lines. The grim implacable machine of empire, not these wild whoops. This is not what Celynen told me they would be like.*

*Whoever they are, I am running for my life from them. A twisting hare. I swerve, but the horses are streaking ahead of me, encircling me. They have slowed now, certain of victory, like harvesters closing in on the last stand of corn where the shivering hare crouches. Grinning.*

*There is an unearthly yell behind me. A rush of wind. I am snatched from the earth.*

Melwas turned swiftly. He caught one glimpse of horsemen galloping over the brow of the hill before Tegan threw him down into the cover of the heather. Hu was already lying there, still and wary as a startled trout in the shadows.

Above their rapid breathing, they heard the hoofbeats of many horses thudding down the hillside. As they swept past, Melwas raised his head to look. He saw the streaming tails of black ponies, small and sure-footed. The riders' blue cloaks were darker than the summer dusk, and waving blue-black hair swung out behind them. They had bows unslung from their shoulders.

Through their flying hooves he saw Cairenn straighten as the horsemen galloped straight downhill towards her. Next moment, she too had seen them and she was running for her life. In an instant Melwas was on his feet, pulling the long, sharp sword from its scabbard. Without pausing to think, he flourished it wildly above his head and raced towards her.

He could have had no hope of reaching her before the horsemen. With a yell of triumph, eight of them swept down the hill around Cairenn and the foremost scooped her up on to his saddle-bow. The whole band wheeled and started to canter back up the slope.

It was then that they saw Melwas charging recklessly towards them. Three of the black-haired men swung short bows from their shoulders, notched arrows to the strings and let fly at him. Too late, Melwas remembered the great shield he had left standing under the pine tree. He flung himself down in the heather and the shafts whistled over his head. It was only a moment's reprieve. The three were galloping down on him, fitting fresh arrows to their bows. He leaped to his feet and swerved sideways to avoid them. Still he was dashing madly for the larger group, which held Cairenn.

It was Hu who saved him. Starting from behind a gorse bush, he seized the leather sling with which he could bring a lark down out of the sky, and fitted a pebble to it. He whirled it round his head, and aimed at the nearest moving target. The leading archer collapsed sideways and tumbled under his pony's hooves. The animal stumbled over him and fell. His two companions could not rein in quickly enough. As they charged into the fallen pony and rider, there was chaos and confusion.

Almost at once, two of them were on their feet, drawing short swords to defend themselves at close quarters. Melwas rushed towards them and they clashed in what seemed like unequal combat. But the boy found that, though he was not yet fully grown, he was already taller than they, and his longer reach was doubled by the huge sword. His first swinging blow caught one archer above his guard and sent him spinning backwards. Melwas leaped upon him and brought the sword down with one tremendous blow across the neck. The man died instantly. Melwas had often wondered what it would be like to kill his first enemy in battle. But now that it had happened, he had no time to think about it. As the blood gushed out, he felt a frenzy of anger possess him. He struck again and again, heedless of a second horseman whose quick sword was lifted above him. Only Tegan, running into the fray in a whirlwind of green, brought him to his senses. She caught the dismounted archer a deep gash across his sword arm so that he dropped his weapon with a cry and clutched the wound. Leaping back to his mount, he turned it with his knees and galloped out of the fight.

Melwas whirled about, parrying the upward thrust of the
third archer, who had risen to his knees and now hesitated,
seeing himself outnumbered, between sword and bow. Again,
it was Hu's sling that decided it. A stone caught him on the
side of the head and he fell, motionless.

But the other horsemen still held Cairenn. Melwas and
Tegan and Hu stood panting and desperate. It was now so
nearly dark that they could hardly make out this larger
group. Arrows still hissed from them, but randomly, no longer
finding their mark. They heard the escaped archer's cry as he
reached his comrades. Then there were more hooves thudding nearer. The three lowered themselves into the long
grass and began to edge away from the scene of the conflict.
The hoofbeats slowed some way off. They could hear the
voices of the strangers, tense, questioning each other.
Distances and directions were becoming uncertain. They
were scattering, searching.

A shout of anger. Someone had found the dead men. There
was a bloodcurdling keening, then a thrashing of bushes.
Melwas tried not to think what would happen if one of them
were caught.

But he would not run from them. With grim determination
he was working his way in a looping semicircle around this
forward group. If he could evade their almost-blind searching, somewhere beyond, one man at least, possibly no more,
was guarding Cairenn.

He never reached them. Behind him, there was a scream
like a buzzard. The hoofbeats were coming back, more slowly.
He guessed, rather than saw, the archers whom he and Hu
had felled, laid over their mounts and being led back with
laments. A cry came from the waiting rearguard, still further
away than Melwas had imagined. The horsemen passed him,
far shadows on the skyline of the slope, and merged into the
gloom. They had quickened their pace, disappearing swiftly
into the valley. He started after them, but soon lost even the

133

distant sound of their hooves. He could not hope to give chase on foot, or track them in the dark.

A wave of weariness washed over Melwas. It had been a momentous day. He had seen the horror of invading Romans encamped in Dumnon. He had nerved all his courage to face death with honour as a sacrificial victim for his tribe. He had fought his first real combat, against experienced soldiers twice his age, and he had won. He had killed his first man. His knees trembled.

*Thin arms, hard as spear-shafts, against my ribs. The reek of breath, like wild garlic trampled underfoot. Insane laughter and cries I do not understand. They are galloping me away towards the farther woods. I struggle and beat at my captor, but he seems hardly to need his hands to guide the pony beneath us. Now I am fighting with the instinctive desire to cling on to him, so that I do not slip under these threshing hooves. There are more horsemen, blue and black and silver in the twilight, alongside me.*

*We make a sweeping curve and stand, suddenly still, on the edge of the trees. Not all the horsemen are with us. I hear a sharpness in the men's voices. Something is wrong, for them as well as me.*

*Grey dusk is settling over the heath. I still see the huge skies, almost emptied of colour. But it is harder to distinguish gorse, heather, grass, bracken. It is the shouts which tell me there is fighting, back where they caught me. Again that surge of pride, like sparks flung up from a fire. Surely there is only one person who would be fighting my captors? It is Aidan after all, come in the nick of time to rescue me. I hold myself tense, muscles gathered to spring out of these imprisoning arms and race to him.*

*Clash of blades. A man screams. How many are the British? What is happening? There is rapid angry talking all around me.*

*Darker shapes are coming out of the gloom. Too slowly, I fear, to be Aidan. He would come swooping up to snatch me away, laughing, to safety. These must be the returning archers. There is something large and heavy, draped over the horse's neck. A millstone seems to fall through my body, crushing me with dread. Not Aidan. Oh, please, not Aidan.*

*It is one of their own. A fierce, exultant joy. And another comes.*

*One of the foreigners slaps me violently, unexpectedly, across the face. It almost knocks me from my seat, but my captor is quick to tighten his imprisoning arms.*

*They are more concerned with their comrades now. I think they are both dead. And my eyes go out beyond them, searching for their killers in the twilight. My friends, surely?*

*The archer who holds me leans sideways to speak to the others. I feel the grip round my waist easing. Now!*

*I leap from the far side of his pony and dash for the woods. I want to scream 'Aidan!' But I need that moment of confusion before the rest know I have gone. I hear my captor yell. And a chaos of shouts echoes his. I don't need to turn to know they are all on their feet or drumming heels into their mounts to storm after me.*

*I cannot see the brambles or branches any more than they can. I am tearing, tripping, crashing through. Suddenly there is silence behind me, then a yell of triumph as the noise of my going betrays me.*

*They are on me, tall creatures of nightmare in the near darkness. I see their teeth grinning. I feel their hands like pincers. I hear their panting breath. I am hurled to the ground. The first man stoops over me; I know what must follow.*

*A single sharp command. Their roars are hushed. Someone is stepping forward. The rest fall back.*

*He looms above me, so that I can see only the thundercloud of his hair. Is he their captain? Will he have me first? I curl my knees in a tight ball of defiance. His hand shoots down and grabs me by the throat.*

*A guttural question. I cannot understand. My neck jerks so, I think he will break it. His knuckles are round the torque Beath gave me, digging painfully into the muscles beneath it. Let him have it. I am not Aidan's wife, though I wear his mother's gift. I bear a loss greater than that. Aidan has not rescued me, so they must have killed him, back there in the heather. Let me die.*

*There is muttering all around me. I am hauled to my feet by that grip on the torque, so that I choke for breath. I think he is showing it to the others in the last light between the trees. The men are angry, cheated of lust and revenge. But they obey him. I am pushed savagely, but with a reluctant respect, back towards the waiting ponies.*

*I try to hold my head high and hope they cannot see my tears coursing in the twilight. Aidan has probably died for me. But I have been reprieved. The golden gift that should have sealed our marriage has bought my life.*

From far away Melwas heard a whistle. It touched the edge of memory. Somewhere, Hu and Tegan would be looking for him. He still had friends.

He tried to shout, but there was surprisingly little strength in his voice. He stumbled back towards the sound. They came to meet him through the gloom.

'You're safe?' Tegan called. 'They didn't get you?'

'Of course they didn't. I'm a warrior of Britain; I can look after myself.'

'You, and Hu's sling,' murmured Tegan, coming closer. 'Who were they, Melwas? They didn't look like that dead Roman.'

'Does it matter?' said Melwas. 'They must be on the same side.'

'But we beat them, didn't we? They ran away.' Hu's teeth grinned in the dark.

'Those others came too soon. It was my first kill. I should

have cut off that archer's head and tied it to my saddle-bow as a trophy. That would have shown Aidan.'

'Men!' Tegan almost spat. 'You haven't got a horse, anyway. And Aidan's going to be furious when he hears about this. You realize the news will now go straight back to the Roman camp that there are armed warriors this side of the Forest? Just when he's planning to surprise them with an ambush.'

Melwas winced. 'He killed a Roman himself. He should be glad there are two more dead before the battle.'

None of them was saying the thing which lay heaviest on all their minds. At last Tegan broke the silence.

'Did you see that thing Cairenn was wearing round her neck? That great golden torque, like a queen's?'

Hu murmured assent. Melwas did not answer.

'I've never seen it on her before. But it wasn't wise. Does she want the whole world to know she's a princess, even the Romans?'

'Why shouldn't she?' Melwas's voice rang out alarmingly over the hillside. He lowered it again as he went on. 'I don't know where she got it from, but she *is* a princess. The daughter of a famous chief of Dumnon. I challenge anyone who holds her to treat her with proper respect.'

'Oh, you nobles!' Tegan snorted in exasperation. 'You're all the same. You can't see further than the end of your proud noses. Do you think a scouting-party would have bothered about a village girl? They leave that sort of thing till the battle's won. But even in the twilight they could see she was a fine prisoner to take. One that Dumnon will pay dearly to get back.'

Melwas stared at her shadowed face, then turned away. 'All the more reason to defeat them tomorrow,' he said bitterly.

'Tomorrow?' There was a nervous question in Hu's voice. 'What's going to happen now? Will Aidan want us back?'

There was a pause. Then Melwas declared, 'I don't care. I'm going to kill the Romans, whether Aidan wants me or not.'

137

'We can't get back tonight,' said Tegan. 'Not in the dark.'

'We can sleep as well under the stars here as at the Silent Fort.'

They retreated to the edge of the unguarded heath and the shelter of the trees.

As they settled themselves down, something dug into Melwas's neck. He felt for it in the dark, expected a twig or a piece of grit. His fingers found the lead pendant, taken from that first dead Roman legionary. He explored its shape, curiously. It was all he had. No hacked-off head, dangling from blue-black hair. No captured weapon, though one might lie somewhere out on the heath. He had not even killed the man whose neck he had taken it from. A pendant of common lead, with the sign of a fish. Was it the symbol of some Roman god?

And Cairenn, with a British golden torque round her neck, was a prisoner of these Romans.

# CHAPTER 10

## AMBUSH

*I* am a princess of Dumnon. I will not show fear.
They have brought me to the changed ground of the Underworld. The wounded earth piled up in embankments by alien spades. How can they have built this mighty palisade, those guard towers, so swiftly? These are not humans.

I am a princess of Dumnon. Hold fast to that.

The light of their torches catches me in the gateway. My skirt is torn, my hair dishevelled. I am covered with leaves and dirt, where they threw me to the ground in the woods.

I must keep my head high.

I cannot help shaking. Surely this is a winter wind, bitter and chilling. Too many eyes are looking at me. Men. Foreign men. I do not need to understand their language to know the jokes they are making.

I will not let my eyes drop.

A murmur of curiosity. The captain of the archers answers them. He speaks their tongue, but his accent is different from theirs. Now the guards have seen the torque which marks me out as different. Something has subtly changed in their attitude. I am no common girl running from soldiers, a thing for their sport. I am noble.

Let me act nobly.

*I am shivering under their stares.*

*Dragged inside now. Even in the dark I see how huge this camp must be. Fires light the alleyways between the tents, more regular than our wandering stars. There are broad roads laid down, but not Arianrhod's curving silver highway across the sky. Their Otherworld is straight, ruthless, relentless.*

*How can Celynen's serpentine druid intelligence hope to influence a people who think in straight lines? They will not listen to us. They have their inflexible Roman laws. They will despise ours.*

*Is this their commander's tent? Is it meant to overawe me? The eagle-headed standard, the plumed helmets, the blaze of scarlet cloaks? I have lived in vaster halls than this, seen shields that are miracles of art, embroidered cloaks woven from seven colours entwined with silver thread.*

*I have lifted my hand unconsciously to show them the torque. This is rare work. British gold.*

*Their chief leans forward. A sentence so sharp it must be a question.*

'Who are you?'

*The word startles me. This is my own tongue. Then I realize it cannot come from this hammer-faced man in the general's breastplate. The voice spoke from the shadows to one side. I turn my eyes and find someone whom I know cannot be Roman. A leather jerkin over a plain brown tunic. A hood that hides his face of shame. Sharp features, like the rat he is, peer out. He is one of us. No foreign inflection in these British words. He speaks my language, for Rome.*

*I hate him.*

'Who are you?'

*And then I realize this was not an echo of his words in my head. He has repeated the question. I must answer.*

*Who am I?*

'Cairenn, Drem's daughter.'

*If only I could have told them I was Aidan's wife.*

140

*Cairenn of the White Fingers. Cairenn who plays the harp, with its lilting British airs that seem to tune themselves best to laments, though we can pipe a march bravely too.*

*Cairenn, daughter of a woman of druid blood. Wise enough already for Celynen, High Druid, to talk with me as though I were a favoured student in his school.*

*Little Cairenn. Last week a child, looking forward proudly to womanhood, yet chafing at the loss of her freedom to run wild.*

*Cairenn, a war-widow before her wedding.*

*I am the hope of Dumnon, to teach her songs and stories to her children, even under the heel of the conquerors.*

*I have missed several questions. They are growing angry. And suddenly I am overwhelmingly tired. I drag the answers out of a weary heart.*

*I do not know why I was alone on the heath. I was lost. I live at the Forest Fort with Idwal Goldenshield, but my true home is farther west. I know nothing of rebels. I do not know who killed your men.*

*I do not know. I do not know.*

*The torque does not save me from a disbelieving blow.*

*I do not know. It was dark. I was alone. No one was with me.*

*I want to shout that it was the bravery of Aidan, the Red Fox. Aidan who will kill you if you venture any further into our beloved land. It must have been Aidan. Who else would risk his life to save me?*

*Is he dead, back there in the darkness? No one will tell me. I dare not ask.*

*A smaller tent. A mattress. A candle. My hands are bound. No woman to attend me. No comb for my hair. No drink but water. This heavy gold collar is all I have to make me believe I was once a princess.*

*A prisoner of Rome. A woman alone, among thousands of hostile men. Bereft of all I love.*

141

Hu woke them while it was still almost dark. They rose, stiff and chilled, with the stale taste of unfinished sleep in their mouths. But immediately Melwas knew what morning it was, the sense of danger and adventure sent his spirit rising and his heart beating faster.

'The ambush!' He reached for his sword. It was still a creature of awe and alarm, rather than a trusted friend.

'And Aidan,' Tegan murmured. 'I'm not looking forward to that.'

'Aidan needs every sword he can muster.' Melwas buckled the too-long weapon on. 'I'm a warrior now. Dumnon needs me . . . And they've got Cairenn.'

Tegan caught Hu's eyes and fingered the blade of her own sword.

They had brought no food, and hunger was sharp in their bellies. There was a keen awareness in all their senses. They knew that this morning everything they touched and smelt and saw might be theirs to enjoy for the last time.

Hu led them swiftly up the hill. He seemed sure of his direction even in the gloom before daybreak. As they crossed the ridge, it was just becoming possible to distinguish sky from earth. The fall of land led down in a long incline to the next river, where the ambush must be set. As they pressed towards it they became gradually aware that they were not alone. There was a tide of movement in the murk, a silent flow of warriors coming down from the heights.

Tegan slowed. 'He won't be pleased with us, but as long as we can hold a weapon he won't send us back, will he?' She spoke as if to convince herself.

'Two hundred is little enough against a whole Roman legion. And if he thinks we betrayed him last night, we'll show him he's wrong. When he sees our daring, he'll know we're as loyal to Dumnon as any grown man.'

Tegan laughed, and gave him a friendly push. 'That's the

spirit, foxcub! We'll show him, you and I!'

The bare heath was giving way to wooded coombes, leading always downward towards the river. They halted where the trees began. There was just enough light to see the dark press of men and the tall figure of Aidan striding amongst them. At his murmured commands the men shuffled into groups, and to each band he gave the order of attack.

Just as he finished, there came the creaking of chariot wheels over the rough ground. Seiriol came riding down the hill towards them. She was standing beside her charioteer, dressed in long black robes bound with gold across her breast. Her grey-red hair flowed loose to her waist and her great sword in its jewelled black scabbard hung heavy against her hip. In her hand she grasped her spear. She lifted it high to greet Aidan. Then, as she ran her gaze over the troops, her sharp eyes picked out Melwas trying to slip inconspicuously into the third group.

'A fine morning to you, Melwas Mighty-Heart!' she called. 'Since you come last to the battlefield, may you also be the last to leave it. But you are only half armed. Do not despise the gifts of Seiriol.'

Her chariot wheeled round to him. She tossed his own spear into his hand and passed down to him his studded shield. Melwas felt the eyes of the whole warhost upon him as he settled it on his arm. The first rays of morning blazed upon the rich design of red and blue enamel, the intricate spirals. He was suddenly aware how much more beautiful and costly this shield was than that of any other man around him. It marked him out as a prince. The thought came to him that if Seiriol had really wished to protect him, she would have given him equipment of less magnificence. Armed like this, he must surely be singled out by the enemy for death or capture.

As Cairenn had flaunted the torque of a princess . . . .

But there must be magic in these marvellous weapons. The

143

very touch of them filled him with new courage. As he grasped the spear in his hands he knew a fierce joy that cared nothing for danger or death. It was as if his whole life had been lived for this moment, this battle, this glory.

Even through the long waiting which followed, this high pitch of expectancy did not leave him. At Aidan's orders, he climbed an oak tree and lay crouched in its branches while the sun climbed into the sky. Somewhere over the hill a Roman legion was breaking camp, loading its baggage train, setting out to march. Unless . . . .

What message had those archers carried back, with Cairenn as their prisoner? Would the Romans now be expecting this ambush?

He listened through the rushing of the river for a new sound.

It came at last, the rhythmic tramp of many feet, hundred after hundred, till it seemed that the whole hill beyond the river was shaking to their tread.

Still they waited. The nearer sounds became muffled under the branches. There was a light splashing through the water, and then hoofbeats on the bank close at hand. Not a movement stirred in the trees around as the advance scouts passed on through the wood. Those last seconds of waiting seemed the longest of all.

Then, suddenly close, there was a harsh word of command, the splashing of many more feet in the river. With a fierce yell, Aidan launched his first wave of attack. After that, time had no meaning for Melwas. Another cry. Another band of young Britons broke from the trees to join the shouting and clash of weapons at the ford. A third cry, and Melwas, pulses racing, leaped from his hiding-place and tore into the sunlight.

He plunged into the water in the midst of a scene of utter confusion. Sheets of silver spray flew through the air in all directions. Bodies struggled and staggered to the thrust of sword and shield. On the further bank Roman soldiers were pouring out of the trees. But they were helpless to join the battle at the narrow ford. They could only line the banks in close-packed ranks, shouting encouragement as they waited for the order to advance.

Melwas charged forward, hacking and slashing with his long sword. He could not remember when he had cast his spear. It was hard to get past the taller Britons wrestling in front of him. Inert bodies rolled underfoot. The shifting shingle gave an unsteady foothold. He dodged round Elaeth, hacking and slashing at anyone coming. Even now he scarcely saw whom he was hitting. Blows hammered against his shield. Only the speed of his sword-arm saved his life. Against a disciplined foe, he fought that morning like a man possessed.

Yet now they were pressing him hard, three stocky, muscular legionaries against himself and Tegan. The reach of his weapon was longer than theirs, but his arm was unbearably weary from the swing of the heavy sword and the jarring blows with which it bit into Roman armour. Its fine blade was blunted and bent now, but still the battle-hardened Romans were coming after him, driving him back. Their short, bright swords were stabbing towards his stomach. How much longer could he continue to sweep those blades aside with his longer weapon before one of them cut upwards under his guard?

Then, with a scream that struck terror into every heart, Seiriol's chariot came thundering out of the woods behind him. With her red hair streaming out behind her and her great sword brandished aloft, she swept into the fight, scattering British and Romans alike. Glittering water shot out from under her wheels. In sudden panic the Romans stumbled and turned. Melwas and Tegan leaped for their lives. Their three adversaries had dropped their swords and were clawing their way towards the bank. With a mighty sweep, Seiriol's sword sliced into one of them and sent him tumbling backwards into the river in a red torrent of blood. Her chariot surged on. Right and left she struck, dealing death and consternation. Legionaries were praying aloud as they struggled for safety. But the grassy verge was so choked with the press of the oncoming army that many men fell back before they could gain a foothold, and were swept away into the deep, swift water below the ford.

The charioteer wheeled her team. The foam-spattered ponies plunged towards the western shore, leaving the echo of Seiriol's laughter ringing down the sunlit river.

There was a strange lull. Melwas found himself standing knee-deep in the middle of the ford with Tegan and a handful of others. For a moment he did not understand. In front of him, the legionaries were ranged shoulder to shoulder, a great host as far as the eye could penetrate under the trees. He could hardly press forward against such a foe. And where were Aidan and the rest? Suddenly, he saw what had happened. The Romans had withdrawn and the British were now an open target for their javelins.

Even as he turned in panic, they began to hurtle through the air. He started to splash towards the shelter of the trees. His movements seemed desperately slow. Now that he could no longer fight, his courage deserted him. Breath sobbed through his trembling lips. Around him, men fell and did not rise again. Some of them he knew as friends. But he dared not stop. In front of him, he saw Tegan stumble, and he thought she was hit. Then she recovered and went on.

At last he grasped the bank. Even as he did so, a new danger broke upon them. Archers on horseback, blue-cloaked like those he had barely escaped the evening before, came bursting out of the trees on the other side of the river. They loosed a flight of arrows at the retreating Britons. The approach to the ford was jammed by the infantry, but these horsemen scorned the shallow water and fanned out upstream and downstream. Their ponies neighed shrilly as the riders leaped them down the banks. Now they were breasting the current, swimming strongly towards the British side. In desperation, Aidan's men gathered up what missiles they could find – British spears, Roman javelins – and cast them at the oncoming riders. But these weapons were soon spent. Only Hu's sling kept up an unflagging defence. There was a breathless pause while the first horses struggled to find a landing-place.

The leading rider suddenly toppled backwards. Blood trickled down his face, though no blade had struck him. Hu took another stone from his pouch and whirled the sling round his head.

Then the valley rocked to Roman cheers as the tide of invading cavalry poured up over the banks and wheeled upon Aidan's band. A rain of arrows joined the hail of javelins.

From inside the wood, a horn-call sounded the retreat. Melwas scrambled to his feet and fled. He saw Hu dropping from an oak branch and tried to follow him, but the swift, brown figure was lost among the trees. He found that Tegan was running at his side. An arrow plunged through the leaves. She screamed, and clutched her shoulder as the blood trickled down her green tunic.

'It's nothing. Don't stop,' she panted.

They ran on, dodging between the trees. Somewhere there must be open ground ahead. The light grew brighter. Suddenly they were out of the wood. Ahead of them, the slope was dotted with British warriors, scattering towards safety. Melwas glanced back. Pursuit was not yet in sight. Without thinking, Melwas began to run uphill, back to the Silent Fort.

But Tegan gasped after him, 'Not that way! They'd soon find us there!'

She turned her face down-river and steadied her run to a long, loping stride. He followed her. They seemed to be running alone, with the stillness of noonday all around them. If they went on like this, they would soon put miles between themselves and the Roman army at the ford. Then they could find a hiding-place to rest, and . . . .

Tegan shrieked. Out of the trees to their right broke a group of horsemen. This time they did not have Hu to wield his deadly sling. It was too late to hide. Melwas and Tegan changed course and ran desperately uphill. With every step they were listening for the thunder of hoofbeats behind them.

On they ran, the breath torn from their lungs with the sound of ripping cloth. At last Tegan ventured a glance over her shoulder. Her knees staggered and she dropped to the ground.

'It's all right, foxcub. They've found bigger quarry.'

The archers had swept in a wide arc up the hillside further west. Flashes of colour told where Aidan's warriors were still fleeing from them.

Tegan was doubled over, her tanned face yellow with pain. Blood was oozing through the fingers she held over her wound.

Melwas went down on his knees beside her. He wished he knew more about wounds, anything. He felt ignorant, frightened.

'Sorry, I can't run any more.' Her breathing was laboured. 'Well, go on, tear me a bandage, can't you? Use my tunic if you're too proud to spoil your own.'

He took his dagger and slashed a strip from the hem of his own. Awkwardly he started to bind the gash.

'Tighter,' she ordered, through clenched teeth.

It was done, though the blood saturated the cloth almost immediately and continued to trickle down her arm.

'Help me up. We can't stay here.'

He supported her to the top of the ridge. Suddenly there was a brightness in front of them. The sound of the sea was in their ears. Below them, a river flowed out on to a pebbly beach. Grey waves came surging up over the shingle and fell back with a grinding roar. They staggered down to it and stood at the sea's edge, letting the rhythmic rush steady their breathing.

'There's nowhere left to run.' Tegan was nursing her bandaged arm.

'Does it hurt?'

'Of course it does. What did you think?' But her usually brisk voice was listless.

'I'm starving.'

Melwas went off to search the beach. He tried to prise limpets off the rocks with his hunting-knife, but they were tightly clamped. He took a stone and broke them open and tore out their soft bodies.

Tegan sat slumped on the stones. He offered her a handful. They both chewed the tough, salty morsels. Tegan swallowed a few with difficulty, then handed the rest to him.

'You have them. I just want to sleep.'

She lay down in the open. Melwas gave her a worried look, then began to search the beach for some shelter. There were caves in the red sandstone, slits of darkness. He tried several before he found one that was dry.

'Tegan,' he said, standing over her.

'Yes?' She did not open her eyes.

'Get up.'

To his surprise, she started to struggle to her feet. He helped her into the cave. She lay down on the gravel floor and closed her eyes again.

Melwas went and sat in the cave-mouth. The sun was laying a broad track of gold across the sea. As the whisper of the waves steadied his breathing, he felt the fear and tension beginning to relax, leaving him curiously light-hearted. It seemed impossible that he could have fought in such a bloody battle and yet sit here, alive and whole, beyond the reach of his enemies. He had not even dropped his shield and sword in his desperate flight. Surely that was something to be proud of?

What should he do now? For tonight, he had shelter and a safe hiding-place. In the morning, he would have to get help for Tegan and find Aidan again.

But first, he must bring his weapons into the shadows of the cave. They lay where he had set them down on the beach, between him and the sea. He walked across and bent to lift them.

As his muscles took their weight, reality returned. His face creased with the pain he had been denying. It was true that he had not been seriously wounded, but all down his left side he bore the bruises where his shield had caught the force of enemy blows. He shifted the weight of it to his right arm. There, too, red pain threaded his wrist which had wielded the great sword for so long. Yet every ache was a source of satisfaction. His own British chief had called him a boy, but the Romans had met him sword to sword, sparing him nothing, and he had lived. Tomorrow this sun would rise for him again.

As he turned back to the cave, he wondered about the ambush. It was over, and he had survived it. Yet he did not think it had been a victory. Many of Aidan's young warriors had fallen. His feet had stumbled over them in the ford. The rest were scattered over the countryside, fleeing for their lives.

And for what? By now the Romans must have poured across the ford to the western bank. They would be following the archers up new slopes of Dumnon. Surely they had, all of them, known how it must be? Could Aidan really have believed that two hundred British warriors could hold back an entire legion?

So what had they gained? It was true it would take Vespasian one day longer to march westward. *One day?* One precious day as a free people: was that all it had been for? That, and the determination that, though they could not stop the Romans from conquering Dumnon, they would make them fight for this beloved soil foot by foot, and hour by hour, to the last drop of their blood?

He looked down the long sweep of the coast westward. Where the red cliffs ended, the estuary of the Salmon River spread a sheet of silver, broadening out to meet the sand banks and the sea. If it had not been for Aidan, the army of Rome would be standing now on its brink. And they were not. They still had to cross the wood between the heath and the river. Unconquered still were the coracles bobbing on the evening tide, the golden pastures by the Quiet Water, the deer-haunted dells of the Great Forest. Ours, for one night more. Aidan had won this. And he, Melwas, had helped him do it.

# CHAPTER 11

## THE PRISONER

Next morning, Melwas woke to a sense of unreality, and then a knowledge of loss. But something of Tegan's old cheerful self had returned. He noticed that she winced as she moved and there was a tautness in her smile, but she declared defiantly that her arm, though stiff, would soon be as good as ever.

They washed in cold salt water, then stood staring out to sea. They were forest-people, marvelling at the grey plains of the Channel reaching away as far as the eye could see, and beyond that still lay the unseen shores of Gaul. Soon the last south-west kingdom of Britain would fall, as Gaul had been conquered.

'Well, foxcub?' Tegan laughed, shaking the water out of her eyes. 'Those Armoricans didn't come across the Channel for nothing. That was a brave fight. We've tasted Roman blood, and we're still alive to tell the tale.'

'What about the others? Did Aidan get away? Where would he go?'

'The Red Fox has more than one hole to his earth. We'd better start looking for him. And food too, before I faint from hunger. I need more than an uncooked limpet.'

Gathering up their weapons, they set out westwards, inland.

Soon they saw a trail of smoke ahead and their spirits rose. Smoke meant fire and food. Melwas realized painfully how hungry he was too. They hurried hopefully forward until a small cluster of huts came into view. No one was about.

Melwas went up to the nearest hut and called out, 'Hey, there!'

There was no answer. The leather curtain in front of the doorway did not stir. Melwas walked across the trodden space between the huts and called again. A lone hen squawked anxiously and scurried away. The huts were silent.

He walked back to the first hut, from which a slender stem of smoke still climbed into the sky. He pushed back the curtain and strode in. The hut was empty. The few coverings and cooking pots it must once have held were gone. The last logs had collapsed on to the fire. Soon they would burn through to a smokeless ash. He poked around, and under the low mud wall of the hut he found a half-eaten, grubby crust of bread. He walked out into the daylight chewing it and tore off half for Tegan. She had found two eggs. In a few moments, they had baked them in the ashes.

'Where's everybody?' Melwas wondered.

She shot a glance up at him from a face bent over the food. 'Can't you imagine? This is war, Melwas. The Romans are here.'

The sheltering roofs of the huts no longer felt secure. Too easy now to imagine the inhabitants fleeing in terror of the Romans' approach. The weight of their fear hung heavily upon the deserted village. Melwas walked outside, away from the dying fire. Even in the sunlight, with Tegan behind him, he felt a chill of loneliness. They were not yet far enough away from the enemy.

They made haste to leave the village and walked on westward, guided by the dancing light in the sky to their left, which showed where the land ended and the bright bay began.

153

Tegan stopped where a brook glinted through a thin screen of alder bushes. On the crest beyond reared the ramparts of the Silent Fort, red against the pale blue sky.

Melwas gave a crow of triumph. 'We're nearly there! I bet he'll be astonished to see us alive!' Already he was splashing through the water.

Tegan grabbed his arm. 'Don't be silly. Aidan won't be there. Now that the Romans have crossed the ford, the Silent Fort will never be safe for us again.'

'He might have left someone behind to tell us where to go.'

Tegan snorted. 'The rest of the world doesn't think you're as important as you seem to rate yourself. Aidan's got far worse things to worry about than what became of us two.'

'You don't know that. And there were lots of others who scattered as we did. He's got to get us all back together somehow. At least he might have left us some signs.'

'Oh, well, if you're set on running into a Roman trap, I'd better come with you to look after you.'

'Thanks!' He strode ahead, offended.

They saw no one, Roman or Briton, over that wide hillside as they climbed. The shadow of the earthworks enfolded them and they slipped in through the southern gate, hands tensed on their swords.

No one challenged them. They relaxed again, in a wave of relief and disappointment. The fort was empty, though for all Aidan's care there were, as in the village, signs of recent occupation. Flattened grass that had not all been combed upright. Missed footprints in the sand. Fresh scores upon the weapon stone. Yesterday, two hundred British warriors had risen in the grey dawn and armed themselves here. Not all of them had lived to see the sunset.

Melwas scuffed his toe in the fallen pine-needles. There was a question he had dared not voice last night. 'What about Hu? Do you think he got away?'

'I shouldn't worry about him. He's uncanny, that one. I think he must have been given the gift of invisibility from the Fair Folk. If he stood still in the shadows, the whole Roman army could march past and not see him. He seems to be able to appear out of the mist and vanish again into the side of the hill.'

Melwas thought of the boy in the brown tunic with the quiet smile. He saw him flitting through the woods like a shadow. Tegan was right. He did not think the Romans would have caught him.

'So what do we do now?'

There was a hesitation. Then Tegan's voice came low and strained. 'I think I know a better hiding-place. At Seiriol's Oaks. They've gathered there before.'

A blaze of fear and exultation surged in Melwas's heart. The heart-stopping grove of his initiation. And the night before, the laughter of men while he lay locked in a hut.

In silence, he walked to the northern wall of the fort and looked over. He drew his breath in a shocked gasp. A new marching-camp of the Second Legion lay in full view of the ramparts.

It was exactly as though they had picked up the camp he had seen before and carried it by its four corners to set it down in its new place. The square of red earthworks. The same lines of brown leather tents, with the same spaces between. Even the cooking-fires sent up their smoke from the same positions. Cold fingers groped across Melwas's heart. An alien mind was creeping across his country like the dark shadow of a cloud.

Unable to speak, he motioned Tegan to join him. She stared down at it. There were tears in her eyes.

*Can British gods have any power in a Roman camp? I still make the age-old chants, instinctive as breathing, when I rise, when I lie down, when I eat the dull food of bread and*

155

*beans they give me. But I am afraid that those I call on have deserted me. All my life I have moved surrounded by their presence, in every tree, every stream, in the spurting milk, in the running horses. I have even found myself talking familiarly with them. I have druid blood. This is their land. We are their people. Nothing that we do is done without them.*

*Not here. I do not know what gods the Romans worship. They are not ours. I press my hands against the earth this prison-tent covers. Surely this is still British soil? Surely our tribal Lords and Ladies are present here?*

*I feel nothing. Can gods be conquered, like people? When these soldiers dug their spades into our red earth and piled it up in fortifications, did they uproot the guardian spirits of this land? Are these ramparts their burial mounds?*

*Can the gods die?*

*No, but they are deserting us. How else could it be possible for the High Dun to fall? For the legions to tramp over Dumnon, swallowing my country into their empire, like a terrifying tide that goes on rising and refuses to turn?*

*Our gods are going. Where I knelt at the Salmon River's edge to plead for their help, there they will come stalking down from the moors, sidling out of the woods, creeping like a mist up out of the marshy hollows. Taking ship.*

*They are leaving us. There must be ghostly craft rocking on the estuary of the Exe. And sleep-stunned seamen who cannot see their passengers. Only the ship settles deeper under this weight of grief. The moorings slip, the tide is ebbing. Down over the silver reach to the last red sandbar and the open sea. Westward, to the sunset, and the Isles of the Blest.*

*Shall I follow them?*

*The general's questions are over. No one talks to me now. They have left me alone, my arms bound.*

*Is the ship of the dead already waiting for me?*

*I grasp a handful of earth in my imprisoned hands and squeeze it tight. Are any of you still here, in your sacred soil?*

*Can't you feel my need?*

*Why did I run from the Forest Fort? I have thrown my life away. I have not found Melwas . . . or Aidan.*

*We British are a disobedient people, who despise discipline; who call folly honour and save our most glorious songs for those who fling their lives under the feet of their foes. We were not obedient to our elders, Aidan, Melwas, I. We did not weigh the cost. We were not sensible.*

*We are true children of Dumnon. This is the sort of people we are. This is how we define ourselves.*

*Celynen is not of our times or our thought. Too grave, too wise, too peaceable. Elsewhere, in the mountains of the west, the druids rant and chant and inflame the British to war. Celynen would make an accommodation with the Romans.*

*The Romans will swallow up Celynen, as they have devoured me.*

*The greasy leather of this tent is like the stomach of a monster. I shall never get out alive. Our gods have left me.*

They fled the fort by the southern gate, keeping low in the long grass. Melwas felt like a mouse running for its life under the shadow of a hawk.

The oak wood closed round them. The sunlight dwindled. The trees grew larger, older, swelling into more fantastic shapes.

Seiriol's grove drew them into its shadows like swallows returning from the sunnier south. Their first warning was the cry of guards hidden in the oak trees beside the track. They were instantly surrounded. These were men from a clan further north, but they recognized Melwas and looked with respect at Tegan's bloody bandage. The two were passed through and came out before the high fence. Tegan hung back, staring up at the huge twisted branches reaching out over it.

'This place is worse than the Silent Fort. I'm scared. It

belongs to the Lordly Ones, not us.'

Melwas summoned up his own courage and strode through the gateway.

He stopped still. The clearing looked utterly different. All sense of mystery had gone. The sanctuary was now a busy camp of war. Wounded men lay in the thin sunlight where the branches of the oaks did not reach. Seiriol and her assistant were moving among them with medicines and salves. Warriors were attending to their damaged gear. A smith bent over a smokeless fire, busy repairing a blade.

It was strange to Melwas to see the carved pillar still standing between the greatest oaks. It looked almost out of place. Most soldiers were walking past it and back again without a second glance. But some peered sideways, furtively, and made a wide detour to avoid it. Melwas found his own head bowing.

A glad cry startled him. To his joy, it was Hu. He came running, light-footed over the grass, calling out to Aidan as he went. There was a smile on his face as eager as if they had been lifelong friends, as though for a moment the two boys were not prince and peasant.

'Melwas! You're safe! We were all sure you must have been killed at the ford. There was no chance to turn back and look. And Tegan! . . . Come in. It's all right, there's nothing to be afraid of.'

Yet Melwas remembered how Hu himself had hurried them both away from here. The battle at the ford seemed to have changed Hu. This was no longer the shy boy who had crept up to drop his salmon by Seiriol's gate and run.

Tegan came slowly inside, but she still hung close to the fence, keeping well away from the pillar and from Seiriol.

Aidan came strolling over, his face surprisingly brimful of laughter. Rieuk, the Armorican druid, was behind him.

'So, you cheated the Romans again? I thought we'd lost you to the Otherworld this time.'

'Not me!'

The Armorican greeted Melwas courteously too, but his dark eyes burned with impatience. 'Aidan, we must decide . . . .'

But Aidan clapped his foster-brother on the shoulder.

'That was bold work you did at the ford, foxcub. I had precious little time to look about me, but I saw you holding back some of their bullies. It was bravely done.'

Melwas glowed. 'Tegan was wounded.'

Aidan gave the girl no more than a glance. Rieuk broke in again.

'Son of Idwal, time is short! Those accursed Romans must be less than a day's march from the Salmon River. If they capture the bridging-place, all Dumnon is lost. What are you going to do?'

The two men moved away, their heads bent in earnest talk.

Hu smiled shyly at Melwas. 'I went back to my village last night. I think they were surprised to see me alive.'

'You went home? What about Crab? Is he all right? Does he miss me?'

'Your dog's fine.' Hu grinned more widely. 'My sister loves him. They go everywhere together. I think she'll be very sad when you take him back.'

'Could I go and see him? It's not very far, is it?'

Hu frowned. 'I don't know. Aidan's given orders that no one is to leave here unless he tells them. Did you see the Roman camp? They're very near. They know they're going to meet opposition now, but they don't know where we're hosting, or where the next ambush will be. It wouldn't matter if they caught me outside; I'm not important, but you . . . .'

He looked meaningfully at Melwas's stiff red hair and the rich sword at his side.

'I'll ask him if I can go,' Melwas said. 'I'll be very careful. I could leave my weapons behind.'

Hu looked Melwas over from head to toe. He said nothing.

159

But there was no time even to ask. The newcomers were given food. Immediately the warrior band was on the move again.

Tegan, to her disgust, was ordered to stay behind and have her wound attended to, and then to help Seiriol with the more gravely injured.

Melwas found himself marching swiftly with the others by forest trails and sheltered coombes. At the head of one valley, Aidan lifted his hand. They waited breathlessly. Along the path below them came a foraging party of Roman soldiers laden with corn. With a cry of triumph the British host swept down on either side of them. Quickly the Romans closed their ranks, shoulder to shoulder. They fought for their lives with a grim determination and they took many Britons with them as they fell. But there could be no escape. They were too few. When none of them remained alive, Aidan's men buried their own dead with honour, then gathered up the stolen corn and bore it back to Seiriol's grove.

Next day they came upon the ruins of a small village. The huts were smoking heaps of ashes and blackened timbers. The little gardens had been plundered of beans and corn.

On the way back, they ran into a Roman patrol on the edge of the wood, and this time they fought with a more bitter edge to their anger. Melwas hurled himself into the fight regardless of his own safety, until Aidan shouted roughly to him to take more care. Melwas obeyed. Grimly he acknowledged that Aidan was right: if he wanted revenge, he must stay alive to kill as many Romans as he could.

It was a short engagement. Seeing themselves heavily outnumbered, the Roman party retreated rapidly, still fighting, towards their camp. And Aidan was not to be lured into such a trap. His call rang out. The fight broke off, and in the space of a few heartbeats the warrior band had dissolved back into the shadows of the wood.

That night they were flushed with success. The wine-horn

went round and they feasted on roast pork, though Seiriol quickly smothered the fires, before the smoke could disentangle itself from the leafy boughs, and Aidan tried to hush the loudest of the singing. They grew more joyful still as the next day went by, and the next, and still the Romans did not break camp. Four thousand men lay pinned down by a band that now numbered no more than a hundred and fifty.

Melwas talked no more about going to see Crab. Each night he returned to the camp to throw himself on the ground and eat and sleep. His world had shrunk to the need to attack and survive. Hu's village, at the end of the forest trail, seemed oddly far away.

The hills were thick with Roman patrols, searching for the rebels. Aidan would allow no attacks on them near Seiriol's grove, but all through the day his men ranged far and wide, and wherever they came across a scouting-party far from their camp, they would cut them down or drive them back and then vanish once more into hiding. Melwas was scratched all over from hiding under gorse bushes, from crawling through the tough stems of heather and from leaping recklessly down from the branches of trees. He bore his first wound, a gash across his left arm, gained when he dashed into the fight from an ambush in which there had been no space to hide his shield. He tried to disguise the pain it cost him to carry that shield the next day.

They grew more daring. Under cover of darkness they crept up even to the earthen wall of Vespasian's camp. They heard the sentry cough, and watched his silhouette against the stars as he paced the raised walk to the corner. They spread out around the four walls. Aidan whistled. At once, all the sentries sprang to attention, with shouts of warning. They were too late. Three of them fell. One by Aidan's spear, one by Hu's sling, and one by the spear of an Armorican. There was uproar in the camp; men shouting, lights blazing, feet running to battle-stations. Outside in the darkness, all was silent. The Britons had gone as swiftly as they came, choking with silent laughter like mischievous boys. They had killed only a few out of thousands, but they were sowing terror among the invaders.

Early on the fourth evening, the sentries reported a Roman patrol approaching Seiriol's Oaks. The warband waited, hardly breathing, their hands on their weapons. The sacred oaks creaked in the wind. Pigs snuffled for acorns. The patrol passed on down the trail. Aidan had ensured that the paths to Seiriol's grove were so lightly beaten that the Romans would never know how close they had come.

It was nearly dark when the patrol came back up the trail. The watchers in the forest passed word back that they seemed to be laden with plunder. There was a stir of anger through the camp. But Aidan would not let anyone go after them. It was too close to their camp. Again, the Romans were allowed to pass unsuspecting.

But Melwas was alarmed. Down that path lay Hu's village and Crab. Had the Romans been there? Had they robbed it? When the danger was over, he hunted all over the camp for Hu, but no one had seen him. Melwas guessed that he had slipped away to find out for himself.

He was on the point of going after him. But it was not so easy now to act alone. Four days of danger and bloodshed had bound him into Aidan's band more strongly than he had realized. Each of their lives depended on their loyalty to each other. Many times these older warriors had risked their lives to save his. It was no light matter to disobey orders and chance betraying their hiding-place.

This time, he found Aidan and asked permission to go. His foster-brother frowned and said, 'You say Hu's gone?'

'I think he must have done. I've looked everywhere for him. He must be worried about his family.'

'Damn him! I gave strict orders no one was to leave this

camp without permission. I need him tonight.' His fingers drummed impatiently on his knee.

'What for?'

Aidan looked up, suddenly wary. Then a familiar laughter lit his blue eyes.

'Why not? You're not as light on your feet as Hu, but you could do it.'

Melwas found his heart racing with an unexplained excitement.

'Do what?'

'Look, Melwas.' Aidan leaned forward urgently. 'I must find out what's going on in Vespasian's camp. He can't stay there for ever. If he's going to capture Dumnon, he'll want to move soon, before the fine weather breaks and the autumn rains set in and turn our Dumnon clay to mud. And the moment he moves, we've got to strike again. He's a long way from base. He's never come this far west before. If we can get his baggage train . . . .'

'But what can I do?'

'I want you to go to his camp tonight. Get inside, if you can. Give me some idea of what's going on. If they're loading baggage, preparing to strike tents; anything unusual at all.'

Melwas swallowed. It was one thing to rush into battle, sword in hand, surrounded by a hundred shouting comrades, but to creep into danger alone and in the dark . . . . This called for a different order of courage. Yet he was proud, too, and glad now that Hu was missing.

He pushed down the thought that Hu had stalking skills he did not possess.

'All right. When?'

'Tonight. Go now. You won't learn much once they're asleep.'

Melwas turned for the gate. Aidan called after him:

'Oh, maybe you'd better take someone else with you. If one of you gets caught, the other one might still get back to us

163

with news. Who'd be best?' His eyes ranged round the oak grove.

Melwas thought quickly. Aidan's warriors sat dicing after the evening meal, or lay at ease on their cloaks, talking in low voices. Which of them would he trust with his life, where one careless movement could mean death for both of them? Away by the huts his eye caught a flicker of green, and he knew the answer.

'Tegan?'

Aidan raised his eyebrows and laughed contemptuously. 'A girl? A strange choice for a prince of Britain!'

'She's as brave as any of the men. And if we have to run for it, she can go like the wind.'

'Please yourself. At least if she gets herself killed, I shan't lose a grown warrior.'

There was a soft footfall behind them. Rieuk the Armorican looked Melwas over thoughtfully before addressing Aidan.

'So. Where is Hu?'

'Melwas is going in his place.'

'Then you've decided to seek news? Good. The men are getting impatient. These little skirmishes are not enough. We need decisive action. If Vespasian will not break camp of his own accord, then we must find a way to tempt him out.'

'You have a plan?'

Melwas left them talking and sought out Tegan. He watched her expression as he told her about their mission. He had expected her to be flattered, but her face crinkled in comical dismay.

'This is a doubtful compliment you're paying me, foxcub. I've no doubt you meant it kindly. But I don't fancy getting myself spitted on a Roman spear without the chance to strike first. I'd rather meet them in fair fight, any day, than go creeping into their camp like a snake in the grass.'

'I don't much like it either. But Aidan needs me.'

'Then I suppose I shall have to go along and keep you out of trouble.'

Tegan could move her arm more freely now, but long swords and heavy shields would have hampered their movements. They left them behind and set out through the woods, armed only with daggers in their belts.

It was a lonely walk. A pale owl flitted silent across their path. The wood was full of rustlings. Once, they heard a deep growling in the shadows. Tegan clutched Melwas's arm, biting back an almost irresistible scream. They hurried past, trembling. At that moment, even a party of Roman scouts would have seemed welcome.

They came out on to grass. The evening was overcast. The thick twilight offered protection, but it also muddled their senses. For a week, these slopes around the Silent Fort had been familiar ground to them in their covert operations, yet now the landscape seemed strangely distorted. Nothing was where they expected to find it. In the end, when they were sure they had lost the legionary camp completely, they almost blundered into its earthworks.

They dropped down into the heather and held their breath. Above them, a dull footfall told the passing of a sentry. They could see nothing from here. With a whispered word, Tegan rose and slipped away round to the back of the camp. Melwas felt terribly alone.

There was nothing to be gained by waiting. Already he could feel his courage ebbing with every heartbeat. He went up the bank with a rush, vaulted the fence, and dropped over and lay still. He expected to hear shouts, the pounding of feet. Nothing happened. The camp was undisturbed.

A burst of laughter came from the men's quarters on the other side. Nearby, a tent curtain moved aside, spilling lamplight on to the trampled grass. An officer came out. Melwas was startled to see a guard, whose presence he had not suspected, spring to attention out of the shadows and salute.

A few words passed in a foreign tongue, and the officer walked away. Inside the tent, another man sat at a table. In front of him was a small slab on which he seemed to be scratching signs with a stick.

There was nothing here worth reporting. Melwas crouched in the darkness and longed suddenly to be back home in the Forest Fort with Idwal Goldenshield. All the old memories came flooding back, of Coel and Crab and all the fireside friends of his boyhood. He pulled himself together. Dare he risk going further into the camp?

He looked at the lighted tent. Not that way, with the guard at the door. And how many of these other tents were guarded? They did not seem to be common soldiers' quarters – they were too quiet for that. He began to edge his way along the foot of the rampart.

A moment later he froze. The sentry was coming back. The measured footfall drew steadily nearer. Now it was like thunder in his ears. Surely the man must feel another living presence so close? The boots passed by along the beaten terrace above Melwas's head. The thuds faded into the night.

He worked his way forward again. Once more he had to wait for the sentry to pass, and then he was close beside the gate. There were more guards here. Two at least. There was also more light. He found himself looking down a wide avenue of tents that cut clean across the camp. In the centre there were still people about, raised voices. This was no place to linger.

Stealthily he turned to go, when his ears pricked with a sudden urgency. That last voice! Surely it had spoken in the British tongue? Quickly his eyes searched the tents. There! That one, which faced the main gate, where the light showed a knot of men with their backs to him. There were Roman uniforms, guarding the door. But inside – could that be the sweep of a white druid robe and the chequered cloaks of

166

British warriors? Here, at last, was something that Aidan must know.

He darted across the open ground to the first row of tents. Between their leather walls the shadows were thicker. He crawled forward over the dew-wet grass. Now he could see better. His heart leaped to his throat. There were three of them, and he recognized them all. Celynen the druid, Bearrach Horse-Thief, and . . . his own father. Not Idwal Goldenshield, who had fostered him from early childhood. But the grave, strong, fearless chieftain who must not recognize his son in public until the day of his manhood.

Sick thoughts whirled through his brain. What were they doing here? Were they prisoners, too, like Cairenn? Had all Dumnon fallen, without Vespasian moving from his camp? Then he remembered: Tegan had said that Idwal was sending ambassadors to sue for peace. But that was days ago. What new errand could bring such men back to the Roman camp now, when night was falling?

Celynen was speaking, and there was something like despair in his voice. '. . . This is not Idwal's doing. The young men are headstrong. They left the Forest without our knowledge or consent. The tribe of Dumnon seeks peace, and we keep our word.'

Melwas could not hear the answer. But the next voice that spoke was his father's, and that too was loud with passion.

'I beg you once again to let her go. You have before you the High Druid of the Forest, the leader of Idwal's warriors, and I myself am chieftain of my clan. Take all of us as hostages, if you will. Only set this one prisoner free.'

His father was pleading for Cairenn.

Melwas edged closer still. Now he could see the officer to whom they were speaking. The cropped hair. The strong, blunt features, reddened with lamplight. He answered in Latin. Another voice, empty of emotion, translated.

'The prisoner's life is forfeit. The general has lost too many

167

men, too much valuable time. Unless you stop this . . . .'

Melwas shifted his position. His foot caught against something. A tent cord twanged. A cry of suspicion came from the lighted tent. He ran.

He lay in the shadow below the rampart with his heart thudding. Men were checking between the tents. Clipped voices called out questions. He scrambled up on to the sentry-walk and crouched again. Too late, he heard through their voices the slow rhythm of approaching feet.

He was trapped. If he made a movement, a last leap over the wall, he would be seen. If he stayed where he was, the sentry must stumble over him. Either way meant death. He lay rigid, choosing to live a few seconds longer.

The feet were three strides away. He could feel the earth tremble beneath his cheek. Then voices called up from the tent-lines. The man halted and turned, replying. In that short moment, Melwas sprang for the top of the wall and rolled over. He heard shouts in the gloom. But he was running. He was free.

It seemed impossible that he should find Tegan in that ocean of shadows. But as he raced on, an arm shot out and grabbed his.

'Dumnon for ever!' she hissed as she drew him into the bushes.

He could not speak. They crept deep into the thickets of the wood until they felt safe from pursuit. Tegan let go of his shaking arm.

'I heard shouts. Did they get you?'

'Not quite. But it was a close thing. Did you see anything?'

'No. Just some mules tethered in a corner. And soldiers who sounded as though they were grumbling or joking, the same as soldiers anywhere. Nothing Aidan would call news. And you?'

He told her of the three Britons he had seen and of how they had pleaded with Vespasian for the release of a prisoner.

Tegan's voice breathed his own fear.

'And we know what prisoner it is that Celynen and Bearrach and your father would offer their own freedom to save. They've got your sister, Cairenn of the White Fingers.'

Melwas heard his own voice crack as he answered. 'I'm afraid it's worse than that. If Aidan goes on attacking, Cairenn will die.'

*They are dragging me out. It is days since I stepped into the light. I have been trapped like a rat in its hole, in the dim lonely tent with the door tied down. Hot when the sun beats down, chill when the rain falls.*

*Yet not solitary enough. Sometimes the guard looks in. A shaved, jowly face between the curving cheek pieces of his helmet. I cannot tell if it is always the same one. All Romans look alike to me. But when I see the leer on that face I thank the discipline of the Roman army which is all that keeps that face from mine, my unprotected body from his. There are boundaries set, but no one sees inside the tent when their hands can still grope me.*

*They took my knife away, and tied my wrists. A bond of shame tethers me to the tent-pole.*

*I was once a princess.*

*Now I am let out, like a dog on a leash, to blink in the daylight.*

*I try to hold my head up and straighten my shoulders. Let me not look afraid, though I am.*

*But as I move, the smell of my own unwashed body wafts over me, and I am ashamed. It is more than a week now since I bathed in the clear stream that tumbles down through the woods towards the Salmon River. A lifetime, it seems, since I was surrounded by the young women of the Forest Fort, dipping and diving in the still pools where the water lies warmest, splashing the silver spray at each other and screaming under the cold sluice of the waterfall. Naked and proud of our bodies, slender and lithe. And slaves ready on the bank to enfold us in towels of soft linen. To massage our wet hair and stroke us with perfumes.*

*I ache for the feel of clean skin, for that tingle of freshness. I, who was often scornful of those other girls, am ripped from their company, cherishing too late what I have lost.*

*I am staled, enslaved, isolated.*

*What have they summoned me for?*

*And now I begin to tremble. It is hard to act bravely when your hair is tangled with its own grease, your dress is soiled, and no one speaks your language. Is this how it ends? A despised barbarian woman, butchered for no reason in a nameless marching-camp they will soon abandon?*

*I was once a princess of Dumnon. I am nothing to them.*

*Why have they let me keep my gold torque? My bound hands lift to touch it. Let me remember Beath's hands giving it to me.*

*'Courage.' A man's voice, low, at my shoulder. My own tongue.*

*My head whips round, astonished. There is only a Roman officer there, his armour a little showier, his helmet more splendid with its transverse crest. He stares ahead, his face unmoving. It cannot be he who spoke to me.*

*But the word has done its work. I will show courage. It is oddly comforting that someone of these enemy men around me cared enough to speak that word so that I could understand.*

*It was just coincidence. Some Latin word that sounded a little like the one I knew. I can have no friends here. This is probably the squad that is going to execute me.*

*They are taking me to that larger tent, in the centre of the camp. Is this where they brought me before, the night I was captured?*

*The centurion is beside me now. Stiff of back, as well as face. He does not look at me. But his hand is under my elbow with a pressure that feels reassuring, rather than invasive.*

170

*The light dims. I have been pushed inside.*

*I hear the cry before my eyes can focus.*

*'Cairenn!'*

*My father. Drem Chariot-Dancer, chieftain of the Red Deer Fort that guards the road west to the moors.*

*My tongue is trapped. I want to cry out with joy, to run to him, but the leash holds me. I am not a free woman. I am a prisoner of the Romans. And I know a heartbeat later that it was not joy in my father's voice, but anguish.*

*My sight has steadied. I can see him now, brown bearskin cloak thrown over his shoulder, beard bristling. And the years of my fostering fall away. I am a little girl. I want to run into his arms.*

*My Roman guards will not let me.*

*There is someone else. Tall, white-gowned. And this time it is my spirit, as well as my heart, that aches. Celynen, his face drawn as if in pain.*

*His voice is quiet, calm, but urgent. He speaks not to me, but to the proudly armoured man I think may be Vespasian.*

*'Let the girl go. She is still a child. She has not even been through the rites of womanhood.'*

*This week, I should have withdrawn from the foster-home of my childhood to a hut in the woods. I should have been taught the mysteries that women know. I should have undergone the trials of courage and obedience. Beath, in the name of the goddess, should have welcomed me into the tribe, fully a woman. Aidan and I should have been betrothed.*

*A harsher voice is turning his words into Latin. That weasel-faced interpreter.*

*A third familiar presence. Bigger than my father, redder of face, more muscular. Bearrach Horse-Thief. And my pride aches for him. The master of Idwal's cavalry. The sword-master who taught a whole generation of boys to fight. And for nothing. That battle will never happen. Dumnon will not defend herself. The chiefs will parley for peace with the*

*Roman empire. We are defeated already. Shamed. Conquered.*

*Not Aidan! Aidan is fighting them. Aidan will not accept shame.*

*Aidan is probably dead. He must be dead, slain on that twilight heath the night they captured me.*

*I have lost the point when the rattle of Latin words flowed back into British. It must be me they are talking about, but it sounds like someone else.*

*'. . . Roman soldiers killed . . . control your rebels . . . this prisoner dies . . . .'*

*I am the carved queen piece in some military board game. Dirty and bound though I am, I still have value. I can be bargained with, for other pieces. The value of love, the price of strategy.*

*Aidan is still alive, still fighting them.*

*The realization leaps through me, like the shock of lovers meeting. What other rebel can there be? And he is killing Romans.*

*My life, or his.*

*The cry is torn from me, 'No, Celynen! Don't betray Aidan!'*

*There is fierce argument now, hoarse pleading. I see my father's eyes begging me for information. Is Melwas here, too? I see it in his despair. It cannot be all for me. I shake my head. Did he understand me?*

*I am hustled away. Behind me the desperate parley goes on. How can my father and Celynen stop the rebels? The chiefs are for peace. Young men are headstrong.*

*I am bundled back into my tent, tied to the pole. I have just a little life left.*

# CHAPTER 12

## REPRISAL

Melwas and Tegan groped their way on in silence. If it had been hard to find the Roman camp earlier, it was harder still to find their way back along the dimly seen paths. Stars glinted between the clouds before they stumbled on Seiriol's grove.

They roused Aidan, and for once his face was grave as he listened to their report.

'He's going to kill her if we go on attacking them.'

'Leave that to me.' But he sounded less confident than before.

He sent them to bed, and they tumbled wearily on to the ground under a rough shelter of hazel branches and fell asleep.

Melwas woke late, to find that Aidan and the others had already gone, leaving him to take his turn at guarding the camp. Even now, he was not free to find Hu. Hidden in an oak tree, he watched the path while the slow hours dragged past. A blackbird whistled at him. A squirrel ran along a bough above his head. Fears haunted him; urgent fear for his sister, a gnawing fear for his friend and for Crab. But he saw nothing more sinister than a weasel in the undergrowth.

At last, at mid-afternoon, a man came to relieve him.

Melwas sprang from the tree. Like an arrow from a bow, he sped away down the path that led to Hu's village, telling no one where he was going.

The year was turning. Already the first yellowing leaves were tumbling down. They lay smooth and new and slippery, making the flying soles of his feet slither, hiding the tangled tree roots. Down, down the path he plunged, and all the time the wood was close and still about him. Round each new twist of the track he expected to see the trees thin out, to hear the sound of voices, the murmur of sheep. But he ran on in an oppressive silence.

At last, above his hurried breathing, he heard a welcome noise. He had met the brook, running now beside the path as the valley narrowed and deepened, hurrying down to the estuary. It could not be far now to the village.

He glimpsed light through the leaves. A grey light, under a cloudy sky. There was open grass. A bitter smell.

Melwas stopped short. He knew at once what it was, but his mind did not want to accept it. The sharp, choking smell of charred wood. A little breeze from the south-west carried the powdered ash towards him and sprinkled it at his feet.

He made himself go forward through the last trees. The Romans had been thorough; not a swathe of thatch, not a standing timber, had been allowed to escape. Everything in Hu's village had been smashed, burned, destroyed.

Melwas walked through the blackened heaps, appalled. His mind begged for hope. What had the villagers done when they saw the Romans coming? Had there been time to escape? Most of all – though he hardly dared to think of it – what had happened to Hu, and to his little dog Crab?

Beside one fire was a scattered pile of white bones. He thought they might be only the remains of a sheep, but he was afraid to look too closely. He hurried past, sick with worry, towards the bank of the brook. Along its margin the still water was clouded with a film of ash. Beside it, the grass grew thick and sweet, feathered with yarrow and the starry blue of speedwells. He stopped and stared, seeing, but not yet believing what he saw. Deep in the green there was a small white foot.

A knot of fear tightened horridly in his stomach. Slowly his hands parted the tall grass stems. It was Hu's sister, Garwen. She lay with her arms twined close around Crab. Her tangled brown hair mingled with the grey fur of the whippet. Both of them, little girl and small dog, lay dead with a wound in their throats.

Melwas put out a hand and touched the cold side of his dearest friend.

'Oh, Crab!' he whispered.

Something crashed heavily into the blackthorn bush beside him. Melwas whirled round, his hand instantly on his sword. Hu stood on the opposite side of the brook. Even as Melwas saw him, he picked up another stone and hurled it. Melwas dodged aside.

'Hu! You're still alive! Stop it! Can't you see it's me?'

A third stone hurtled through the air. Melwas threw up his arm just in time, and it caught him bruisingly on the bone.

'Hu! It's Melwas! I'm your friend.'

Hu turned away, but only to search for more stones. When he had gathered a small pile, he began to aim them once more at Melwas, his face expressionless. Melwas backed away from the water's edge.

'Don't be a fool, Hu. Come over here and talk to me. Look, I'm on your side. I'm very sorry about Garwen, but I didn't kill her. It was those Romans . . . .'

The stones kept coming, one after the other, with monotonous regularity. The only relief was that Hu was hurling them from his fist, not his deadly sling. It was as though he was too hopeless even to kill Melwas accurately.

'Please! Hu! I need your help. There's my sister, too. The Romans have got her. I mean as a prisoner. But they're threatening to kill her . . . What about the rest of your people? Did they manage to escape?'

The only answer was a stone that whistled dangerously close to his ear. Gradually Melwas was forced back, leaving a widening space between himself and the little girl and Crab. They looked lonely like that – two small, still figures in the grass. Tears blurred his vision. Across the water, Hu kept up his silent barrage of hate.

Melwas called once more, pleadingly. 'Why be angry with me? What have I done? It's not my fault . . . .'

His voice faltered. He had spent his first night as a warrior, sheltered here in this village. Hu's family had fed the rebels, and brought food to them at Seiriol's Oaks. Melwas remembered how proudly he had rejoiced over his reddened sword. He knew now why Hu hated him; he had shed Roman blood, but it was Garwen and Crab who had paid the price for it. There was nothing he could say.

Slowly, his heart aching for lost friendship, he turned and walked away. Hu could have killed him then. It only needed one stone to strike the back of his head and it would have been all over. But the blow never came. The stones fell short, thudding into the grass behind him. Hu stood on the other bank, throwing on and on as if his arm had lost the power to stop. But there was no real anger in his movements, only a dull despair. He seemed to have forgotten what he was throwing at.

At the edge of the wood, Melwas turned for the last time. He watched Hu heave his final stone. Then the boy picked up a flat-bladed bone and began to dig. There was already a little patch of freshly turned earth under the rowan trees. Melwas felt the tears slide down his face. He remembered the little girl smiling shyly up at him, and thought of her body lying under the dark earth. There was no druid to perform the last rites. He wished desperately that he could go across and help Hu. But it would be no good.

176

He wondered what Hu would do with Crab. Somehow he knew that it would be all right; Hu would not take away from his sister the friend that she had loved. It comforted Melwas to think of his little dog laid to rest still hugged in loving arms.

It seemed a long way back. The paths were quiet with new-fallen leaves. The first touch of autumn chilled the air. He walked with head bent and heavy steps. In the end he had to be challenged twice before he shook himself awake to the sound of the sentry's voice. The man, who had recognized him anyway, grinned as he passed.

'Too much beer for a young one? Where did you find it? Or is it some girl you've been chasing? Looks as if you could do with a good night's sleep.'

Melwas mumbled a reply and went on through the gate into Seiriol's grove. The clearing was calm and quiet in the late afternoon. Wounded men lay silent, tired by pain and idleness, waiting for Aidan and his comrades to return. Seiriol herself squatted by the door of her hut, brewing herbs and watching him through the smoke. Melwas avoided her. He could not bring himself to talk to any of them. Even Tegan took one long look at his face and, for once, kept silent. A heap of branches had been gathered for the cooking-fire. Melwas took an axe and started savagely to split the boughs.

Towards evening the men began to troop back into the camp in small bands. For once they were not supporting bloodstained comrades, nor speaking by their grave faces of brave men killed. Today there was a suppressed excitement about them. Aidan was laughing as he entered Seiriol's hut, with Rieuk close behind him. Melwas threw down his axe and ran after them. All the fear and sorrow of that day flared into anger against all of them, especially against Aidan.

He halted in the doorway. Seiriol still squatted outside, watching, saying nothing. Inside, the hut was dim. Aidan was

177

tossing back a cup of wine. Rieuk paced anxiously to and fro, saying,

'But can it work?'

'Of course it will. Tomorrow, or the day after. Vespasian must be impatient to move. He'll believe it.'

'Aidan!' Melwas's voice called sharply from the doorway.

Aidan looked round. 'Oh, it's you, Melwas. What do you want?'

'I went to Hu's village. It's been burned to the ground. Everything. There's nobody left. Only ... Only ....' He choked. 'Hu's sister is dead. And Crab. The Romans killed them.'

'Did you find Hu?'

Melwas shook his head wordlessly. He could not describe what had happened.

'Bother. That boy was more use to me than a dozen warriors.'

'What are you going to do about Cairenn?' The question sounded more like an accusation.

Aidan shifted uneasily. He did not seem to know what to say. Melwas rushed on.

'It's her life they were bargaining for. I heard my father pleading for her.'

'We don't know that. You're only guessing. They never mentioned her name, did they? Cairenn might have escaped from those horsemen before she reached the camp. She could be safe across the Salmon River by now.'

'You *know* it's her! The Romans are cruel! Just because the villagers helped us. I expect Crab tried to fight the soldiers off, and Garwen stayed behind to try and stop him. Those beasts killed both of them. A little girl and a whippet. And if they've got Cairenn hostage and we go on attacking their patrols ....'

Rieuk's voice broke in from the shadows.

'You are not alone in your sorrow, boy. There are many in

this camp who have lost parents, brothers and sisters, children even. We shall avenge them all, down to the last drop of Roman blood!'

'Why aren't you listening? As long as Cairenn's a prisoner, there mustn't *be* any more fighting. Not till we've rescued her. Can't you understand? That's why Vespasian's holding her. He said if one more Roman soldier dies, then she dies too.' He went suddenly pale. 'What happened today? Where have you been? Did you kill any of them?'

Aidan answered. 'As it happens, no. There's been a change of plan. We're tired of waiting for Vespasian to march out and meet us in the open. So we now want him to think that he's beaten us. We're still watching his camp and his men very carefully, but we've not touched one hair of a Roman head today. And we shan't ... until they move. And then ....'

He looked across at Rieuk, and the two of them laughed long.

'Then it's not too late? There's still a chance! We can break into their camp tonight and rescue her.'

'Don't be stupid, lad. Successful or not, such a raid would give us away. Vespasian would know for certain that we're still here. No, Melwas. She'll have to wait. She'll be safe enough until the battle. When we hit their marching column, we'll rescue her anyway.'

'But you can't leave it till then! Anything could happen to her before that.'

'You worry too much. Cheer up. We'll sweep the Romans out of Dumnon, and carry off Cairenn and their baggage-train into the bargain.'

'You're not being serious, you're just playing games. She's your foster-sister! You were going to marry her!'

'Be careful what you say! Do you think I don't care what happens to her? But this is war, Melwas. The future of Dumnon. I'm fighting to win.'

179

'By the time you've won, half the people you fought it for will be dead!'

Melwas stormed out of the hut, his cheeks burning with rage. Outside the troop were gathering round the fire for supper. Melwas was hungry too, but he would not stop. He strode across the clearing and threw himself down behind the trunk of an oak tree. The meal began. He could smell the roasted mutton. His mouth watered and his stomach growled. But still he would not join them. The image of Crab and Garwen lay between him and them, sharp and cruel as a drawn sword. He sat on, with his arms folded and his eyes staring ahead, bright and angry.

Leaves rustled. Tegan stood beside him, holding out bread and meat. 'Seiriol sent you this. I'm sorry about Garwen and Crab.'

He hesitated for a moment, and then took the food from her without a word. She sat down, a little distance away, and watched in silence while he ate. When he had finished, she said quietly,

'So what are you going to do about Cairenn? If you're thinking of trying to get into the camp again to rescue her, I'd come with you.'

'I don't know,' he said bitterly. 'What good would I do? You've seen their camp. How would I ever find her among all those tents? And if I was caught and had to fight my way out, she'd die anyway. Aidan's right, curse him. There's nothing any of us can do until they march. And by then it may be too late.'

Tegan did not answer for a while. She reached out a hand and laid it briefly on Melwas's shoulder.

' We'll think of a way. And you can count on me to help.'

He was woken in the middle of the night. Warriors were springing up all around him. Melwas heard Tegan's voice in the darkness.

'Wake up, Melwas. It's happening! Aidan's scouts say the legion's getting ready to break camp. We're setting an ambush before dawn!'

The night was alive with hurrying figures, whispering eagerly, moving in silent haste to buckle on their arms. The news went flying through the camp, like a warm wind thawing a frozen wood into bubbling motion.

Melwas, running across the grove, came upon Seiriol. She was standing before the pillar, in the dim, red glow of the smothered fire. He heard liquid trickling from something between her hands on to the grass. He stopped, afraid to disturb her.

'Is that you, Melwas Mighty-Heart?' she said, not turning round.

'Yes.'

'They're all in too much of a hurry. There are some things they have forgotten. Even Rieuk, who uses the names of our gods when it suits his purposes.' She sighed, and her voice sounded older than he had ever heard it. 'Still, I do not suppose it will make much difference now.'

She swung round to him, with the sword heavy against her side, and her smile was young and magical as ever.

'Be brave, Melwas. You hold our future in your hands.'

He did not understand what she meant, and there was no time to ask. Seiriol had been wrong. He stayed beside her while the troop halted and formed a circle. They did need her blessing, though they listened impatiently to her torrent of prayers. Then they were on the move, slipping away through the darkness to set their ambush.

It was no easy task for Aidan. He did not know what route Vespasian would choose next morning. And he did not have Hu to guide them through the night trails of the forest. They stumbled through a darkness that showed no stars.

Aidan made the best plan he could. By the first grey light of morning he halted them in the fringes of the wood overlooking the Roman marching-camp.

'This way, we can't make a mistake. Either they'll come west towards us, over this ridge towards the Salmon River, or they'll go north, and we can take them from behind. And remember, it's their baggage-train we're after. I know you're all eager to cut as many Roman throats as you can, but we can't do battle with a whole legion. Now, hide yourselves well. They'll have scouts in plenty about, and they'll be on the look-out for trouble.'

The dawn was chill, with dampness palpable in the air. Melwas crouched in the branches of an oak tree and squinted up through the leaves at the overcast sky. He could feel the nearness of approaching rain. He tried to imagine the red sandy soil being churned into mud underfoot. He hoped it might hamper the heavily equipped Romans more than the Britons.

There was a restlessness among those around him. He felt it in himself. This was what they had been waiting for, hoping for. Yet, now it had come, they knew it would be their grimmest fight yet. And Melwas feared for another life, beside his own. To take his mind off Cairenn's danger, he made himself think coldly about the possibility of his own death in battle. Was it true that the Otherworld was a marvellous island where no one ever grew old and all wounds healed, where there was always feasting and fighting and song? He decided it was not really death that frightened him, only this *waiting* to die.

The wait for action was shorter than he had expected. Already the camp was astir with orderly bustle. Tents were coming down. Squads of men were forming up, each with their equipment slung on their backs. Horses were being saddled and led out of the picket lines. It seemed incredible to Melwas that six thousand men should go about their work so swiftly and efficiently, as though every soldier in the camp knew beforehand what task he had to do.

Suddenly it was done. The legion was formed up in ranks outside the camp. The last officers rode out through the gateway, leaving behind them only the yellowed squares where the tents had stood, the blackened rings of fires, and the walls of freshly turned earth thrown down again, abandoned and empty. With a quick tightening of his stomach, Melwas saw this long river of men begin to flow. The Second Legion Augusta was marching west.

*Now the fear intensifies. I should have been prepared for this, but I was not. When the Romans caught me, I thought my life had stopped. In my shrouding tent I performed the waking, noontide, evening chants, but I never saw sunrise or sunset. I waited for death, or ransom. I expected it would happen here. I did not question why the Roman legion had halted before they reached the Exe.*

*Now their march resumes, and I am still alive and still their prisoner. Will they wait till the last cart is loaded, the last foot soldier drawn up, and kill me then, leave me behind, unburied, with their rubbish? Will these raw red earthworks serve for my grave-marker?*

*It is fitting. The goddess has put her hand on me. As she is conquered, so should I fall with her land.*

*There is no one to rescue me.*

*But no, I am not to die yet, it seems. Still more humiliation. I am loosed from the tent-pole, only to be lashed to the back of a cart.*

*Huge though this marching-camp is, I never realized till now the full might of the Roman army in Dumnon. I see them now, drawn up ahead of me, already positioned in lines abreast all up the slope. Some officers on horseback, the wings of cavalry, and a sickness rises in my throat as I remember those little, black-haired, blue and silver archers, too eagerly round me as I lay defenceless on the ground.*

*There is a considerable wagon train, pack mules, great*

engines of war towed by straining teams. What will they do to my people, these instruments of death?

I storm against the gods of the sky who have smiled on our invaders. Surely they could have lashed the ground with rain, churned up the mud, flung floods up over the banks of every river? Dumnon is no place for wheeled traffic, for heavy wagons. Only the lightly bowling wicker chariots of our chiefs can skim these tracks, and even then we must take to the saddle in winter. If you loved us, Lords and Ladies, you could have prevented this. What have we done to anger you?

But the day is fine and the country fair, and the Lords of the Otherworld smile on these strangers as they trample the tracks westward, all scarlet and silver, with the drums banging and the standard-bearers strutting their foreign gods with a face of grinning pride beneath their bear-masks.

Would that living bears would leap out of the woods and rend them.

They are on the march now. Up over the crest. The strong rope that is Rome is uncoiling out of the camp, length upon length, hundred after hundred. I wait for the jerk on the cable that will tow me in their wake.

A shout. I stumble, though I have been hours awaiting this, till my legs are already tired. I see the whip in the mule-driver's grip, and flinch. Am I any more to him than a pack animal?

We are on the move, we the unglamourous chattels in the footsteps of the army, with a frowning rearguard behind us, impatient at our progress. I never imagined foot soldiers would march so fast. How many miles will they drag me before we can halt? I am spattered with dirt already from the wheels I must follow too closely.

I should be glad. I am being taken back into a country that is familiar. The woods of the west where I grew up. When we top this ridge, surely I shall see the flash of the Salmon River, the glimpse of blue hills where my mother still waits for my coming.

184

*She does not know she has lost two children. If Aidan is dead, did Melwas fall with him?*

*It is too much effort to lift my eyes to the high skyline. Last time I looked, it was still impossibly far away, and the hill steepening. They will not wind and curve, these Romans; they live by relentless straight lines. So they assault the slope as if they could see already the Exe on the other side and Idwal's Forest Fort, and aim for them straight as a spear.*

*My lungs are labouring. I must fix my eyes on the ground just ahead, each step discovered as the shadow of the cart passes over it and on. Quartz glints among the wheel-churned sand, briefly in sunlight. The grass is trampled on either side by ranks of hobnailed boots widening the track across the heath. Have they cut a swathe like this through the young men of Dumnon, too?*

*The gorse will resist them. Surely even Rome cannot flatten everything in its path. It brings a little smile to think of them swearing at scratched flesh.*

*Did Aidan score deep wounds before he died?*

*'Too many Roman soldiers killed . . . .' Who but the Red Fox could have done this? Perhaps, just perhaps, Aidan is still alive.*

*And my steps quicken to distant drums. Have I the right to hope?*

*A few more paces and reality dashes my spirits to the ground. An entire Roman legion on the march. Every soldier, every weapon, every horse. Vespasian himself. What could even the bravest of British rebels do against this?*

*I study the tailboard of the cart I am tied to. Every knot in its planks. The folds of the leather tent, still dark with dew, which cover the contents. There is a rattle of metal beneath, the roll of wood that thumps against the side when the wheels jolt. I do not know what it carries. Weapons for killing? Food for life? I marvel at the load each legionary shoulders. Even the spades with which they will dig the next camp and claim another swathe of Dumnon for their empire.*

*My gown was crimson once. It is reddened again with the flung dirt of a baggage-cart.*

*The wheels before my eyes judder and stop. The air is full of shouts, of flying turf, of horses' hooves.*

Squadrons Melwas did not recognize came first, marching up over the ridge to the pulse of drums. Behind them came the Roman cohorts of the legion, red cloaks warm and brave in that grey morning. The cluster of standards glinted coldly, the alien eagle and the laurel wreaths and the gilded bull's head. Vespasian rode with his officers. And fanning out on either side of the column, the wings of auxiliary cavalry, flashes of blue and black and silver, ranging warily over the hillside with eyes alert for trouble.

Up over the hill they marched. The watchers held their breath, lest even a leaf should tremble under their hands and betray them. Aidan let all these pass unchallenged. The legion passed over the crest of the ridge and disappeared down the long descent towards the Salmon River. And now at last the Britons could see what they had been waiting for, and it became hard to still the movement of their eager hands towards their weapons.

Almost at the end of the column came the baggage-train. Teams of oxen strained to tug huge instruments of war, whose use the Britons hardly dared to guess at. Great implements of wood, leather and iron; gigantic, sinister. Behind them came sweet-faced mules laden with panniers or pulling smaller carts. Here were the more familiar loads of tents and stakes and sacks of food. Drivers walked alongside them, goading the animals on. And bringing up the rear a formidable guard of auxiliaries marched shoulder to shoulder, their eyes fixed steadily on the file of animals hauling its way up the hill in front of them. Even here, the column was flanked by breastplated cavalry outriders.

The attack was swift and silent. There was no ringing war-cry from the crest to warn the front of the column, which had long since dropped out of sight. At one soft call from Aidan, the Britons were on their feet and dashing downhill to hurl themselves on the baggage-train.

Melwas ran at full stretch. He glimpsed the cavalry wheeling to the defence, the glitter of lifted swords, the black sheen of horses' legs. But he was through before they could reach him, and racing across open ground towards the carts. Pack animals were backing and jostling in confusion. In front of him, a soldier drew his sword. He had no chance to use it. There were a hundred warriors around Melwas, felling the drivers, seizing the mules' heads, and dragging them away.

Melwas grabbed at a halter and pulled. There was no time to look round and see how close the rearguard was. He could tell by the roar of approaching shouts that they must be pounding up the hill behind him. Horns were sounding the alarm.

It was so desperately slow. The mule dug its heels in and refused to budge. In a panic, Melwas beat it with the flat of his sword. The animal leaped forward and the cart began to roll over the heather, gathering speed. Ahead, the cavalry was reforming in a murderous line.

'Oh, come on!' begged Melwas. A cold sweat broke out on his brow.

The wheels skidded. The cart lurched, and stuck fast in loose sand. What fools they had been to think they could get away with all this weight of baggage! They should have brought torches and burned it where it stood.

The cavalry were bearing down on him at the gallop. Behind him, a renewed clash of iron and cries of pain. The rearguard had reached the carts, and the Britons still there were fighting for their lives. Should he leave his mule and run for it, hoping to cut his way out through the horsemen sweeping towards him? He threw a last desperate glance

187

around him. What he saw then drove everything else from his mind.

A leaderless mule was careering over the heather, dragging a cart behind it. At the rear, tied to the tailboard by her wrists, was Cairenn. She was half-running, half-stumbling in her long gown, desperately trying to keep her feet. She had seen him, and she was shouting to him, but amid the braying and clangour and cursing he could not hear her. He dropped his mule's bridle and dashed towards her. A Roman soldier seemed to leap from nowhere, barring his way. Melwas swiped at him with his sword, saw him topple sideways and did not stay to see more. There were other footsteps running beside him. He wheeled round, sword raised. It was Tegan.

'After her! You can do it!' she panted.

The cart slowed in a tangle of heather. Melwas was gaining rapidly on it.

'You cut her free. I'll guard both of you,' Tegan shouted.

Melwas slashed at the rope with his sword. It snapped, and Cairenn pitched forward into the heather. He pulled her to her feet.

'Run!'

The nearest horseman was galloping down on them. Tegan dashed to intercept him, and he reined in too late. Melwas saw his pony strike the abandoned cart breast-high, sending his rider flying headfirst over it. A second was bearing down fast. Tegan struck out at him bravely and he swerved aside. A third followed hard on his heels. He closed with Tegan, blue and green meeting in a clash of sparking iron. Before Melwas could reach them, the horseman swayed slowly backwards, clutching a reddening wound in his swordless hands. He dropped heavily from his horse.

There was a moment's silence. Then Tegan gave a little moan and slipped to the ground at Melwas's feet. He stared down at her in astonishment. She lay with her green eyes open and the Roman sword clean through her breast.

'Tegan!'

Melwas never knew afterwards whether it was his own cry or Cairenn's that echoed so desolately across the hill. It seemed to go on ringing through the morning, out beyond Dumnon, out across the seas, out to the furthest Isles of the Blest.

And then there was no more time to mourn. Another Roman soldier was almost on them. But before he could close with Melwas, he gave a convulsive leap and toppled back, his helmet spattered from his bloody eye-socket. There was a moment's silence. Melwas turned. A small figure in a brown kilt stood in front of the woods, reloading his sling.

'Hu?'

It was only a moment's respite. More horsemen were thundering down on them, hacking and slashing at the scattered Britons. The Roman infantry were forging their way uphill in a solid mass, felling every warrior in their path. There could be no escape. With the strength of despair, Melwas raised his sword for the last encounter.

A wild shriek pierced the uproar. In front of him, a horse reared. In spite of the danger, Melwas spun round and a sudden joy seized him. Seiriol's chariot was sweeping across the hillside, swift and fierce as a hawk swooping to the kill. Her yells rang above the din of battle and her red hair streamed free in the wind. Horsemen were scattering in terror as she whirled down on them.

Only Melwas was slow to move. The wheels hurtled towards him, leaping on stones. He saw Seiriol snatch Cairenn off the ground and deposit her on the wicker floor. The chariot was rattling past him. He sprang for it. There was no room for four. He dropped his sword and clung on as the charioteer wheeled her team.

Seiriol caught his arm in an iron grasp. With her other hand she seized the goad and spurred the straining ponies towards the crest. Melwas twisted round. The archers were steadying their frightened horses. A flight of arrows sped after the departing chariot.

They were rushing towards a line of abandoned carts. At the very last moment the charioteer reined back. Cairenn and Melwas were unceremoniously tumbled off on to the grass.

'Save yourselves, while I save Dumnon!'

The wheels lurched and spun back towards the fighting. As the pair sped towards the oncoming cavalry, there was another bloodcurdling yell.

'Call yourselves warriors? On, you Britons, on! Turn and fight with these soft, southern men! Would you yield them the breadth of a sword, of a finger-nail, in the land of your fathers' gods?'

Her mocking laughter screamed towards them. Even then the auxiliary cavalry would have reined aside from her if they could. But the impetus of their downhill charge swept them on into the path of the chariot like a river in spate. The piebald ponies struck them at full gallop. With an upheaval like the meeting of two swift torrents in flood, the chariot was thrown into the air and overturned. Seiriol, like a great crow, flew through the sky on the black, spread wings of her robe. As she dropped, for a moment she hung helplessly across a horse's mane. Then red hair, red blood, spattered the red earth around her where she fell. The flailing of horses' hooves threshed the life from her body and pounded on.

Her charioteer dropped the reins and made to leap down, ready to die there beside her mistress. But out of the battle came Rieuk, running for his life. He pushed the charioteer back, scrambled aboard and goaded the team into a gallop. Like sleet before a gale, they burst through the Roman column and streaked away, on, on, into the north.

They left behind a wild confusion of riderless horses and injured men. Melwas seized Cairenn's bound arms and pulled her to her feet. He whirled her round.

190

'Quick! The other way!'

They raced back towards the mule-train, where the abandoned animals and carts were jammed together in a hopeless tangle. Here, too, the ground was littered with bodies. Melwas cast his shield aside and threw himself under the nearest cart. Cairenn followed, wriggling as fast as her long skirts and bound wrists would let her. In a few moments they were out on the other side.

It was strangely quiet. All the fighting was on the southern flank. Suddenly, incredibly, escape seemed possible. They sprinted away through the long grass. No cry followed them.

The woods were still a long way off. Melwas knew he could run faster than Cairenn. It was the hardest thing he had ever done to slow his pace to hers.

It could not last. There was a swift darkening of the skyline. If the rearguard had seemed formidable, it was now as nothing, as the main body of the legion came pouring back over the brow of the hill in annihilating strength. They came at a run, and with them more contingents of cavalry, sweeping past the infantry, straight for Melwas and Cairenn. Horses wheeled in a flurry of black hooves and red sand. In an instant, a ring of swords surrounded them.

Melwas expected to die then. It was Cairenn who saved them. She drew herself up, noble and tall, with the royal torque of twisted gold about her throat. She stood her ground. Her still, proud, frightened face stared back at the horsemen without flinching. They looked from her to Melwas, and hesitated. He was smaller than she was. He had lost his great shield and spear. Hard fighting and rough living had so spoiled his fine clothes and Seiriol's dressing of his hair that he looked again more like a boy than a warrior. Only the long sword in his hand and the bandaged gash on his right arm told a different story. That, and a new darkness behind his eyes which would never leave him.

But Melwas did not know this. He heard their leader rap

out an order. He grasped his sword two-handed to swing it in one last, defiant blow. But before he could raise his arms, he was seized from behind. His weapon was taken from him as easily as if he were a baby playing with a stick.

# CHAPTER 13

## SENTENCE

*D*elight and despair in a single moment. Aidan is alive. Aidan is here with me, but in a Roman war-camp. Now Aidan will certainly die.

*My eyes cannot feast enough on him. There is no one in the world I longed to see so much.*

*I cannot bear to look into his sky-blue eyes and inflict on him the knowledge that he cannot save me.*

*There are so few of them. A knot of eight. The warrior pride of Dumnon looks incongruous here, beaten. Hair once stiffened with lime droops from hanging heads. The blue tattoos of war paint shadow faces darkened by defeat. They have been robbed of the weapons that made them men. The hammered shields gorgeous with the metalsmith's art. Aidan's sword, five times forged, wickedly edged, with the twists of its welding twining like water-snakes down its long blade. Even their buckled armour has been stripped from them, so that their tunics hang beltless. Only the richness of the coloured weave they wear and the length of their hair marks them as more than slaves.*

*Aidan will not look at me.*

*There is a sword-cut on the side of his head, through the red hair. My body jerks at my bonds as I long to run to him, staunch his wound, put my arms round him, comfort him.*

*It is not fatally deep, I think, though the blood still drips. A death-blow would have been less cruel.*

*I want to give him hope, but there is none. Roman pride has been sadly damaged – someone must pay for it.*

*Lift your head high, Aidan. Laugh at death. You will die for Dumnon.*

*Not on the battlefield, amid yells and the clash of steel. Not with horses galloping and trumpets braying. Not with the chants of druids standing on the hillside to call down the gods to our aid.*

*His princely glory is gone. He is shackled and shamed. They will execute him like a common criminal. Where are the bards to sing of it?*

*Look at me, Aidan. I love you. If I live, I will tell your story.*

*But will I live? I think the sentence will fall on all of us.*

*Is this what is breaking your heart, Aidan? Your grief for me?*

*Smile then, and raise my head high, though I want to fling myself down on the bloody grass and wail my anguish. Do not let him see I am afraid, too.*

*There is only one of them who is lifting his chin, with a flash in his eyes still. Melwas.*

*Astonishment. My little brother. He almost rescued me.*

The mud was cold to sit on. Melwas squirmed uncomfortably, hunching his shoulders against the thin rain that had been falling for hours. The ropes bit into his arms. But at least when their Roman captors bound them to the stakes they had allowed them to squat down. He looked sideways, through lashes pearled with raindrops, along the line of fellow prisoners.

There were eight of them. Himself. Elaeth. Five others. And at the far end of the line, Aidan. Melwas's heart grieved for his foster-brother. Aidan, who had challenged the whole tribe of Dumnon to follow him to war. Aidan, whose laughter had lit the fires of hope. Aidan, for whose smile young men would proudly die. He sat now, his red head, dark with rain, bowed over his knees.

They must be all that was left. Did that mean that two hundred of the finest young warriors in Dumnon lay dead? Tegan, he knew, was dead. Seiriol was dead. Only Rieuk had escaped, galloping away into the north to some last rallying of the druids. Could anyone else have survived?

They had failed. The Romans had brushed them aside, reached the Salmon River, and dragged their British prisoners with them. They had established their camp now on high ground overlooking the Red Quay, within a bowshot of the Great Forest.

Was Idwal still at the Forest Fort, and Beath and Coel? Was life somewhere going on as normal? How could it be?

As soon as they had arrived, the legionaries had unpacked their shovels and begun throwing up earthworks, hammering in stakes, until they had another camp just like the two before it. Rome was here in the heart of Dumnon.

The prisoners shivered in the rain. All except Cairenn. They had led her away, still bound, and shut her up in one of the tents. Melwas counted the slopes of glistening leather. He thought it was that small one, down near the corner.

A group of soldiers passed, their helmets dulled and their red cloaks sodden. He could not understand what they were saying, but he could tell by their faces that they were hating this British weather. One of them kicked out at Elaeth as he passed.

At the end of the line they stopped and stared down at Aidan. A second soldier caught up a fistful of his red hair and tried to pull his fingers through it. Even in their camp at Seiriol's Oaks, Aidan had kept himself dressed as a prince, combing his lime-washed hair into a sunburst glory. Now, rough hands seized hold of it, dragging his head this way and that to roars of coarse laughter.

Red rage swept through Melwas. His hand grabbed for his sword before he realized he had none. Shocked, he saw Aidan as he had been a week ago, his bright blue eyes as quick to flash anger as laughter. In Idwal's feasting-hall, Aidan might have killed a man who laughed at him. With one last cuff that knocked him sideways, the soldiers dismissed their captive and walked on.

Aidan's head drooped. His mouth trembled. He might almost have been about to cry.

Melwas looked away. He could not bear it. Was this how all the others felt? Had they ceased to be men, now that they were prisoners? Had they lost the will to resist, along with their weapons and their freedom?

There were soldiers still working, even in the rain. He could not understand what they were doing. They had dragged eight tall timbers into the camp, and to each of these they were lashing a shorter length of wood in the shape of a rough cross. Melwas watched them uneasily. He felt those crosses had something to do with the prisoners, but he could not imagine what they were for. Unconsciously his eyes dropped to the pendant he had once taken from a Roman soldier, the leaden charm with the sign of the fish, which he did not understand.

Another soldier was approaching. Melwas would not look at him. The boots stopped in front of him. The man squatted down until his face was level with Melwas's.

'Boy.'

The word was in the British tongue. Melwas's anger flared. Were the Romans capturing his language, too? It was a broad-shouldered centurion, a hated foreigner using British words to tell British warriors he had taken away their freedom. The boy shut his mouth tightly and would not look up.

The centurion leaned closer. 'You Christus man?' His voice was low and urgent.

It was not the true British tongue, but Armorican, thickly accented. He must have picked up a few words in Gaul.

'I don't know what you mean,' Melwas muttered. 'I'm British.'

The man's hand reached out and grasped Melwas's pendant. Then from the neck of his own tunic he drew another. Melwas's eyes widened in recognition. It was the same. He shook his head defiantly.

'I took it, from a Roman soldier.'

The centurion's eyes blazed. 'You kill him?'

Melwas's hands made an instinctive movement to protect himself, before the rope stopped them. 'No. He was dead already when I found him. It wasn't in this battle. It was a week ago.'

The man stared. His eyes saddened. He touched the pendant again, then his hand dropped to his side. 'I think from Festus. My friend. He Christus man, too.' Still he looked into Melwas's face. 'I want hate you. But Christus say no.' He managed a smile and shook Melwas by the shoulder. 'Too small. Festus good soldier. No boy kill him!'

Rage shook Melwas. 'I've killed Romans!'

The centurion's face filled with pity. His voice murmured lower, 'You know Christus?'

Melwas shook his head again.

The officer looked around warily, to see if any other Roman was in earshot. 'My captain now. Emperor's son. Very brave.' His eyes seemed drawn to the end of the line, where those carpenters were at work on the timbers. He spread his arms wide like the beams. 'He die on cross like that. For us.' His eyes shone darkly back at Melwas. 'Too small! You brave. Christus help you.'

A commanding voice called. 'Justus!' The centurion jumped upright. He slipped his own pendant out of sight. For a moment his hand rested on Melwas's head, then he straight-ened his back and marched off.

Melwas watched the centurion go. He crouched on the damp earth, remembering the shadow under the pine trees at the Silent Fort. The dead Roman soldier, clutching this sign with his last breath. It was strange. Justus must have known that another of Aidan's band had killed his friend, and yet his face had shown pity.

He looked the other way, to where those huge lengths of timber lay on the ground. What word had Justus used? A cross? His captain Christus had gone to his death on one. But how did someone die on a cross? He pictured the cross-beams holding up a roof and frowned. Was it a form of hanging or burning?

A Roman carpenter turned away from the beam he was working on. He emptied out a bag. Even from here Melwas could see he was counting out huge nails. He could not reach to hold the pendant at the neck of his tunic, but he felt the edge of it against his skin.

The rain had eased to a light spatter. Someone else was coming along the alley between the tents. Soles squelched on the wet earth. Melwas turned with little interest and stared in disbelief. That white robe . . . .

'Melwas.'

He had not imagined it. This voice was truly British, potently familiar, deep and musical. It was a voice that opened memories of childhood. Of Idwal's hall. Of Maytime sacrifice and Samhain fire. Of druid chanting at the summer moonrise. Now it was Melwas's turn to feel like crying. The voice and face were Celynen's.

The tall druid stood over him. His eyes were grave and deep with understanding. As Melwas's head shot up he stud-ied the boy's face thoughtfully. Then his gaze moved on steadily, along the line of prisoners. Their eyes stared back at him, some dull, without hope, some suspicious, even accusing, others pleading. Only Aidan did not lift his face at all. Celynen's eyes came back to Melwas, and he nodded slowly, as if reaching a decision.

'Listen well, Melwas,' he said. 'They have allowed me only a short time.'

Another centurion, in charge of the prisoners, was standing close behind him. Melwas did not think he understood the British tongue. He was a grey-haired man of middle age, with a plain blunt face. Last night he had checked their bonds. Melwas remembered those hands moving over him. He had not been gentle, but neither had he been vicious, like those others who had pulled Aidan's hair. Just a soldier doing his job.

Celynen spoke fast. 'Vespasian is a hard man, but he is just, according to his own laws. He does what the Roman Empire demands. He will not pardon you, but he has granted me permission to make the last farewells. To send you to the Otherworld with the blessing of our tribe and our gods.'

Melwas gazed up at him. He knew what Celynen was trying to tell him. They were going to die. He had been expecting it. But there was something else that he did not understand. An expression in Celynen's eyes, more urgent than pity. He managed to hold his voice steady for one question.

'When?'

'Tomorrow. At dawn. They are making the crosses now. They will nail you to one by your hands and feet, and stand it upright in the ground. You must hang there till you die.'

Melwas felt himself grow icy cold. For the first time, he envied Tegan. If only he could have died on the battlefield like that, with one swift thrust of the sword. But to have survived for this . . . . He licked his stiff lips.

'And Cairenn?'

His eyes begged Celynen for hope. But now the druid's face darkened.

199

'She, too, must die. We pleaded for her life, but the Romans are angry. You cost them too many men and precious time. That's why they didn't kill you on the battlefield. They mean to make your deaths a warning to others. They will leave your bodies hanging on a hill for all to see. But at least it will not be a cross for Cairenn. We pleaded with him to behead her.'

The centurion cleared his throat warningly.

Celynen stretched out his hands and laid them on Melwas's head. He began to intone the old, old prayer for dying warriors, soon to voyage out to the last Islands in the West. As the chant flowed over him, the beautiful, heart-rending words unlocked the gates of grief, wounding and healing in the same breath. Melwas felt himself caught up, transported, as though he could be in Paradise now. Then there was a sharp prick on his left thigh. He winced. The druid's fingers tightened strongly about his skull, forcing him to look down.

Beneath the shadow of Celynen's sleeve, a small razor, wickedly sharp, lay in the lap of Melwas's tunic. Quick as lightning, the boy closed his knees, shutting it from the centurion's sight. The druid's grip relaxed. He ended the prayer. Melwas looked up at him, but hope must have shone too brightly in his face. The answering glare so terrified him that he was shocked sober again.

The druid moved on. The centurion followed close behind. Celynen stopped for a few words with each man, and rested his hands on each head with the last blessing. Melwas watched him closely. Nothing more fell from his sleeve. He reached the last prisoner.

'Aidan.'

But here the centurion stepped swiftly forward. Celynen was hustled away. For the leader of the rebels, there would be no favours. The Red Fox would have no contact, no comfort, no mercy.

200

Melwas knew he must wait for nightfall. But it was hard. He had let the razor fall to the ground, hiding it under the folds of his short tunic, and now he was terrified that he would lose it in the mud. He wanted to keep feeling it for reassurance, but even this was dangerous with so many soldiers about. The Romans were exhilarated by their victory. They had crushed the rebels, received the submission of the Dumnonian chiefs, they had set up their standard at the bridging-place of the Salmon River. All Dumnon would be theirs. As they passed these last few barbarians huddled in the rain, they jeered.

Towards evening the clouds parted, releasing a bluebell sky and a rich smell of wet earth. The prisoners were brought food. Melwas was young enough to eat hungrily of corn porridge and onions, though his stomach craved for meat. The others, too hopeless for hunger, tasted the strange food once and pushed it away. Melwas longed to share his secret with them, but he dared not. As it was, he was terrified that the Romans would read the hope in his face, that he alone of the prisoners would not look as though he faced the certainty of death. He waited in an agony of impatience for the stars to come out.

The crosses were ready. They might have looked no more sinister than door-posts, if only he had not been told the truth. He tried to stop himself imagining the nails, the ring of cruel faces, the time when his courage would run out but the pain would go on. He felt he could not bear to spend another hour so close to those crosses. He tried to imagine this Christus who had gone to such a death willingly. Where did his courage come from?

The soldiers had gone back to their own quarters. The harsh, unmusical rhythms of their speech died to a murmur from behind leather walls. Stars pricked through the grey cobweb of the sky. Sentries paced the walls. Melwas wondered despairingly if it would ever grow dark.

201

He must have dozed. It was much colder. The damp had got deep into his bones, making him shiver uncontrollably. But it was black night at last.

He sat up in a panic. How long had he slept? Was the night already half over and the dawn approaching fast?

He fumbled for the razor. His bound hands brushed across crushed grass and sticky earth, finding nothing. He heaved himself sideways, feeling the mud smear across his legs. Still his hands groped vainly. Sweat broke out over him. His heart was racing like a bolting pony. Where, oh where, was the razor? It could not be any further away than this. Surely he had not moved his position so far?

*Ow!* Sharp pain slashed his finger. But he was too glad to care. His shaking hand curled round the razor and held it tight. Gripping it between his fingers, he began to work the strands of rope across the blade. It was awkward work, and he nicked his wrist several times, but Celynen had given him the best edge that ironsmith could set. The job was done more quickly than he had dared to hope. He was free.

He crawled to the next man. This was the moment he most dreaded, when a cry of surprised joy might bring disaster. Inside his head, a voice was screaming at him not to risk it. Just to find Cairenn, set her free and get away. But the man had seen him.

The dangerous moment passed in silence. Melwas could feel the desperate hope in his companion's tense body as he worked on his bonds.

Soon they were all free. Aidan was the last. Without a word, the Red Fox rose to his knees. Stealthily he began to lead them away, making for the outer rampart of the camp. The others followed, bent double in the darkness. Melwas had already started towards Cairenn's tent. He stopped and stared after his companions in horrified surprise. He dared not shout to them. Instead, he ran on tiptoe until he had overtaken Aidan and grasped him by the shoulder. Keeping his voice to a low whisper, hoarse with urgency, he hissed,

'We can't go yet. Cairenn's still here. We've got to take her with us, or they'll kill her.'

Aidan's face was a pale blur in the darkness. He gave a moan of suppressed anguish. Melwas could only distinguish the words 'I can't . . . !'

Then Aidan knocked his hand up and twisted out of his grasp. Running double, he made off into the darkness, with the other six behind him. They were within earshot of the sentries, only steps away from Roman tents. There was no way Melwas could stop them. Night swallowed them up.

The ground seemed to give way beneath Melwas's feet. His world reeled. Aidan had gone. He knew the fear of utter lone-liness. And he knew also a bitterness fiercer than he had ever felt before. If Aidan had seized the razor from his hand and stabbed him where he stood, he could not have done worse. Aidan had left him alone in the Roman camp. Alone with six thousand of the Second Legion Augusta. Alone with those crosses.

The night remained silent. There were no shouts from the walls. Melwas was doubly angry at that. Angry because they had got away with it. They were outside. They were alive. They were free. He could picture them running joyfully over the open grass, while he was still here in the camp, risking death.

He walked almost recklessly to the line of tents where he had last seen Cairenn disappear. He forgot to count them as he passed. Was it this one? He lifted a tent flap cautiously and peeped in. He could see only blackness, but it had the feeling of emptiness, of inanimate objects. There was another tent beside it. Inside, the same unbreathing silence. He let the flap fall.

Suddenly he stiffened. A guard was approaching, leather boots swishing slowly on the grass as he paced his rounds. There was no time to hide. Melwas held his breath. The guard strode past.

When he had gone, Melwas let out a long sigh of relief. But instantly a new fear seized him. When he reached the end of the avenue, the soldier would come to the line of stakes where the prisoners had been tied. Once he discovered their absence, all hope of escape would be gone. He must be stopped.

Quick as a polecat, Melwas darted silently over the grass after him. In his hand he gripped the razor. He was aware of a strange reluctance. He must have killed several men in this last week, in the heat and shock of battle. But this was different. To creep up on an opponent in the darkness, without warning, from behind; this was not how Bearrach Horse-Thief had taught him the proud warfare of the Britons. But he had no time to think of another way. He was on his own, in a new and terrifying world. And he had to save Cairenn.

It was neatly done. The razor slid across the throat. The man fell with only a little bubble of sound.

Melwas dropped the razor. He knew it was stupid. He still needed it to free Cairen. But he could not bear to keep the thing in his hand. Could it be the pity of one Roman centurion that had made him this weak?

He dared not take such a scandalous risk with both their lives. Nerving himself to grab up the bloody razor again, he raced back to the third tent.

'Cairenn?' he whispered.

He felt a human warmth in the darkness even before she whispered back.

'Melwas!'

Even now, she was calm and steady. Had Celynen warned her? She asked no questions as he cut her free. Silently they lifted the tent flap and slipped out into the star-pricked night. The grass was wet and cool against their feet as they paused by the last of the tents. Ahead of them was an open space and then the wall. A sentry paced along the rampart.

'He'll see us,' hissed Cairenn.

Melwas did not move. The sentry passed. They dashed across the open ground and up the bank. The palisade of stakes was hard for Cairenn to manage. Melwas heaved her up.

Below them in the camp, a furious shouting broke out. A guard must have discovered the prisoners' escape. There were lights moving fast, soldiers with torches, tossing huge shadows behind them as they ran to the empty line of stakes. The sentry on the wall spun round.

The hunt was fanning out, torches streaming through the camp, like fire through thatch. Melwas gave a last push and felt Cairenn tumble over the wall into the darkness. Then he, too, sprang for the top of the palisade.

The sentry saw the movement. His spear sang through the air and thudded into the fence, pinning Melwas to the wood. The boy opened his mouth to scream. The pain he was expecting did not come. Footsteps were already pounding towards him before he realized that the spear had struck not flesh but the cloth of his tunic. He let go with one hand and wrenched himself free with a sound of tearing fabric. Now he hung wildly by one hand. The sentry was almost upon him. Melwas's free hand scrabbled for the top of the wall. With a last desperate effort he heaved himself up and pitched over. He struck the bank with his shoulder and rolled on down into the ditch.

Cairenn had waited for him. She was beside him now, running as hard as she could. There were shouts ahead. The cries from the camp had alerted more guards patrolling outside. With their senses heightened by danger, Cairenn and Melwas dodged to one side, crouched in the undergrowth, swerved again and ran on.

The shouting faded behind them. Below them a glimpse of firelight was reflected in the wide river from the huts clustered round the Red Quay. The Forest was close. That way lay Idwal's dun. Home. But it was on the wrong side of the

Roman camp. There could be no escape that way. They ran on, down-river, into the night.

# CHAPTER 14

## THE RETURN

'Where are we going?'

Cairenn broke the silence at last, gasping painfully for breath. Melwas had been asking himself the same question. All night they had fled south, through the grey dawn and into the morning. They would have to stop soon. They were pushing now through damp woods, where the wild rose-hips were turning red. Far below them the tide was creeping up over the glistening mud flats of the Salmon River. Oh, if only they could have been on the other shore, losing themselves in the wild, blue lands of the west, in some steep-sided coombe where the Romans might never come! But this side of the river was gradually becoming familiar.

'I think I know a place. It can't be far from here. We'll find somewhere to rest, and with luck there should still be some food there.'

The wood was deceptive. From a distance each stand of oaks, each deer path, seemed to awaken memory. But always, as Melwas came closer, he found he was wrong. It was not what he was looking for. Still, this wood was not large, not like the limitless tracts of the Great Forest. Soon he must find a landmark. Perhaps at the top of this slope . . . .

A terrified squealing stopped them in their tracks. Cairenn

and Melwas looked at each other with scared, questioning eyes. Suddenly Melwas laughed.

'The pigs! Seiriol's pigs! I'd forgotten they'd still be here.'

'What's wrong with them? They're frightened. Listen to them.'

The squeals were cut short. Suddenly men's voices shouted, alarmed and urgent. War-cries rang through the forest, followed by the clash of weapons and yells of pain. Brother and sister stopped, petrified.

Next moment, a man broke into view, crashing through the branches towards them. The first thing they saw was the gaping wound in his head, before they recognized through the curtain of blood that it was Elaeth, Melwas's fellow prisoner. Hot behind him came a Roman soldier, with sword raised to strike again.

Melwas sprang forward to help, racing up the wooded slope with his chest bursting in the effort to get there in time. He saw Elaeth turn desperately. Then the two men were locked together in a panting struggle.

He reached them too late. Groaning, the men fell apart and sank to the ground. Melwas approached the Roman warily and looked down at him. He was already dead. And Elaeth too, pillowed on the green moss of the forest floor.

Cairenn came up the slope more slowly, pale and trembling. Through the trees they could see now the high fence of Seiriol's Oaks, and behind they sensed a curious emptiness. Wisps of dark smoke rose, staining the air between the branches. Inside, it was utterly silent.

They walked cautiously around the fence to the entrance. The gate had been torn from its hinges and flung aside. The grove was a scene of devastation. The sacred oaks were hacked and despoiled, great branches severed. One tree-trunk, thicker than a bull's carcass, had been felled, crushing the fence beneath its sprawling branches as it toppled. Melwas backed away in horror at the thought of the gods' outrage.

The huts were in ruins. Fires had been lit everywhere, but the damp wood had burned sullenly, and blackened heaps still breathed foul smoke. There was no sign of the pillar of carved heads.

Even in the presence of such devastation, Melwas felt his heart lighter for that, as though the dawn had dissolved a dark dream.

It was only a small consolation. Everywhere there were bodies. Roman soldiers and British warriors, who had died in combat. Wounded men of Aidan's band, who had been slaughtered where they lay. Men and pigs butchered. The grove held the stillness of death.

Melwas came close to the first body. The face was a red ruin, unrecognizable, and he felt his stomach heave. He knew too clearly now how that wound had been inflicted, with a grinding thrust of a Roman shield-boss. He walked quickly past.

But Cairenn was not so easily deceived. With a cry of anguish she threw herself over the body.

'Aidan! Aidan!'

Melwas turned back, sick with disbelief.

Cairenn crouched there, tearing her golden hair, rocking and keening aloud her grief.

'Oh, Aidan, my heart, Red Fox of the Forest, brighter than sunset on the western waters! The sun has gone from our skies and the stars have fallen!'

Melwas listened helplessly. He wanted to cry out to her,

'No! He wasn't like that. You don't know. He wouldn't risk his own life on a cross to save you.'

But what good would it have done to tell her that now? She would not have believed him.

*He thinks I grieve for the love of my life. For the flash of laughter in Aidan's eyes. For the arms hard on the grip of his horse, arms which should have held me tight. For the children*

209

*of his my womb will never hold.*

*And so I do grieve, and tears are torn from me for what will never be.*

*Yet I knew, from the time we found he was not in the fort for the Council, that this was his fate. My grief was prepared an age ago. Even without the druids, I have been through my ordeal of initiation, isolated from my tribe, surrounded by horrors. This is my return. These are the blood-rites that make me a woman.*

*I think I always knew that he did not love me as I loved him. It was my good fortune that I was young, beautiful, a chieftain's daughter. Aidan was certainly not ill-pleased to be marrying me, but nothing more. His eyes did not follow me about the hall as I moved. He did not hang moonstruck in my company, when he could be playing war-games with his friends. Sodden with love as I was, I did not care. It was enough that when he smiled at me the strings of my guts unloosed. That I could hug in the night-time the knowledge that he would soon have my body. That other girls envied me.*

*I was young and in love.*

*I am old now, ancient as the goddess looking upon the ruin of her children. Could it have been otherwise? Was Celynen wise to capitulate? The goddess is in me. Did I demand blood?*

*No, Melwas. I keen for a deeper love, for my country, my tribe, my land. For the circles of our houses, and our spiral art, and our wheeling horsemen. For the faces of children turned up to me to hear the stories of Dumnon. For the broken harp-strings. What shall we be when our language is lost to a stranger tongue, and our legends die? When our streets are straightened and our dreams disciplined? I weep for Dumnon, Melwas, and the love of my life.*

Melwas walked on through the grove, making himself count the bodies of the British who had died in this last stand. Six. And Elaeth outside made seven. They were all dead. All the prisoners he had freed from the Roman camp. He was the only one left alive.

The Romans had found the sacred treasure-hoard in the pits under the oaks. But they had not got far with it. It lay spilled in the grass, where they had dropped it. Rich cups, swords and brooches, priceless gifts offered over the years to the awesome gods whom Seiriol served. Aidan had given his life to stop this sacrilege.

Or had Aidan himself come here seeking, not safety, but the treasure of the gods, and the weapons in Seiriol's huts? Melwas let the booty lie.

On one of the fires he found at last the remains of the pillar. It had been hacked into pieces. The heads still showed as shapeless, blackened lumps in the half-burnt wood. They were not only mouthless, but eyeless now, and more malignant than ever. In their downfall they terrified him more.

He looked back and saw with relief that Cairenn had risen to her feet. She pushed back her tumbled hair and smoothed her stained crimson gown. He watched her face struggling for composure. Presently she looked up at him. When she spoke, her voice had changed. It held that brisk, elder-sister note which he had not heard for so long.

'Come along, Melwas. We can't stay here. We shall have to find somewhere else to rest. Anywhere will do, as long as it's away from here. Then tonight we must steal a boat and cross the river.'

They should have gone straight downhill then, towards the estuary. They could have found some secret hollow of the woods and slept in safety while the long hours of daylight passed. But that way lay the ruins of Hu's village. Melwas could not face passing it again.

'There are villages down that path. Too many people. We might meet more Romans. Let's find a quieter way.'

He led her through the trees. Thrushes sang to them and squirrels ran along the branches over their heads. They met

211

no signs of human life. They stumbled on till they seemed to be walking without reason. Twice Cairenn said that they should stop, but Melwas shook his head obstinately. He felt that he had not yet reached the end of his journey, but he could not remember what it was.

They came out of the wood on to open grassland near the top of the ridge. Then Melwas knew at last what had been drawing him. The Silent Fort reared its ramparts above them, and the tops of its pine trees brushed the cloudy sky.

Cairenn looked at Melwas, but said nothing. They passed into the shadow of its walls and crossed the causeway to the gate. Inside, it looked just as Melwas had first seen it. Silent. Empty. Only the wind rustling the dry grass. And still that sense of something waiting for him under the knot of pines. He went forward, gripping the fish pendant in his hand, with Cairenn following. From the shadows a grey figure rose and watched them come. It was Celynen.

The druid's smile was brilliant with relief when he saw them, but after the welcome embraces his face became old and sad.

'Thanks be to the gods, you're safe! Where are all the others?'

'Dead.' Melwas heard his own voice speaking the word, and realized that he had never fully believed it until now. It was too great a loss, too final. He looked slowly round him at the wide, grassy space within the fort, which had held so many eager warriors, and repeated wonderingly, 'They're all dead! Every one of them! There's only me left.'

The druid sighed heavily.

'I feared it would be so. That you and Cairenn escaped is more than I dared to hope. But you're a long way from safety yet. I've a boat standing by to take you across the river. A guide will meet you and take you into the western hills. There you'll find a hiding-place for the winter. Beyond that, no one can plan in times like these.'

Cairenn asked, 'What is it like now at the Forest Fort? Is Father safe? And Idwal and Beath? What will the Romans do to you all, now we've escaped?'

'Your father and your foster-parents are unharmed, thanks be, as yet . . . Here, I've brought some food. After that, you must sleep while I keep watch. You must be ready to move at sunset.'

Melwas ate hungrily of the cold meat Celynen had brought. But Cairenn was uneasy. She took Melwas aside and murmured, 'Look at Celynen, Melwas. There's something very wrong, I'm sure of it. You can see it in his face.'

'Well, how do you expect him to look? Aidan's dead, isn't he? Our next chief, and all the best young warriors of Dumnon with him. How do you think *I* feel? You wailed loud enough yourself.'

'No. It's more than that. Didn't you see it in his face when we came? Before you told him the news?'

'Celynen knows things, without needing to be told. He must have guessed when he saw we were alone.'

'This is worse than grief. Celynen couldn't grieve for Aidan more than I do. And death is not the end; he knows they've all gone to feast in the Otherworld. But look at his face now.'

He followed her gaze. The druid was standing a little apart from them, staring out over the rampart to where the Great Forest rolled a dark tide across the northern hills. His face bore the marks of deep anguish.

Melwas got to his feet. 'What's the matter, Celynen? What are you hiding from us?'

Cairenn joined him. 'It's the Forest Fort, isn't it? Something happened after we escaped. What have the Romans done there?'

Celynen stayed silent. Then Melwas spoke, and his young voice was hard and commanding, as Aidan's had been.

'Tell us, Celynen. Tell us now.'

The druid turned slowly to face them.

213

'You do not know what you are asking me. If I were to tell you, it would give you no peace, now or any night hereafter. It is a thousand times better that you should cross the river and go away into the west not knowing.'

'You *must* tell us. They're our people. Our friends, our blood. We have the right to know.'

'Yes, you have the right. Aidan would have said that. But do you have the courage to bear the knowledge?'

'Try me and see.'

Celynen looked at him long and hard, then sighed.

'I believe you do. Yet my heart is heavy because of it. It is a decision I would far rather have taken upon myself, and sent you away still fearing but unsure. But I cannot do that. You have become a man. Neither Idwal nor I nor Cairenn can take that away from you now. Perhaps Seiriol was wiser than us. So listen like a man to what I have to tell you.

'As soon as he discovered your escape, Vespasian sent troops to the Forest Fort. They came marching in, drums beating, even though it was the middle of the night. When they found all our young warriors were gone, they seized the boys. Every boy from the dun of Idwal Goldenshield.'

The druid's voice faded in Melwas's ears. He saw the Forest Fort. He saw fat, cheerful Coel, struggling to learn bardic poetry, snoring in the hay beside him. He saw the boys who had practised sword-fights with him on the chariot-field, who had raced him on the hunting-trail, charged him in wild games of sticks and balls. He tried to picture all that shouting and jostling and laughter, silenced for ever. He remembered the hammers thudding on the crosses. The blood drained from his face.

'Unless you are recaptured, they will die. For Aidan, and for you, and for all the other rebels and the blood you shed.'

'But they can't do that! We were the ones who fought the Romans. They can't kill the other boys for what *we* did!'

But he saw Hu's little sister and Crab, with the spear-wounds in their throats. He knew they could.

'I warned you, Melwas, that this news was not for your peace. And not for mine, since it was I who set you free.'

'They shan't do it! I shall go back. I'll tell them that Aidan and all the rest are dead now. The rebellion's over. When I'm dead too, they'll have had their revenge.'

He must not let himself imagine that cross. He found he was holding on to the scrap of lead with its sign of the fish as never before.

They had forgotten Cairenn. Now she said simply, 'Then I shall go with you.'

Celynen and Melwas whirled round, horrified.

'No!'

'No, no, Cairenn of the White Fingers. Not you. Melwas is a man now. It breaks my heart to let him go, but I can't stop him, and he wouldn't forgive me if I tried. I too have my own bitter road of life to tread. So have you.'

Melwas said quickly, 'What's it got to do with you anyway? You're not like Tegan. You never fought them. You even tried to stop us. Why should you die for that?'

She went on calmly, as though neither of them had spoken.

'I must. There's no other way. Do you suppose Vespasian will take your word for it that Aidan is dead? You think you're a man, but to him, you're just a boy. He'll only crucify you with all the others.'

She lifted a white hand and fingered the coil of heavy, twisted gold about her neck. 'But I am a princess of Dumnon. I wear the torque that Aidan's parents gave me, that should have been the token of our betrothal. Could even a Roman general believe that, if Aidan were alive, he'd let me go back to face execution at the hands of Roman soldiers? Only when I myself stand before Vespasian and tell him they are all dead, will he know for certain that it must be true.'

There was a bitter silence. Melwas thought helplessly of all the things he could have told her about Aidan, things he had

215

vowed never to say. The moment passed, and the time when he might have argued with her slipped by for ever.

At last, Celynen said slowly,

'You are a man, Melwas. But your sister is a woman, and a queen among women. You are both your father's children.

'Listen. There is a land the Romans cannot conquer; there is a land their feet will never tread. It is the land of free hearts, unvanquished. Rich are its harvests, sweet are its apple trees. There, there is always wine and feasting and music of the harp. We three shall meet there, when we have passed over the dark waters.'

Cairenn and Melwas looked about them. Heather was brushing purple round their feet, still blinded with teardrops of dew. Clouds of mist breathed up from the rain-soaked woods. Across the broad estuary the tide crept forward in a silver flood. Above their heads a skylark poured down song, soaring into the sky up and away beyond their seeing for ever. A stiff-legged deer stole from the edge of the wood and sniffed the autumn.

As in a dream, the brother and sister walked to the gate.

# CHAPTER 15

## TRAVELLERS

Behind them now, that first, heart-sinking moment when the raw walls of the Roman camp appeared on the horizon. Behind them, the startled shouts of recognition from the sentry, the rush of guards to seize and bind their unresisting arms. They had been pulled roughly through the gate. They were prisoners again.

It seemed that every soldier in the camp had heard of their return. Hundreds upon hundreds were pressing forward, packing every avenue, jeering, whistling, shouting loud-mouthed abuse. Coarse hands thrust out to paw at them as they passed. The foxglove colour flamed high in Cairenn's cheeks, and Melwas burned with helpless anger. He did not need to understand Latin to guess what insults they were hurling at her.

The centurion rapped out an order. The escort closed in around the prisoners, and the soldiers reprimanded fell back. The noise was more subdued, but still a grinding murmur of ill will and ugly jokes rose from either side all down that long street.

In the centre of the camp, in the commander's tent, Vespasian sat waiting for them.

At last Melwas stood before him and raised his eyes. He

had been afraid on the long trail back from the Silent Fort. He had been afraid at the first sight of the Roman camp. But now it was too late for fear. He had made his choice, and he was glad. He met Vespasian's eyes defiantly.

The face he saw was ugly, square-jawed, with a bulbous nose. The eyes were not as blue as Aidan's, nor would they ever be as quick to laughter or to anger. They met his with a steady thoughtfulness. Some of Melwas's defiance ebbed away. He felt a stab of envy for those crowds of Roman soldiers outside the tent. Men might not love this leader with the same fierce energy with which Melwas had loved Aidan, but they might trust him longer.

'What brings you back, boy?'

A different interpreter translated the words. Melwas hated this one too. He should have been a little weasel of a man, looking the part of a traitor, but he was not. He was a little short, perhaps, for a Briton, and a trifle too plump, but sleek and prosperous-looking. Smooth, grey hair; a fine, curling moustache. He was a man who might have drunk wine in Idwal's hall, or hunted with Melwas's father, and not seemed out of place. Melwas detested him all the more for that.

He wished it had been Justus, speaking a few halting words in that thickly accented Armorican tongue which the people of Dumnon understood. At the thought of the grey-haired, square-shouldered centurion, of the fatherly look in his face when he said 'Too small' to him, a rebel who might have killed his friend, Melwas put up his hand to the pendant that linked them curiously together.

The silence was lengthening. Melwas spoke out bravely:

'Celynen says you've taken all the other boys from the Forest Fort. You can't do that. They haven't done anything to deserve death. Idwal offered you peace. If you must have revenge, then kill me. Aidan the Red Fox is dead, and the warriors who followed him, too. I'm the only one left alive.'

The interpreter translated with none of Melwas's passionate emotion, almost apologetically. Vespasian frowned.

'The Red Fox is dead? Idwal's son? Am I supposed to believe that? It would be a small loss to him to send a youngster like you to his death, while the Fox goes free to raise a new warhost against me.'

'If you don't believe me, go to Seiriol's Oaks. You'll find their bodies there. Celynen promised he wouldn't give them a burial before you saw them.' He couldn't resist adding, 'And you'll find the remains of your Roman patrol, as well. They went down fighting.'

'You'd like me to put my head into another noose; one of your confounded ambushes, in your treacherous British forests. This Red Fox is cunning, but Vespasian's not yet such an old fool as that.'

It was Cairenn who answered him then, lifting her golden head. Her voice was high and strained, but she held it steady with an effort, like a charioteer whose hands are firm on the reins of a frightened horse. Melwas watched her proudly.

'Aidan the Red Fox is surely dead. I am Cairenn of the White Fingers, princess of Dumnon. If Aidan were alive, I should be his bride now. Instead, I have come back of my own free will, to lay my neck under the Roman sword. If I do this, and the Red Fox does not stop me, then you may be sure that Aidan, Idwal's son, has gone to the Otherworld before me.'

Vespasian rose from his seat. He looked from the brother to the sister.

'A girl and a boy! Is this how the British fight against the empire of Rome? Is this the warhost that has delayed my legion for a whole week? Gentlemen, what shall we do with such dangerous rebels?' He paused. 'You, boy. They tell me you were captured on the battlefield yesterday. You speak as if you have followed this Red Fox from the beginning. Have you really fought against a Roman legion?'

'It's true! I fought your Roman soldiers. I think I may have killed some of them, too. And I'm glad of it!' Though even as he said it, the words rang strangely in his ears. He was no longer sure that they were true. 'Crucify me, if you must, but let the rest go free. I'm the last of the rebels!'

As the interpreter relayed the words in Latin, Cairenn turned and smiled at him, a long, warm, loving smile, as though she knew it would be for the last time.

And so it was that neither of them saw the quiver of mirth that trembled in Vespasian's face and passed itself on into wide grins on the faces of his officers. They only heard his sharp word of command and saw the straight-faced guards step forward to lead them away.

Summer had gone. Rain fell heavily from low skies as the marching column of the Second Legion Augusta squelched its way eastward through the mud of Dumnon. When the British winter was over, they would return. They would build a fort of stone above the Red Quay. They would rule the west.

For now, Vespasian could send booty enough for a triumphal parade through Rome.

The column passed below the Silent Fort. Melwas's eyes went up for a last look. Clouds hung low on the summit, veiling the pines. But its walls still brooded darkly over the land. He wondered if the ramparts would be standing like that when the might of the Roman Empire had rolled away like the clouds. Then he pulled his good British rain-cloak about him and huddled lower in the saddle. At least, on this journey they had been given mules to ride.

He looked sideways through rain-fringed lashes at Cairenn. She was sitting coldly upright. It seemed to him that Cairenn had changed since their capture. She had not bothered to pull her cloak up over her head, and her hair was drenched and flattened with rain. She, who had always been so particular about her dress and her hair. She looked almost as though she were *trying* to make herself as miserable as possible. Melwas rode closer.

'It may not be so bad. We'll come back one day. And it's not as if we were ordinary prisoners now. Being a hostage is something different. As long as Dumnon stays peaceful, the Romans will treat us well.'

Cairenn did not answer.

'Don't you want to see Rome? I do. Just think of it. Sailing across the Channel, travelling right through Gaul, crossing the mountains into Italy. And Justus says when we get to Rome there'll be huge buildings made of stone, each one as big as the whole Forest Fort! And they've built rivers of stone up in the sky to bring them drinking-water. Justus says we'll probably be taken to see the Emperor. He might . . . .'

Cairenn burst out passionately, 'I hate them! I hate them!'

'Who? Justus, or the Emperor?'

'The Romans! All of them! Why couldn't they have left us alone? Why did they have to come and take our land and kill our friends and spoil everything? We were so happy as we were! But what do they care about what they're destroying? If I could get hold of a sword, I'd like to kill every one of them with my own hands.'

'I don't understand you. You were the one who was always on at us not to fight. You said that Celynen was right, and we should make peace. You said . . . .'

'What does it matter what I said? What does anything matter any more? Aidan's dead, and the Romans killed him. I shall never forgive them. Never.'

*I hate the Romans. They are taking my country away from me. They are taking me away from my country.*

*I cannot believe I may never see it again. My eyes devour the slightest details. The proud purple heads of thistles turned hoar and grey, shedding past glory as insubstantial down as we brush past. Mist coiling above the brooks in the valley bottoms. The rain-beaded cradles of spiders' webs hung from*

221

*the heather.*

*I fear the lightness in that sky over the sea that will bear me south to Gaul and Rome. Its promise of sunshine mocks my misery. Better this rain on the hills of Dumnon, which nursed me like a mother's breasts.*

*A savage weaning. An army of men, brutal, military, marching me away from everything I love. The sandy track weeps red under the mules' hooves. The raindrops on my cheeks are all the tears I have left to weep for Aidan. My heart is empty, even of grief. They have left me nothing.*

*Nothing but the silky feel of the wet west wind on my face. Nothing but the dark red flash of a bedraggled squirrel running up that oak tree. Nothing but the scream of the buzzard perched in the tree-tops. Nothing but the scent of the gorse. The Romans cannot kill my memory.*

*Somewhere out of sight red cattle are lowing as they swing in a long line from the morning milking to lush pastures. I was raised on their milk. They will always be part of me.*

*There is a flicker in the woods. A peasant girl, her arms full of firewood, shrinks back into the shadows, torn between curiosity and terror. We pass her by. She will survive. Girls like her will inherit Dumnon.*

*I am a princess. I am a hostage. I will lose my country.*

*We are coming in sight of another river, a widening estuary. Ships at their moorings. The very beauty of our coastline betrays us, giving our enemies anchorage.*

*Will the hills be able to resist them? Will the Romans set their signals on the tops of our tors and our highest headlands? Or will the mists roll round and confound them, the mires enmesh their stumbling feet, the Fair Folk entrap them amongst the standing stones? Will the Legion find its way westward to my father's fort and the Land's End?*

*I cannot imagine my country perpetually under the Romans; the druids dead, the songs silenced, the roads straightened. I cannot imagine what my people will become.*

222

*Yet Melwas chatters as though this were not our tribal tragedy, but some great new adventure.*


Melwas sighed. Sometimes he found his sister very hard to understand.

The centurion Justus was riding ahead on a fine black mare. He waited while they caught up with him. Melwas looked up at the Roman officer hopefully. There were so many things he needed to learn before they got to Rome. He pointed emphatically at the horse.

'What's that?' he asked, raising his eyebrows.

Justus looked surprised. 'Horse,' he said, in the Gaulish language which was nearly like Melwas's British tongue.

'No. What do *you* call it?'

The centurion was still puzzled. Then he threw back his head and laughed.

'*Equus!*' he said, grinning broadly and slapping the animal on the withers. '*Equus.*'

A happy light broke over Melwas's face. The word stirred in him memories of an older speech of the British people, still heard in forgotten corners of the countryside.

'*Echos?*' he said.

'*Ita vero! Equus. Equus.*' The centurion nodded vigorously.

For a moment the two of them stared at each other, as all the new possibilities dawned upon them. Then they broke into uproarious laughter. The Roman began to look about him. He drew his sword and waved it in the air.

'*Gladius.*'

And his spear.

'*Pilum.*'

His shield.

'*Scutum.*'

One by one, Melwas repeated the strange words after him, with growing delight.

Justus turned to Cairenn, who was riding sullenly beside

them. He grasped Melwas's arm and turned him to face his sister.

'*Soror*,' he said, pointing at Cairenn. 'Sister.'

Melwas shook his head warningly. But the centurion was smiling at Cairenn and pointing back at Melwas.

'*Frater*,' he said to her.

Cairenn stared back at him in mutinous silence. The mules walked on. Melwas and Justus exchanged glances.

Slowly, she brushed the mingled rain and teardrops from her cheeks. With an effort, she managed a faint half-smile.

'*Frater*,' she muttered, as though the word had been wrenched from her. 'Brother.'

The rain still fell about them, but up ahead pale sunlight glinted on the eagle standard. All across the heath the bracken was beginning to glow a deeper gold, and the forests of Dumnon redder yet. The spiderwebs were beginning to glisten with diamonds.

Melwas turned his head, to what he was leaving behind. He scanned the woods, searching. He knew it was impossible that he would see a small, brown-haired boy in a rough kilt, yet he could not help hoping still. Hu had survived. He was still here. Would he always be here, whoever ruled, as much a part of Dumnon as the red deer?

Side by side with a Roman centurion, the brother and sister rode forward on the long journey that would carry the children of Dumnon to Rome.